The Cat Kin

As a child Nick Green landed a tiny part in the John Madden-directed serial *After the War*, and wondered about an acting career. Sadly, that *was* his acting career. Eventually he ended up reviewing children's books for a book club, but decided it would be more fun to write them himself. *The Cat Kin* is his first published novel. He now lives in Hertford with his wife, young son, and cat.

'An excellent debut . . . a gripping adventure.'
Amanda Craig, *The Times*

The Cat Kin

Nick Green

ff

faber and faber

With thanks to Thomas and Greg Cooke, Alan Cumming, Joanna
Devereux, Janice Swanson and Kevin Mansfield. A great big purr
to Jackie Morris and Hannah Stowe. Special thanks to Shirley
Davis and to my editor Julia Wells.

First Published in Great Britain in 2007
by Faber and Faber Limited
3 Queen Square London WC1N 3AU

Printed in England by Mackays of Chatham plc,
Chatham, Kent

A CIP record for this book
is available from the British Library

ISBN 978–0–571–23481–3

2 4 6 8 10 9 7 5 3 1

For Marcia

1

Vermin

When Ben got home from school he found something good, something bad, and something worse. The bad thing was that he had lost his front door key. The good thing was that he didn't need it, because the door was already open. The worse thing was, it was not merely open but smashed off its hinges.

Ben felt sick. He stood in the lobby until the silence convinced him that whoever had done this was not inside the flat. He went in and turned automatically to shut the door. Unable even to do this, he wandered in a daze to the fridge and got himself an orange squash. He was sitting on the sofa sucking the glass when he heard Mum's feet in the corridor. A very loud swear-word echoed off the bare plaster walls.

'Ben! Are you okay? Ben!'

'Mum.' He stood up as she ran into the lounge.

'What did –' Mum was silent for about thirty seconds, her lips pressed white. Then she exploded like Vesuvius.

'How dare you? How dare you? Who do you think you are? Who? *Who?*'

She went on in this fashion until Ben heard himself stammering, 'I'm sorry, Mum.'

Her eyes nailed him. 'What? Sorry? Why are *you* apologising? Why are *you* saying sorry?'

Ben didn't know. He shook his head. Tears were fighting to get out and it was taking all his strength to stop them. Mum balled her fists and glared at the splintered door.

'Stanford. Damn Stanford!' She used a string of words Ben never even thought she knew. 'I can smell him all over this. It stinks of him!'

She dealt the ruined door a kick.

'Mum.' Ben looked at his hands. He was *wringing* them. Up till now he'd only ever done that to his swimming things. 'Mum, sit down. I'll put the kettle on.'

'That's it. That really is it. I'm calling the police. He's had it now. They'll pin it on him even if he was fifty miles away.'

Ben filled the kettle, all he could do, while she paced the lounge like a caged animal. He noticed that, although she was shaking the telephone as if it were a weapon, she was not dialling. He poured hot water onto the teabags and heard the phone slam down. Then the bathroom door slamming shut. Then the sound of Mum crying while trying to make no sound at all.

She was not going to call the police. Because, of course, they had just found out what happened when you did.

Ben could barely recall the lost golden age (really just a couple of months ago) when Stanford had been merely a word on a letter, and not a name to place alongside Hitler and Satan. That first letter had gone into the bin since it obviously didn't apply to them. *Dear valued tenant*, blah blah. *We regret to inform you that the tenancy period of your flat is due to expire subject to Clause 18c of your agreement. We must therefore request that you terminate your occupancy by 30th August* and so on. With these jaw-breaking phrases it seemed to be saying that the tenants in the block had to move out. But Mum wasn't a tenant. She and Dad had bought this flat from the landlord, Stanford and Associates, four years previously. So that was all right.

Ben forgot about it until another letter hit the mat one frosty Saturday morning. It was from Stanford and Associates. It offered to buy the flat back for a certain price. Mum spluttered into her grapefruit juice.

'Are they mad? We *paid* thirty thousand more than

that!' She laughed as if it were a joke and tore the letter up, then ranted about it morning and night until Ben learned to tune out. He had other things, like his homework, his sadistic French teacher and the brand-new pinball machine at the arcade to worry about. A short while later Mum got a phone call Ben didn't hear, except for her very loud 'No thank you!' at the end.

Then the aggro started. Someone's burglar alarm went off all weekend, driving them bananas. Mum finally went looking for it, found it belonged to the nearby derelict factory and used the bread-knife to cut its cable. Some days later, piles of rubbish began collecting in their tiny garden. Eventually Ben spotted a bunch of teenage boys dumping bin-bags over their wall and peeing on the flowerbed. He fetched his camera and they scarpered.

One evening Ben took a phone message from a Mr John Stanford. He wanted to stop by and 'discuss the sale'. Somehow he booked himself in for the Friday. Mum flipped at first but decided, in the end, that if this guy had trouble hearing the word 'No' then he could come round and read her lips.

John Stanford was tall with sandy blond hair. He wore a smart suit. His smile was bright, revealing hidden wrinkles in his young-seeming face. Following him into the flat came a tree-trunk of a man ('This is Toby,') not at all suited to his name. Stanford laughed and joked about the weather and shook Ben's hand. He asked Mum if she wanted a cup of tea. Taken by surprise, Mum said yes. Stanford sent Toby into the kitchen. Mum looked on, flummoxed, as this huge stranger made tea in her kitchen with her cups. He didn't know where anything was, either, so there was much banging of cupboards. When she said, 'I'll do it,' Stanford seemed not to hear.

'What about you?' he said to Ben. 'Lemonade?'

Ben had his bearings by now. He said, 'No, thanks.'

Toby brought the tea and a plate of biscuits, which he placed near Stanford. Mum grimaced as she sipped hers. It clearly had sugar in it.

John Stanford settled down to business. He said he would increase his initial offer on the flat. Mum reacted as if he'd spat at her. Stanford lit a cigar, ignoring her grunt of distaste.

'Mrs Gallagher.' He spoke in a clipped, polished way. 'This property isn't nearly so desirable as you think. Not with kids running amuck and leaving litter everywhere.'

Toby slurped his tea in the silence. Stanford allowed smoke to curl up around him.

'Tell you what. I'll give you till midnight on Monday. You can call my mobile. After that, my offer drops by a thousand every day I don't hear from you. So think about it, Mrs Gallagher.' Mum's face had no colour in it. Stanford's wrinkled with another smile. 'At least do it for your son.'

'Leave him out of it!'

'It wasn't I who brought him into it. All I'm saying is that this area is growing less and less like somewhere I'd want to raise my own children. And the longer we wait, the less desirable it's going to be.'

He laid his still-burning cigar upon a cushion, one that Mum had embroidered herself. When he picked it up, a black crater gaped in the fabric.

Mum told him to leave. Stanford finished his tea and biscuits and nodded to Toby. The men breezed out as smoothly as they had arrived. Mum burst with a shriek of rage. That was when they'd called the police, who did precisely zilch, as far as Ben could make out. And now they had no front door.

'Look out, Ben!'

He'd already seen the danger. He hammered at the button and the flipper winged the steel ball before it could plummet into oblivion.

'Yay, Gallagher!'

He cradled the ball in the right flipper, let it roll and flicked it at a deflector. It rebounded into a multiplier zone and buzzed around like a trapped hornet. His score piled up. He kept a weather-eye on it. Not too much. Not today.

Ben's reputation as a pinball wizard had spread like head lice around his school, and beyond. The new craze for the old-fashioned machines meant contests were a regular thing. Ben's advantage, aside from quick reflexes and an unusual ability to watch the ball no matter how fast it ricocheted around, was that his father was obsessed with the game and had even built a pinball table from scratch, which he kept at his own flat.

'Come on, Ben,' Alistair urged. 'Make us rich. You're destroying that sucker.'

Other friends chipped in with cheers of encouragement. Glancing to his left (and a fair way up) he caught Cannon's eye. Cannon – real name William Canning, nickname a no-brainer – gave him a warning wink. Ben carefully sent the ball into a low-scoring area.

Normally he wouldn't dream of doing this. He hated the idea of letting everyone down. Many bets got placed on these games and most people here had a couple of quid on him winning, as usual. But Cannon had offered him twenty pounds to throw the match. ('You've got to make it look real,' the huge boy insisted. 'I want you to *almost* win.' *And I want a titanium front door and a Kalashnikov*, Ben had thought at the time, *but it ain't gonna happen*.) However, Cannon had been, well, *insistent*, so Ben reluctantly decided he could stay in one piece and give Mum the money towards the new door – he planned to slip it into her purse so she wouldn't know it came from him.

'Hit the reactor again. The reactor!' Rajesh gibbered, jumping up and down.

Ben fired the ball at it and missed, deliberately. He thought how dumbfounded everyone would be when he lost on his favourite table. It was called Fort Osiris and the setting was secret agents storming an enemy's lair. How this scenario related to the abstract way the ball spasmed around the board, he couldn't guess – but the concept appealed to him.

Groans swept the arcade as he let himself drop the ball. He had one more shot left.

A droplet fell from his nose and splashed a red star on the bathroom's decorated tiles. Just then Mum rustled in through the cardboard barrier they'd rigged up as a substitute door. He knelt, dabbing up the blood with a tissue. Mum wouldn't want her mosaic of a giant seashell stained – she'd slaved over that every evening for two weeks.

'Sweetie! What happened to you?'

'Football accident.' He sniffed, trying not to bleed in front of her. 'I bumped into the goalie.'

'Are you sure?' Mum peered at him. The bruises on his face were already darkening. 'Have you been playing with those yobs from school?'

'We don't *play* . . . we hang out.'

'You're lucky your teeth aren't hanging out. I can't afford dentists as well as carpenters, you know.' Mum tutted, then hugged him. 'At least you're brave about it.'

Later, tucking into his fish fingers, he felt her eyes on him again.

'Ben. This isn't about . . . You aren't doing that pinball nonsense still?'

'Of course not.' Ben drank quickly from his water glass. What an idiot he'd been. As his last ball rolled harmlessly towards the gully, a reflex had taken over and sent it hurtling back up the board. His safety margin vanished in a barrage of lights and he had beaten his opponent's score by a measly 200 points. And then, outside the arcade, Cannon had beaten him up.

Mum picked at her Marmite on toast, about the only meal he saw her eating these days. She looked tired and hollow-cheeked as she continued to give him suspicious glances.

'I won't have you doing it, do you hear?'

'Mum! I stopped ages ago.'

'Good. So how are you spending your free time now?'

Ben tried to think. If you took out school and the arcade, his mind was a blank.

'I've got the computer. I like time by myself.'

'You need to get out more. And I don't mean with

those bus-stop kids. The leisure centre's just down the road.'

'We do enough swimming at school.'

'Do something else then. The man who takes my self-defence course is starting tae kwon do classes for kids. Why not try that? It'd be a great way to meet new friends.'

Ah. Now he recognised the signs. She'd been looking for a chance to suggest this.

'I don't need to learn self-defence.' He winced as a bit of ketchup stung his cut lip.

'Ben, I'm not nagging,' said Mum. 'I worry, that's all. This time it was the front door. Next time . . .'

'Oh yeah. Like a kid with a bit of kung fu could duff up Stanford's heavies.'

'Not exactly.' Mum held his gaze. 'I don't mean a big thug like the one who came here. Stanford would be sneakier than that. He bribed those yobs to dump litter in our garden. That mightn't be all they're prepared to do.'

'Mum!' She was scaring him now. 'Okay. I might check the class out. If you want.'

'Only if you want.' She touched his hand across the table. 'We'll be all right, Ben. No one's going to force us into anything. This is our home.'

It hurt to smile.

2
Anything but Ballet

The highlight of the dog's morning had been nosing inside a bin, so when the cat appeared it was like winning the Lottery. A mongrel, part Alsatian, part hearth rug, it hurtled along the gutter two strides behind a ginger streak. The cat leaped onto the bonnet of a blue Volkswagen, its fur standing in spikes as if frozen by an icy wind.

The dog barked in triumph, making experimental jumps at the car. The cat retreated up the windscreen, hissing and arching like electricity. Half-crazed with joy, the dog got its front paws on the bumper.

It recoiled as if stung by a spark. The cat had flashed across the bonnet and clawed its nose. More horrified than hurt, the dog ran in circles, yelping. The door of the nearest house opened and a lanky, brown-haired girl ran out.

'Oi! Pack it in, fleabags!'

Sensing that the fun was over, the dog slunk away.

'Ssshh, Rufus. It's gone.' Tiffany Maine scooped the cat off the car. Rufus changed from feline fury to fluff-bundle, squinting with pleasure as he let himself be carried baby-style into the house. He gave Tiffany's hand a sandpapery lick.

Cats didn't, of course, do this. Cats didn't care for people the way dogs did. Cats were selfish and cold, neither giving love nor welcoming it. What rubbish. Tiffany got cross when she heard people saying that. If any dog was more friendly, more needy, or more doting on humans than her cat Rufus, she had never met one. But still people refused to see it, purely because they didn't expect to.

'Tiffany! Do shift yourself. We'll be late.' Her mother was calling up the stairs, not noticing Tiffany right behind her, getting a free hair-styling from Rufus's tongue. 'Oh, you're there. Shoes on? Where's your coat?'

'It's the first day of spring.'

Her mother tutted. 'The year has no business going by so fast. Peter!'

'Hang on. We're about to break a world record here. Five, six . . . aha!' Tiffany's father hurried downstairs, both hands bristling with mugs. 'Tiffany, unless the dwarves are visiting I think *seven* cups in your room is excessive.' He vanished into the kitchen.

'Come *on*, Peter.'

'Cathy, the hospital won't fly away if we're five minutes late.'

'But he'll be waiting.'

Dad swept into the hall with a jingle of car keys. 'It's a good job then that *I* was ready half an hour ago. Tiffany, put the creature down, he's not coming.'

The hospital's logo was the face of a crying child forever on the point of cheering up but, Tiffany noticed, never quite managing it. In spite of this the place felt less like a hospital than a huge playhouse. A helter-skelter stood where the receptionist should have been and a shiny red bus looked as if it had wandered in off the street. Only the unnaturally clean smell made her uneasy.

They still knew the way to Lion ward blindfold, even though Stuart had been living mostly at home these past months. He had enjoyed learning to use his electric wheelchair, pretending to be a comic-book super-villain, and Tiffany had been glad to help out in her own way. Not many big sisters were actively encouraged to thump their little brother repeatedly on the back every day.

Tiffany had once had tonsillitis for a whole fortnight

and had feared she would never get better. But Stuart had been ill for two years. Shortly after he turned six he had begun to fall down a lot in the playground. He complained all the time that he was tired and kept getting terrible coughs. Soon he was walking strangely; then he had trouble walking at all. Tiffany had watched at first with pity, then impatience, then horror when she realised this was no silly phase. Looking back, she believed Mum and Dad had always known far more than they had told her. She'd had to work out for herself what was happening to her brother.

Tiffany reached his room first, creeping her hand round the door. She heard Stuart's cry of delight above the burble of Sunday morning television. He was sitting up in bed, pale but grinning, waving a deck of cards.

'Best of three!' he demanded, by way of saying hello. The pack was Superhero Top Trumps, an old favourite. Tiffany settled on the bedside beanbag and shuffled the cards. Stuart sighed. Probably, he had spent all morning arranging them.

'What have we here?' Dad came in with Mum. Their smiles were like floodlights: bright and not quite realistic. 'No tubes, no machines? Have we got the right room?'

'Yeah.' Stuart grinned. He looked unbearably pleased to see them. After hugging each in turn he lay back on his pillows, as if the effort had exhausted him. He seemed weaker than usual, Tiffany thought. And a lot pudgier than he used to be. The doctors had said that the medicines they gave him might do that. Still, he perked up when he saw the packet Dad was tearing open.

'Tortilla chips! Gimme, gimme.'

'These'll have you back on your feet.' Dad tossed the packet over and Stuart scrabbled for the ones that fell out. With some kids it was chocolate or crisps, with others it was the kind of toffees that tear out fillings. With Stuart it was spicy tortillas.

Tiffany munched one. 'Hey. These are pretty good.'

'They're – mmmm – magic!'

'What did you expect?' Dad put on an affronted face. 'Your mother only buys from the Tesco *Finest* range, the Sainsbury's *Taste the Difference* range or the Waitrose *Look on My Works, Ye Mighty, and Despair* range.'

'How are you feeling, sweetie?' Mum's smile hadn't lasted.

'They gave me the buzzy vest yesterday,' said Stuart. 'That's pretty cool. It beats you lot thumping me on the back.'

The buzzy vest was a device that vibrated Stuart's chest to help clear out all the gunk, because he couldn't take deep breaths or even cough properly by himself.

'You should come and listen,' said Stuart. 'When I sing with it on I sound like a robot.'

Mum looked worried, as if she had missed something important. 'They make you *sing*?'

'No, silly, I just do.' Stuart laughed, then half-coughed for about a minute and went white. When he had recovered, he and Tiffany played Top Trumps. As usual, she tried to lose. Stuart found this tiring too. Holding the cards, he had once said, was like lifting bricks. Mum and Dad chatted to him, reeling off lots of news that even Tiffany found boring. Soon they began to run out of things to say. Kids, she could have told them, didn't do small talk.

'You'll be home in a jiffy,' said Dad. 'I spoke to Dr Bijlani and he said he's never seen anyone with M.D. shake off an infection so fast.'

'Peter,' Mum whispered, not so softly that they didn't all hear.

'So when we leave here on Tuesday, you might just be coming with us.'

'Brilliant!'

Mum cleared her throat. 'What Sanjeev actually said was . . .'

'Cathy, just because he's a doctor doesn't mean he's the expert.'

Even the crunch of chips briefly stopped.

'I think you'll find it does,' said Mum.

'What I *mean* is,' said Dad, somehow raising his voice and speaking more quietly at the same time, 'they don't know everything. They always cover themselves. It's like being optimistic is against the law.'

'But there's no point in — never mind.' Mum clamped her mouth shut as if she had more to say, but not here.

Tiffany caught Stuart's eye. The joy that had sparkled there when they arrived was fading. He had turned away from his parents to gaze at the ceiling, cool blue and painted with clouds.

'Physical strength eighty,' he murmured. 'The Mighty Thor.'

'Thirty-two. You win.' Tiffany gave him her card.

She blanked out the car ride home. It was like a film she had seen too many times. Mum's lines went something like, 'You always make it worse by getting his hopes up,' and Dad's character always said, 'But people get well faster if they believe they will.' Tiffany was the silent extra no one ever noticed.

She found proper solitude in her room. It didn't last.

'Tiffany,' Mum called, 'your kitty is curled up on your clean laundry. Sort it, please.'

Cat and clothes were piled on a kitchen chair. The prophet Muhammad, she knew, had once cut off part of his cloak rather than disturb a sleeping cat. Resigning herself to a less blessed life, she nudged Rufus aside and took the slightly hairy laundry upstairs. Her mood sank lower when she saw her black ballet leotard. Thursday was coming round again. She couldn't fake a sore toe for the third week in a row. It had taken only a few lessons to unmask ballet as evil. Once she had loved watching ballerinas flit around on television. Now she hated it the way chickens must hate watching eagles. She was too tall, she was too clumsy; her pirouette resembled an out-of-control shopping trolley.

And then she remembered something worse. She had PE tomorrow.

'Mummy. I think I've got a cold coming,' she sniffed. Mum was preparing dinner.

'Oh, shame. Do you think you'll be well enough for school?'

''Spect so.' Tiffany nodded bravely. 'I don't think I should do gym though. Can you write me a note?'

'I don't hear you sneezing.' Dad had materialised in the doorway.

'It's just a tickle in my throat right now.'

'A tickle. But it'll be worse tomorrow?'

'Yes.'

'I see.'

Mum already had pen and paper in hand. 'Who's it to? Mrs Farmer?'

'Miss Fuller.'

'So, let me get this clear.' Dad stroked his chin. 'Your little brother is fighting muscular dystrophy on one side and pneumonia on the other, while you are laid low by a sniffle that isn't even detectable to the outside world . . . oh, fine, fine, whatever.' He retreated before Mum's stare into the safety of the lounge. Mum scribbled the note defiantly and handed it over.

'Best play it safe,' she said. 'After all, you don't want to have to miss ballet again.'

Ugh. It was like rolling a boulder uphill. 'Don't I?'

'You *love* ballet!' Mum tweaked her nose.

Tiffany flinched. 'I don't. It's embarrassing. And I wish you wouldn't do that.'

'What's got into you?'

'It's just horrible. My joints don't even bend right.'

Dad's low whistle drifted in from the lounge. 'Funny how these discoveries always come to light *after* the money's been spent.'

'Well.' Mum mixed gravy in a jug. 'You should go. Thursdays are Mummy and Daddy time, remember.'

'Mother! I'm not a baby.'

'Sorry, sweetheart. It's not that we want to get rid of you. But we do have a lot on our plate. If we know you're having fun doing something of your own, we can catch our breath once a week. Do you see?'

'You want to get rid of me.'

Something boiled over on the stove. Mum rushed to it, blowing and mopping.

'It's just a Thursday thing, Tiffany,' she sighed through the steam. 'Is it so much to ask?'

Tiffany stalked out of the kitchen. 'I am *not* doing ballet.'

The local paper crumpled beneath her on the bed. She scoured the Classified columns in rising despair. A watercolour painting club? She might fancy trying that, but none of them met on a Thursday. Girl Guides? Get lost. Junior Fitness Club? PE by another name. And kickboxing was right out. Her annoyance gave way to misery. She was too much of a weed even to give her parents one evening alone. Maybe she could develop an illness herself and get packed off to hospital. No. That was a horrible thing to think.

She turned the page. Hmm, tae kwon do . . . was that the paper-folding one? She wouldn't risk it. Tiffany kicked her pillow in frustration.

A ginger missile launched from the top of the wardrobe and splashed down on the duvet by her head. Rufus looked peeved at being granted such a soft landing. Startled only for a second, Tiffany hugged him to her. Here was a real gymnast, martial artist, ballet dancer, you name it. He could have done any class he liked (well, maybe not the painting club). Sad, she gazed into his amber eyes. It seemed that the only talent she had was loving her cat.

She glanced down at the newspaper. There was a tiny advert in the corner that she hadn't noticed before. It was shaped like a pyramid.

Cat Kin

Explore your feline spirit
Cat lovers and the curious all welcome

That sounded more like it! Not a stupid PE lesson. A proper club. People like her talking about their pets, sharing tips, swapping pictures maybe. She did wonder why the meeting place was Clissold Leisure Centre, but only for a moment. It was probably just a good place to hire a room.

Rufus was testing his claws on the newspaper. She tore out the ad before he could.

3

The Grey Cat

Echoes from the squash courts perforated the dry, processed air. Sports centres made Ben nervous. No doubt the smell of chlorine awoke memories of clutching the poolside as a toddler. Now, crossing the lobby, he was even more anxious than usual. He couldn't help thinking about what might be happening at home.

It was a stupid thought. It was not as if he could offer Mum the slightest protection if Stanford should appear again in a cloud of brimstone. She might cope better if he wasn't there. At least they had a door now. It was light, flimsy wood, unpainted; easy to break, cheap to replace.

The muscle-bound man at reception noticed him, the way a bull in a field might. Ben found himself whispering.

'Tae kwon do?'

The man tilted his shaven head, possibly meaning *Go that way,* more likely trying to ease cramp. Ben bruised his hip hurrying through the turnstile.

While he changed into tracksuit trousers and T-shirt he wondered again why he was here. Perhaps Mum thought it would take his mind off things. It was true that she always came home cheerful from her own self-defence class. But given the choice he would be at Dad's flat, taking on the master himself on his home-made pinball machine, ignoring the furious neighbours who banged on the ceiling.

He wished Mum would swallow her pride and give Dad a call. Raymond Gallagher would tell Stanford where to go. Yet she had made Ben swear not to mention their problems to Dad. It was a tough promise. Dad always asked Ben questions. He wanted to know how Mum was getting along, if she needed anything, did she seem happy in her new job at the organics shop. If pressed for details, Ben would have to grit his teeth and say 'Fine,' over and over.

He left the changing area and climbed the stairs to the upper level. A girl with wavy brown hair was lingering by one of the small halls. She wasn't dressed for sports and looked awkward in her jeans and black coat. It was the only free hall so Ben decided to wait there too, leaning on the other side of the doorway.

The girl kept glancing down at Ben's trainers. He was wondering if he should say hello when the texture of the air changed. He turned.

A grey-haired woman stood there, dressed as if for yoga. He hadn't heard so much as a footstep and yet there she was. No taller than him, with neat features and eyes between brown and green, she might have been seventy or younger than fifty – her wiry build made it impossible to guess.

'Are you here for the class?'

'Yes,' said Ben and the girl together.

'How do you do. I'm Felicity Powell.'

She seemed to be waiting for something. Finally it clicked.

'I'm Ben.'

'Tiffany,' said the girl, breathlessly. 'Erm, is this –?'

'Hmm.' The woman looked them up and down. 'I was expecting a few more. We'll wait.'

She padded off down the corridor. Ben blinked and she was gone.

Minutes passed. Just as he was thinking he had made a mistake (what mistake, he wasn't sure), the woman reappeared with several kids shuffling ahead of her. None wore martial arts gear and only two looked dressed for sports. A couple of them exchanged hesitant glances as if they already knew each other, if not to talk to. A girl in a blue gym suit had a newspaper tucked under one arm, and one boy, round-faced and wearing an anorak, was carrying a flat case like an artist's portfolio. By the time they reached the hall he looked deeply confused.

'Welcome to my class. My name is Felicity. You can call me Mrs Powell.' The woman did not smile. The group edged closer together.

'There's been a mix-up,' said Mrs Powell. 'This hall has been double-booked. We're going to move elsewhere.'

Without another word she led them down to the lobby. Feeling something wasn't right, Ben glanced back up at the balcony. A line of youths clad in white tunics were filing into the free hall. It was the tae kwon do class.

Before he could blurt out that he had joined the wrong group, he was stepping through the glass doors into the evening light. Why had they come outside? The girl in the black coat trotted to keep up with Mrs Powell.

'Excuse me. Where are we going?'

'To my studio, Tiffany. I live just here.'

Ben was sure he'd misheard. Not Theobald Mansions? Uh-oh, she was. She was heading for the flats that lurked next to the leisure centre. These blocks were long overdue for the wrecking-ball. Brown as old blood, broken-windowed, painted with pigeon muck; the idea that they might harbour life would be beyond the wildest dreams of NASA's scientists.

Mrs Powell unlocked the main door and went in. Ben followed the girl into a hall webbed with graffiti. He climbed a staircase that reeked of cigarettes and urine. The others were drawn along behind him, their footsteps resounding off the walls.

Where was Mrs Powell taking them? Who *was* she? And why in the name of sanity were they still following her? Fear rose in Ben's throat. This was not normal. Not normal at all. He tried to relax. One old lady had to be fairly harmless. Whoever she was, she couldn't abduct seven kids. Not alone.

It was only when Mrs Powell had opened the door to the top-floor flat and was ushering them inside, and Ben was actually *stepping* inside, into this stranger's home, that the thought struck him like a thunderbolt: maybe she *wasn't* alone.

Even as he woke up to what he'd done, he heard the door lock behind them.

Cobwebs, queasy smells, the mouldering skeletons of small animals underfoot – these were just some of the things he expected to find and did not. Fright gave way to surprise. Mrs Powell's flat was bright and spacious and spotlessly clean. She led them into a room that could have swallowed the lounge at home twice over.

It was one big wooden floor with not a carpet, chair or speck of dust to be seen.

'This is my studio. Find a space and sit down.'

Something about her voice made obedience automatic. Ben sat cross-legged.

'Not like that. Kneel. Sit on your heels. That's it. Hands on the floor in front of you. Don't slouch. Good. From now on, this is what *sit* means.'

Mrs Powell sat likewise. She surveyed them, moving her head, not her eyes.

'You may be wondering – ah. Jim has decided to join us. You are honoured.'

A cat trotted into the room, bead curtains rustling in its wake. It had the sort of coat rich women used to kill for: lush, smoky grey, dappled black in a leopardish pattern. It clocked the group with one crystalline glance before settling near Tiffany like one of the group. That was when Ben realised. The strange way they were kneeling was just how the grey cat sat.

The round-faced boy scrambled to his feet.

'Sorry, Miss. I think I'm in the wrong class –'

'Sit down.'

The boy folded up again.

'Do you know what I teach here?' the lady asked.

In the hush Ben could hear buses rumbling down the main road. Tiffany raised a hand.

'Mrs Powell . . .'

'Yes?'

'It's to do with cats, isn't it?'

'It is to do with cats.'

Tiffany beamed and went on staring at the grey cat, her eyes wide and shining as if the animal were made of solid gold and not hair. The oriental girl in the blue gym suit raised her rolled-up newspaper to get attention.

'That's not what I heard,' she said. 'I thought it was a kind of t'ai chi.'

That opened the floodgates. Soon everyone was talking, firing off questions as fast as Mrs Powell could ask their names. A girl called Cecile thought Cat Kin was a London nature trail. A tall boy, Yusuf, who spoke like an American, said he was after the Big Cats Conservation League. Nobody could agree. Daniel, a small black kid in glasses whom Ben vaguely recognised from school, had been sure he was joining a dance group. And Olly, the boy who'd tried to leave, had for some unfathomable reason believed he was going to an art class to draw animals. Why he had thought it would take place at Clissold Leisure Centre, Ben never discovered.

'You appear confused.' Mrs Powell's voice brought instant hush. 'And yet all of you are right. What you will learn at Cat Kin is somewhat akin to dance. It isn't unlike t'ai chi. And it will bring you closer to nature. Even Oliver here isn't totally off the mark: we will be copying an animal. What we shall do together is *pashki*.'

Mrs Powell stood up in a single fluid movement.

'Pashki. One of the most ancient disciplines of body and soul. For more than –'

'I've never heard of it,' put in Susie, the oriental girl.

'You are about to,' said Mrs Powell softly. Ben got the feeling that only a very foolish person would interrupt her again. 'You all know what yoga is? Perhaps you have heard that many movements in yoga are inspired by the animal kingdom. In particular, cats. You've seen how cats stretch and flex themselves – ah, speak of the devil.'

Her cat was reaching out his long, wicked claws, shivering in ecstasy.

'Cats do this to maintain their physique. Unlike humans, cats don't need to go to the gym. You might say that Jim is his own gym.' She didn't smile. A few in the group laughed nervously.

'Long ago in Egypt,' said Mrs Powell, 'people worshipped the cat. They called it Mau – for obvious reasons. The goddess was named, variously, Bast, Pakhet, or Pasht.'

'Excuse me.' It seemed Tiffany couldn't help herself. 'That's where we get the word "puss" from, isn't it?'

Ben tensed, but this time the interruption was welcome.

'Yes! Look, Jim, we have a cat scholar among us.'

The grey cat actually turned his head towards Tiffany and his tail flicked. Ben squirmed involuntarily. That animal gave him the creeps. And all this kneeling was making the arches of his feet hurt like crazy.

Mrs Powell began explaining how the high priests of Pasht developed pashki as a form of worship and exercise. Ben found it hard to pay attention. He'd never had a pet of his own, but he liked taking his aunt's Labrador for walks down in the West Country. Cats, on the other hand, left him cold. Worse than cold.

And now Mrs Powell was bringing Jim round to each of them in turn.

'You see his forehead,' she said. 'Ordinary tabbies have these markings too. The patterns make a clear M shape. M for Mau. After more than four thousand years, the original cat is still among us.'

Hands reached up to caress the fur. Mrs Powell stopped by Ben.

'You can stroke him,' she said. 'He won't scratch.'

Ben shook his head.

'What's the matter?'

'I don't stroke cats,' Ben said, hoping no one else would hear. 'They always give me electric shocks.'

It was true. His friend Rajesh's moggy only had to brush his bare arm for him to feel the crack of a tiny whip of fire.

Mrs Powell peered at him for a few seconds.

'Yes,' she said, 'they can do that occasionally. Poor you.'

Ben made a non-committal sound.

'You don't like cats?' said Mrs Powell.

'Not really.'

'Why is that?'

Ben shifted in discomfort.

'I don't like the way they stare,' he replied, knowing as he said it that Tiffany was staring at him. 'They always seem really . . . I don't know, selfish. Chilly. They're not like dogs, are they?'

'In what way do you mean?'

'Dogs, well. You look after them and they love you back.' He was beginning to sweat. 'Cats don't care. They can't help it, it's how they're made. I'm just not a cat person.'

This evening was light-years away from what he'd had in mind. He yearned for the simple violence of tae kwon do. Mrs Powell was silent a moment.

'That's fine,' she said. 'So you hate cats. I've known many cats who hate cats. Take the tiger. He won't let another within three miles of him. Unless love is in the air.'

She set the cat down and it trotted back to its place by Tiffany. Ben could feel Tiffany's look turn hostile, as if she'd been personally offended by his words. Mrs Powell settled into her sitting-cat pose.

'Yoga,' she said, 'is about becoming one with yourself. Pashki awakens the part of yourself that is like a cat. For cats have much to teach us. They are proud spirits yet calm. They live in the present, without worries beyond it. Cats are pools of serenity that may surge up in storms. They are weightless clouds that can quicken to lightning.'

The grey cat chose that moment to yawn and wander back to the bead curtain.

'Jim? Leaving us already?'

Jim ignored her completely and disappeared into the room beyond. A smile stole over Mrs Powell's face. She began to recite:

I heed no words nor walls
Through darkness I walk in day
And I do not fear the tyrant.

'The words of Akhotep,' she said. 'A poet of ancient Egypt. What he observed then still fascinates us today.'

Ben's legs were really killing him. He would have moved but he didn't want to attract any more attention. Several others appeared equally uncomfortable, especially Tiffany. She looked desperate to get up, her face struggling to hide the agony her knees must be feeling. He bet himself that she cracked before he did.

Mrs Powell told them to stand. She demonstrated a couple of stretches, like the ones her cat had performed. They made Ben's hamstrings twang, but helped to shift the ache in his legs. After that the lesson appeared to be over. Mrs Powell went from person to person, collecting money. Ben handed over the five-pound note he had saved, thinking of the fish and chips he might have bought.

He hurried out, leaving Mrs Powell chatting with Tiffany. They already seemed thick as thieves, those two. Cats were evidently like football: some people were just obsessed. Not that he'd ever use a cat as a football, he wouldn't go that far. He was merely glad his first and last pashki lesson was over.

On the stairs he heard Mrs Powell call after him.

'See you next Thursday, Ben.'

'Uh-huh.' And he whispered to himself, 'Not if I see you first.'

He had reached the scuzzy hallway when her voice floated down:

'You won't.'

He was so unnerved that he almost forgot to pick up his stuff from the leisure centre.

'Oh the shark has, *tam ta-daa*, pretty teeth, dear . . .'

Ben walked more slowly as he drew near home. Someone was singing.

'And he shows them, *ta ta-daa*, pearly white . . .'

Suddenly wary, Ben stepped behind a parked yellow van and shaded his eyes. The evening sun was flaring off the shop windows in Albion Road.

A figure in a pale suit strolled into view. He could only have come from Defoe Court. Where the flat was. A passing lorry blocked the sun glare and he saw the man clearly. It was John Stanford. By a silver car parked on the pavement he fumbled for keys.

Ben's heart was sticking in his throat like a chunk of gristle. Stanford had come while he was out. He cursed himself. He should have stayed at home – stood behind the door with his cricket bat. If anything had happened to Mum . . .

'On the sidewalk, oh yeah, Sun-day morn-ing . . .' Stanford clicked his fingers, opening the car boot to put a carrier bag inside. 'Lies a body, oozing life . . .'

He got behind the wheel. The engine gunned and music sprang from powerful speakers inside. A big band sound.

When the shark bites . . . with his teeth, dear . . .

The song grew fainter. The instant Stanford's car accelerated round the corner, Ben dashed down Defoe Court and into his block. He beat on the flat's unpainted door.

'Mum!'

She opened it, startled.

'What's wrong?'

'Are you all right? What did he do?'

'Who? What did who do?'

'Mr Stanford. He was here!'

'No, he wasn't.'

'Outside! I saw him.'

Getting his breath back, Ben explained. Mum sat down, sucking thoughtfully on a chocolate wrapper. When he told her about Stanford's singing, Mum gave a bitter smirk.

'I never figured him for a Frank Sinatra fan. Likes to do things his way, I suppose. Well, I don't know why he was snooping around, but he didn't come in here.'

'Maybe he was hassling someone else.'

Mum shook her head. 'All the neighbours have gone. Haven't you noticed how quiet it is now? We're the only ones left in these flats.' She touched the tiny scar at the corner of her eye, something she always did when she was sad. She'd cut herself late one night, four years ago, walking into a door when coming home in the dark.

'We could leave, too,' Ben burst out. He was sure he'd had a bright new idea. 'Sell the place properly to someone else and get away!'

'Berk.' Mum poked him, not unkindly. 'Who's this

mystery buyer with piles of cash and half a brain cell? You couldn't give this flat away. And we can't rent anywhere, and we can't buy another flat on what Stanford would pay us. We have no choice except –' she gripped his hand, '– be brave.'

That night, Ben lay awake in the streetlamp-stained darkness. The words of Mr Stanford's song writhed like maggots in his head. For a second, hiding behind the van, he had been sure they referred to his mum. The horror of that thought was still with him. Every passing car was the silver saloon. Every creak was Stanford's footstep in the hall.

He had long since despaired of sleep when his restless mind washed up some other words. He could not immediately remember where they had come from, but they brought a strange, lonely kind of comfort.

I heed no words nor walls
Through darkness I walk in day
And I do not fear the tyrant.

He slept.

4
Only Nature's Own

'I want you to imagine,' said Mrs Powell, 'that you are balancing on top of a thin wooden post. The post is no wider than your wrist and is as high as you are tall. If you wobble, it will sway and tip you to the ground.'

Tiffany sneaked one eye open. Her fellow pupils stood, like her, on tiptoe, one foot overlapping the other. Cecile was already tottering. Tiffany shut the eye quickly as Mrs Powell glided past her.

'Now you see a second post, just as tall, just as thin, one stride ahead of you. Beyond that is another post and beyond that, another. See that row of tall posts in your mind. You are standing on the first.'

Tiffany heard a sharp breath as someone almost overbalanced. It was getting harder to believe in the sturdy wooden floor underfoot.

'When I say,' Mrs Powell went on, 'take a single

step forward onto the next post. You *must* tread precisely on the top. Anything else will make the post bend and you will fall.' She paused for two of Tiffany's heartbeats. 'Step now.'

Tiffany placed her right foot blindly ahead of her and brought her left foot to join it. She was steady. She could feel the imaginary stake beneath her, trembling but upright. Slowly she breathed out. There was a thump as somebody fell. It was followed by another.

'Ugh.' Olly picked himself up. 'Have I only got eight lives left now?'

'It's really hard!' whined Cecile.

'Back on your post. Start again. Eyes *shut* please.'

Although Mrs Powell snapped at them like a games teacher, Tiffany didn't mind. She couldn't remember enjoying a physical activity so much. She was also adding to her (rather small) circle of friends. Once she'd found the confidence to introduce herself properly, she'd recognised several of the class from her year at school, although none of them had lessons with her. Susie seemed nice and chatty, and Olly promised to be a laugh. Tiffany had proudly told her parents that she'd found a suitable Thursday-night amusement, and that her expensive, neglected ballet leotard would finally get some use.

Not that pashki seemed anything like as energetic as ballet. Their lesson last week had been almost totally still. Mrs Powell had taught them cat meditation. One technique, Pur, involved crouching like a Sphinx and trying to make a strange rumble in your throat. Deep meditation, or Omu, meant curling up with your legs just so. This had caused amusement at first, but in a room with Mrs Powell no one laughed for long.

Arriving at that second lesson, Tiffany had been surprised to find Ben the cat-hater still among them. No, that was unfair. He must be open-minded or he wouldn't have come at all. She wondered what had happened to change his attitude. This week she'd even tried saying hello to him. All she got back was a grunt. Still, he had seemed pretty wrapped up in his thoughts.

Today's challenge was Eth, or cat walking. There were, Mrs Powell said, nine rudiments of pashki that every novice had to learn. Eth was the third.

'When you have mastered one step,' said Mrs Powell, 'take another. You should be able to walk from post to post without swaying. Don't hurry. It takes time to come.'

To an outsider, it would look as if they were merely walking along the floor. Yet people were finding it incredibly difficult. Olly had fallen three times and Yusuf had to keep windmilling his long arms to stay upright. And he kept catching Susie's eye, making her grin stupidly until both of them were giggling.

'Eight out of ten for effort, Suze,' said Yusuf, his

American accent even stronger than usual. 'But one out of ten for impressing the boys, you know?'

Daniel was compact and obviously pretty agile, yet even he was getting frustrated. Tiffany couldn't believe it. *I'm the only one doing it well*, she thought.

Or had she thought too soon? To her surprise (and slight irritation) she saw Ben taking one step, another, then a third, lowering each toe with the precision of – well, a cat. His closed eyes, under their strong, dark brows, were a picture of serenity, spoiled only when he walked smack into the wall.

Tiffany couldn't stop the laughter spurting out of her, unfortunately just as he turned her way. He glared. But everyone was chuckling a bit and Mrs Powell was trying not to.

'Do this,' Mrs Powell called to Ben. She made a great show of rubbing her fists against her mouth, the way a cat licks its paws. 'It says you don't care. When a cat makes a mess of things, dignity pulls it through.'

'Thanks for that,' Ben muttered. He checked to see if his nose was bleeding and gave Tiffany another black look. She was sorry she'd laughed. Despite her twinge of jealousy, it would be a shame if he got the hump now, just as he was getting into it.

'Now you see why cats have whiskers,' said Mrs Powell. 'But that's for later. We're going to get this Eth walking right.'

She stood in a corner of the studio and crossed to the far window. Everyone stared. She had covered the space in a twinkling, without seeming to move fast at all. And she had made no sound.

'Your feet are getting there,' she said, 'but you're thinking like bipeds. Cats are four-limbed. When you walk, your arms should move too. Don't swing them. They are your forelegs. Tiffany, come and demonstrate.'

It took a moment to sink in. She was being chosen. If her PE teacher ever singled her out, it was only to show her up as useless. Terrified and delighted she joined Mrs Powell at the front.

'Eth uses all four limbs.' Mrs Powell angled Tiffany's arm so the others could see. 'The cat's pace is a diagonal pattern in four beats. Right fore, left hind, left fore, right hind. Nature has no better way of moving over the ground. Tiffany, show us.'

She pictured the tall posts in her mind and took a few steps. She found that by thinking of Rufus and how he walked, the rhythm flowed naturally to her legs and arms. Her hands were like paddles, pushing the space behind her.

'A perfect example,' said Mrs Powell. 'Everyone walk the posts again.'

Having two extra things to think about wreaked havoc with most people. Yusuf managed three steps before getting muddled. Daniel did five and Susie, with gritted teeth, reached six. Olly couldn't stop falling over, eventually getting the giggles so badly he had to sit gasping by the wall. But Tiffany let herself glide across the room. She widened the gap between the imaginary posts, until she was no longer stepping but striding. Her pace quickened, she pivoted from tiptoe to tiptoe, as light and bouncy as a spring.

Those ballerinas could keep their pirouettes.

'I'm home!'

No one answered. Tiffany looked in the lounge then the kitchen. Rufus ran to her with a *mrrp* of welcome. She put her stuff in the washing machine, found herself a cereal bar and wandered upstairs.

'Anyone in?'

The study light was on. Mum and Dad were squashed on one chair at the computer.

'It's really, really great, that class,' said Tiffany. 'It's sort of like dance and a bit like yoga, only miles better. And it's been around for thousands of years but only a few people know it now. And I'm good at it already. Most of the others were falling over but I can do Eth now which is cat walking and it's so weird, you hardly even feel like you're moving but you are. And that lovely silver cat likes Parmesan cheese.'

'Did you have a good time, sweetheart?' Mum murmured. 'That's lovely. There! See?' She pointed at something on the screen.

'Okay, give me a chance to read it.' Dad frowned at the monitor.

Tiffany draped her arms over their shoulders and hung between them.

'What are you looking at?'

'I may have found something interesting,' said Mum.

'Is it to do with Stuart?'

'Can you back-page?' Dad asked Mum. 'Show me the article you found first.'

Oh well. At least they weren't telling her not to interrupt. Curious, Tiffany stood behind them and tried to read through the gap.

On the screen was an article from the *New Scientist* magazine. It talked about a Dr J. Philip Cobb and his research into traditional ethnic remedies. There was a fair bit of fluff about his life, which she skimmed over: as a child he'd mangled his arm in some accident that killed his mother, while they were travelling in Asia. His father took him for treatment in England, but the muscle in the bad arm never grew properly. That was when the article got interesting. Cobb had grown up to study biology and herbology. He searched for nutrients that could repair muscles damaged by accident or disease. This was the hook that had snagged Mum's internet search (she compulsively trawled Google for the phrase 'muscular dystrophy').

'And look, Peter,' said Mum. 'He has his own company that makes these treatments. There's a link.'

She clicked on it.

'Cathy, I'm not being negative, but if there was some new wonder drug wouldn't the hospital know about it?'

'Maybe not,' Tiffany put in. 'Pashki is wonderful and no one knows about that. In the lesson today –'

'It's not a drug. It's a supplement. You don't need a prescription. Ah, *finally*.'

The screen blossomed with a colourful homepage. The banner headline appeared in leafy letters: *Only Nature's Own*.

'I like their name,' said Dad. 'Shame about the acronym. O NO.'

'Can you be serious for a moment?'

Mum clicked around until one page made them all lean forward. It showed a toffee-brown pill jar with a striking orange label. A panel popped up beside it.

'"Panthacea",' Dad read. '"A revolutionary new formula that combines traditional Asian medicine with the latest research." Well, that covers all bases, doesn't it?' He read on. '"Proven in trials to stimulate muscle growth in tissue-damaged areas. To be taken as a dietary supplement with meals."'

'I don't think you say Pan-*thay*-se-ah,' said Tiffany. 'It's probably Pan-tha-*saya*.'

'And see here, Peter. "All natural ingredients".'

'So is deadly nightshade.'

Mum tutted.

'I don't think they'd last long if they sold people deadly nightshade,' she said. 'Look, you can buy a first course of four bottles for sixty pounds. That's no more expensive than some vitamin pills.'

She was already clicking *Add to shopping cart*.

Dad drummed his fingers on the desk.

'All right. But we are not getting carried away. We've been here before. I shall check with Dr Bijlani, and if he agrees we let Stuart try it for a few weeks. And expect nothing. Are we clear?'

'Yes, yes. Peter, I need the credit card number.' Mum clicked and typed and clicked. Her left hand had clenched into a fist.

Tiffany drifted to her room, where she and Rufus read another chapter of *Gormenghast* before she put herself to bed.

Another Monday, the same old ordeal. Shuffling into the school gymnasium Tiffany took deep breaths. Miss Fuller had set up the apparatus.

'Heck,' muttered Avril. She was another girl who tended to get pigeonholed with Tiffany under Weeds,

Whiners and Weirdos. 'If she makes us do another relay race I'm calling in dead next week.'

'Say I'm dead too,' Tiffany whispered back. Her nervousness had an edge today. At pashki she had started to feel strong for the first time ever, and it made her wonder. Perhaps in this P.E. lesson she might turn in a half-decent performance.

However, she was also worried that Mrs Powell's classes were playing tricks on her imagination. Late on Saturday she'd heard Mum and Dad talking in their bedroom. She never had before. So either they never normally talked, or her hearing had improved. Both explanations seemed unlikely. Then there was last night. Going to the bathroom in the dark, she'd avoided stepping on a drawing pin. It was only afterwards that she realised she couldn't possibly have seen it with the lights off.

Miss Fuller blew her whistle. The class sorted into four teams – as usual, Tiffany and Avril were amongst the last to be chosen. Her team mates set off one by one and Tiffany tried to memorise the course. Balance beam, wall bars, monkey bars and ropes, then over the gym horse they flew like contenders for Olympic gold, the girls rosy-cheeked and grinning, the boys making out they were marines. It was depressing, it was sickening, it was . . . whoops, it was her turn.

She crossed the balance beam. That was easy. At the

top of the wall bars she looked down and froze. She had never climbed so high. Somehow she got down and reached for the monkey bars. Heaving and whip-lashing her way from one rung to the next, she knew, by halfway across, that she wasn't going to make it. Her arms were paralysed. She dropped to the floor. Staggering to a rope she tried to climb it. Four feet up she lost all feeling in her shoulders and with it, her grip. Down she slithered, the rope burning her palms and the insides of her knees.

She landed on the mat in a heap. A hand pulled her, none too tenderly, to her feet.

'That was a lame effort, wasn't it?' said Miss Fuller. Uneasy laughter rippled through the gym. 'Chin up, nothing's broken. Do it again.'

Tiffany could only stand there, trembling, sucking her scorched fingers.

'What am I going to do with you, Tiffany Maine?' Miss Fuller looked to heaven. 'Okay. Go and sit it out. I'm thinking of getting your name engraved on that sicky bench.'

If she cried, she was dead. Dead. It was as simple as that. She trudged to the bench and sat down, hug-ging her knees, cold and yet boiling hot as if she had a fever.

Miss Fuller whistled and yelled at the class, driving them on round the course. Tiffany sat in the corner and stared at her. Hatred knotted in her stomach.

That was a lame effort, wasn't it?

'I should be in that hospital bed,' she whispered. 'Not Stuart.'

And now it was impossible not to weep, silently, into her fists.

5
Death Ray

It was a scene he saw every day, in some form or other: three boys crowding a smaller one against the playground fence. As usual Ben paid no attention, more interested in saving the last of his ice lolly from falling off its stick. The bullies whirled and twitched in a mockery of dance moves.

'Hey, Forrester! Show us some crazy steps.'

'Make the floor burn, Danny-boy.'

'Oh, leave off me!'

Ben looked without thinking and saw Daniel from Cat Kin, trying to stop a much bigger boy from snatching his glasses. In the same moment Daniel, hunting desperately for a way out, recognised him. Oops. Ben stood still, torn. Presumably the bullies were only in Year Seven, but they were all Ben's size. Cowardice fought briefly with shame and lost. He walked towards the group.

'Hey, Daniel,' he said. 'How's it going?'

'Not that great.'

The boys stopped their jiving.

'Ooo,' said one, 'is this your dance partner?' He poked Daniel, who lashed out with his fist. The boy squealed in fake terror and moonwalked away.

'Hang on,' said his friend, fingering the studs in his eyebrow. 'You're Gallagher, aren't you? The pinball guy.'

'The pinhead?' snorted the third, a boy whose face would have been quite handsome on a toad.

'Yeah, right,' grinned Eyebrow-studs. 'It must be tricky playing with those tiny balls.'

The boys cracked up. Ben tried to make the most of his extra inch of height.

'Do you know a quicker way to earn easy money?'

That got their attention. 'What you talking about?'

Ben pointed towards the strip of bare concrete that served as a football pitch. 'You see that guy playing in goal?'

'The really big fella?'

'Yeah. That's Cannon. I play pinball, he bets on me, he rakes it in. I get a share. It's simple.'

'Oh yeah?' Eyebrow-studs chewed his gum. 'How much?'

'He'll tell you himself,' said Ben. 'Go and talk to him. Ask how much money he won on me. He might even let you join the syndicate if you say you're really good friends of Ben Gallagher.'

As the three boys hurried eagerly towards Cannon, Ben grabbed Daniel by the arm and pulled him away.

'This is going to be ugly. I don't think we want to watch.'

On the far side of the school they found a fire escape to sit on. Half-hearted gang warfare was taking place around the burned-out car across the street.

'So what was that about?' asked Ben.

''S'nothing.' Daniel flicked a bottle-top, sending it bouncing down the steps. 'Ed Orlando and his mates trying to wind me up.'

'Looks like they succeeded.'

'They tease me for going to Dance class,' said Daniel.

'What fun for them. When do you go dancing?'

'I don't. I do pashki with you, remember?'

'Then why . . . ?'

'I *was* going to do Dance,' said Daniel. He took a deep breath. 'My dad was really off the idea at first. He only caved in so I'd stop bugging him. But there's no way he'd let me do pashki. He'd say it was New Age tosh. I haven't told him that's what I really do.'

'Have you tried?'

Daniel sucked his teeth in impatience.

'He's a *builder*. If he can't pile it up or knock it

down, it doesn't exist. Or it does exist but it's for pansies. Which is worse. He's happy to let me sit beside him in a JCB or a crane, but if I want to learn swipes and freezes I'm on my own.'

'Swipes and –?'

'I mean it *is* Street Dance, not flippin' ballet or something. That's if I did it. Which I don't. But everyone thinks I . . . look, it's complicated, okay?'

Ben nodded vigorously.

'So how about your dad?' said Daniel. 'Does he mind?'

Ben scratched rust off the banister.

'I haven't got round to telling him,' he said.

The pub windows framed a glorious sunny day. Cyclists in dark glasses and string tops freewheeled down Church Street to the sound of birdsong and police sirens.

Two steaming plates descended like UFOs.

'You don't get a nicer Sunday roast than in the Rose and Crown,' said Ben's dad. 'Not even my gran did better. Thanks, love.' He winked at the waitress.

Ben attacked his lamb ravenously. Normally he ate the Yorkshire puddings first, but not today. Dad savoured every mouthful as if he were at the Ritz.

'So how's tricks, Ben?' he asked. 'Seems like nothing goes on with you lately.'

Ben stuffed a hot potato into his mouth.

'Did your mother get the fuse box sorted?'

'Mm-hm.' Ben had to strain to remember that particular problem.

'You know I would have done it myself. If she'd let me.'

'I know.'

Dad was an electrician.

'Well then . . .' Dad glanced guiltily around him and, with a cheeky grin, re-filled Ben's empty coke glass with some of his own beer. 'How's your game? Or shouldn't I ask?'

'It's okay.' Ben sipped at the beer. He didn't get the taste at all, but pretending to like it made Dad happy.

'I suppose I shouldn't encourage you. Still, everyone needs a hobby. And you don't get hurt playing pinball.'

Remembering Cannon, Ben could have disagreed. But he knew what Dad meant. Before meeting Ben's mum, Raymond Gallagher had been a semi-professional boxer on the Hackney circuit. Though he had been, in his own words, an extremely average fighter, with as many losses as wins, he remained proud of his 'magic jab', a fast punch that could come out of nowhere to send opponents reeling into the ropes. It was this handy if unreliable weapon that had briefly earned him the nickname Death Ray.

'Benny? Is something up?'

'Just tired. School . . .' Ben made vague gestures. And then it all came out. He had to say something or never speak another word again. Over the next twenty minutes Ben whispered, stammered and choked out the story of John Stanford. By the time he had finished there was no beer left.

'And then Mum got this letter yesterday,' Ben went on. His lunch was cold and he had a splitting headache. 'Stanford's taking us to court over breach of something or other. Mum says he's bluffing but I can tell she's not sure. I don't think she knows what to do.'

Dad's face was stone. He tapped an unlit cigarette on the table.

'And I told her,' Ben went on, 'that she should call you, but she ignores me. I said, if Dad was here he'd knock Stanford's head off.'

'What did she say to that?' Dad asked, after a pause.

'Nothing. Just gave one of her laughs that make you feel about two inches tall.'

'I remember them.' Dad stared for a while out of the window. Then he leaned forward and squeezed Ben's arm. 'Ben. She's had a rough time. And there are some things . . .'

He didn't finish. They sat in silence. Dad got another beer for himself and water for Ben. Finally he crushed the unsmoked cigarette into the ash tray.

'Listen, Benny,' he said. 'This prat Stanford, you don't worry about him. He knows he's in the wrong, or he'd have got the law involved long ago. He's all bark and no bite.'

'But he smashed the door. And he really scared Mum. And,' Ben glanced out of the window, 'he's been creeping around. I saw him near the flat.'

'Stanford and Associates,' murmured Dad. 'I know where they're based. Islington somewhere.'

He stared into space.

'Dad?'

'I'd tell my solicitor to write him a rude letter,' said Dad. 'But it'd end up in the bin. No, Stanford's a bully. Bullies speak one language.'

Ben felt hope and alarm swilling round inside him.

'You can't go round there and beat him up. He'd get the police on to you.'

'Not him. Anyway, I don't like to hit people outside of boxing rings.' Dad fell silent and pulled out another cigarette. He grimaced and put it back. 'Sometimes all these thugs need is the fear of God putting into them. I've seen it a hundred times.'

'What are you going to do?'

Dad ruffled Ben's hair.

'Never you mind. You stop worrying. And Lucy can stop worrying too. I might not live there right now, but I bought that flat with your mum and I still have fond memories. And you're more important still. No one messes with my family, understand?' Dad downed his drink and pushed back his chair. 'No one.'

Mrs Powell's ten-minute sequence of stretches usually lasted a year or so. Hunched in a Long Reach, Ben felt his shoulders about to catch fire, and began to wish that he'd stuck with his original plan never to attend a pashki class again. (Why he did keep coming back, he was still not absolutely sure.) After that came more punishing poses, Arch On Guard, Scratching Tree and Falling Twist, until Ben was one of only two left standing. Despite the agony in his calves he wouldn't let himself wobble. Out of the corner of his eye he was watching Tiffany. He would crack when she did.

At last Mrs Powell showed mercy and let them rest. Ben lay flat on his back, too tired to check if Tiffany was doing the same. Then came a fresh mystery. Cecile and Olly were sent to fetch some paper-wrapped bundles. These turned out to be slabs of grey clay. Ignoring all questions, Mrs Powell handed them out: 'Press it over your face.'

The clutch of the clay on Ben's skin was cool and refreshing. It made him feel once again that everything, somehow, would be all right. He eased the clay off to see a perfect mould of his features, eyes closed and calm. After that they had to queue outside Mrs Powell's bathroom to wash the silt from their pores and eyebrows. When Ben returned to the studio, the clay moulds of their faces were gone.

The class sat before Mrs Powell. Ben knew the routine now: this was her pashki lecture. Last week she had begun to tell them of the 'Mau body', which she claimed was the invisible, feline part of one's self. It was all Greek to Ben (or at least, ancient Egyptian), but in his relaxed state he was happy to listen.

'In most human beings,' said Mrs Powell, 'the Mau body is no more than a cat-shaped spark in the soul. In others, it burns more brightly. With training we can feed it, until it fills our whole being. Turn your heads to the right.'

Mrs Powell pointed to the cork noticeboard. A poster showed two outlined figures: a sitting cat and a human. Down the centre of each ran a line of six coloured dots. Cat eyes.

'The Mau body springs from six points of power,' said Mrs Powell. 'Call them catras. Each catra channels a particular kind of energy and appears in a different zone of the body. Balance is Ptep and resides in the head. Agility springs from Ailur, in the base of the spine. Face front and close your eyes.'

Ben did so. A speck of clay was gumming one eyelash.

'Picture the colour blue. The blue of a clear evening sky.'

She paused. The studio whispered with breathing.

'Draw the blue together. Squeeze it to a point. It becomes richer, sharper. It is burning blue.' She waited. 'A blue fire against the blackness. Stare at it. Stare at it. It is the eye of a cat.'

Relaxed though he was, Ben flinched. As she spoke it appeared like a waking dream: a blue cat's eye, staring back. Fear came sharp as a bee sting and he had to blink. The first things he saw were Mrs Powell's eyes, and these too were fixed on him.

'You saw it?' she said.

Ben nodded.

'It scares you?'

'No,' Ben lied.

'Interesting. All right,' she said to the others, 'you can open your eyes now. What we have been visualising is the head catra, Ptep.'

'I got purple splotches,' confessed Olly.

'Not all of you will succeed at first,' said Mrs Powell. 'But you have learned the principle. We invoke each catra as an eye of a particular colour.'

'What do they do?' asked Cecile.

'They do not *do*,' said Mrs Powell. 'They just are. We try again.'

She made them picture a red eye, which she called

Oshtis. Heat welled in Ben's stomach. Kelotaukhon, smouldering copper, brought a tingle to his throat. The golden Parda cut through the dark like a sun, filling his chest with light. He found he couldn't look at any catra for more than a few seconds. Those glowing irises spooked him more than any cat's gaze.

'Good,' said Mrs Powell. 'Some of you are getting there. We will try an experiment. I need a good subject.' She cast about. 'Ben. No, sorry Ben. Tiffany, we'll use you.'

Ben had a sense of being elbowed aside.

'Now there's a surprise,' he whispered to Olly.

'Hey,' Olly breathed, 'as long she doesn't come near me, I'm happy.'

'When you're finished talking,' said Mrs Powell. She stood before Tiffany. 'As I explained, Ptep is the head catra, governing balance. The cat's main senses, such as sight, hearing and smell, reside in the face catra, Mandira, which is green. But what happens when we combine them?' She knelt. 'Tiffany, begin. Let it all go black.'

Ben found himself hoping Tiffany would mess up. It was childish, but he couldn't help it. He'd been enjoying today. Though the catra exercises rattled him, he had started to suspect, to his astonishment, that he liked pashki even more than pinball, and that he might get just as good at it. Yet Tiffany was chosen, as usual.

Jim wasn't the teacher's only pet.

'Hold the blue Ptep in your mind, Tiffany,' she said. 'Now. Summon your Mandira. Let the green eye appear.'

Tiffany's eyebrows twitched in concentration.

'Now, Tiffany,' said Mrs Powell. 'Bring the blue eye and the green eye together. Head and face, head and face. Let them merge. Become one. Hold it.'

Mrs Powell raised her hand. Ben craned forward. The hand crept towards Tiffany's face and came within six inches.

Tiffany opened her eyes. 'Hey! That tickles!'

Mrs Powell turned to the group.

'Did you see? Cecile, tell me. Did I touch her?'

'No.' Cecile was slack-jawed. 'She never even touched you, Tiffany!'

Voices chorused in agreement. Mrs Powell made her try it again. This time Tiffany reacted to a single finger passing by her head. To everyone's amazement, she sneezed. Ben didn't know what to think. If this was a conjuring trick, it was a clever one.

'It's almost like I've got . . . whiskers!' gasped Tiffany.

'You have.' Mrs Powell gave one of her rare smiles. 'Your Mau body has them, and you have helped them to appear. Mau whiskers work like an extra sense, reaching beyond your head.'

Susie snorted. 'That's impossible.'

'Implausible,' said Mrs Powell. 'Like everything else in nature.'

At that moment Jim trotted into the studio. Mrs Powell *miaowed* at him. Swishing his tail, he padded through the bead curtain into the kitchen, leaving a trail of clammy grey paw prints.

Mrs Powell sighed. 'What's *impossible* is training your cat not to go sitting on the modelling clay.'

Clissold Park stayed open on these early summer evenings. Ben had an urge to wander around the ponds. He didn't like admitting to himself that he was putting off going home. The flat was no longer a cosy place. Mum had grown so snappy.

He stroked his face. The last part of the class, learning to develop Mau whiskers, had left him light-headed. When he fused those blue and green eyes in his mind, had he really felt the air stirring to life? Imagination could do a lot. Yet it was as if musical strings had been strung to his skull, each buzzing with its own note. And those notes had translated to pictures in his head, as if he were *seeing* the whole studio as a landscape of vibrations. He could see (feel? hear?) the people around him, blurred shapes through a fog, growing fainter with distance. For those brief moments he could have run blindfold around the room. Had Mrs

Powell hypnotised the lot of them? Or was it something more?

Wandering by the deer enclosure, where a baby-faced doe nosed up to the wire, he toyed with his mobile phone. Dad had hinted that Thursday might be D-Day on the Stanford front. Ben had been half-expecting a call all afternoon. His voicemail was empty. He selected *Dad* and pressed the green key.

Brrrr brrrr

He let the deer nuzzle his fingers through the fence.

Brrrr brrrr

Dad hated a ringing phone. He always picked up by the third ring.

Brrrr brrrr

Ben looked at his watch. Five to eight. Too early for Dad to be at the pub. The phone continued to ring. Might he be eating out? There was always the possibility – galling though it was – that Dad had a girlfriend.

Brrrr brrrr

He moved his thumb to the red hang-up button.

'H-hello?'

'Dad!' Ben grinned. 'Did I get you out of the bathroom?'

'Er – yes.' There was a moment's silence on the line. 'You okay, Ben?'

'Yeah, great. So . . . any news?'

No answer. Ben started to feel uncomfortable.

'It's not a bad time to call, is it?' he asked.

'No, no, Ben. It's just . . .' Dad cleared his throat. 'I guess you want to know if I spoke to Mr Stanford.'

The line was thick with static. No, not static. But Dad's voice sounded odd. Slurred. As if he'd had a lot to drink.

At eight in the evening?

'Hello?' Ben held the phone more tightly.

'I'm here.' Dad's breathing rasped in the earpiece. 'Ben. I have to tell you something important. Listen. You and your mother can't stay in that flat. You must get out. I can put you up at my place for a while.'

'What? But Dad –'

'Ben, this is important. Tell your mother to accept Mr Stanford's offer. Sell the place and cut your losses.'

Thell the place. It sounded like *thell*. *Cut your lothes*.

'Dad? Dad, what's wrong?'

'I'm sorry, Ben. I really am. I made a mistake. Try to help and I only make things worse. I'm . . . I'm not much of a dad, am I.'

The concrete path seemed to wobble under Ben's shoes.

'What happened? Did you go round there? What did he say?' A horrible thought took shape. 'What did he do? Did he –'

'Don't worry about me.' Dad paused a moment.

'Stanford had this guy with him. A big bloke. I wasn't about to start any trouble with him there. I wasn't.'

A big bloke. That caveman Toby.

'Did he . . . hit you?'

Dad made a sound, like a shred of a laugh.

'I'm okay. Still here.' He went silent for a while. 'People mend.'

Ben sucked in deep breaths. He knew that as soon as he turned his phone off he would throw up all over the footpath.

'Dad . . . We've got to tell the police.'

'No!' There was something in Dad's voice he had never heard before. Fear. 'No, you can't do that. I'm not going into details. Stanford made it clear. You tell Mum to take whatever he's offering and pack her bags. Tell her. Do it for me, Ben. Or I won't sleep at night.'

'*Dad?*'

'I'm sorry, Ben.' Raymond Gallagher's voice sank to a whisper. 'I'm so sorry.'

6
Feline Faces

'Hurry, slave-girl. Fetch me my drink.'

'At once, your Excellency.' Tiffany bowed before the electric wheelchair as Stuart trundled into the living room. 'Will it be nectar, ambrosia or Ribena?'

'Naah. Ginger beer,' grinned Stuart.

Tiffany skipped into the kitchen and opened the cupboard, to see Dad's hand-written sign inside the door: *Cups are a renewable resource.* She banged the cupboard shut with her head and grabbed two used glasses off the draining board. Today was better than Christmas.

It had all happened so quickly. Three weeks ago the first batch of Panthacea had arrived through the post. Dad had been suspicious of the bottles at first and wouldn't even let Mum taste one of the chunky green tablets herself. But Stuart's doctor Sanjeev had no objections.

'I am being sceptical of miracle powers,' he said. He had read about Panthacea, and warned them that it was probably no more than a cocktail of A, D and B-complex vitamins, with added herbal ingredients 'for that all-so-important ethnic street-cred'. This put Mum's nose out of joint, so she showed him an article where Panthacea was championed by an Ayurvedic doctor.

'As you know, Ayurvedic healers focus on prevention rather than cure,' she said.

'Very wise, I am sure,' said Dr Bijlani. 'So, if you visit this doctor with a broken leg, does he say, "Ah, well you shouldn't have gone skiing"?'

Such comments aside, he was sure that the supplement would do Stuart no harm. 'And I am seeing people get better swallowing nothing but sugar pills and clever advertising,' he said. 'The mind is a most exquisite healer.'

Perhaps the doctor was right. Still, after just two weeks of taking the tablets (which he said tasted bitter) Stuart was able to play for longer, talk without getting out of breath and even climb into his wheelchair by himself. He was more cheerful and his pneumonia had cleared up. It probably helped that Mum and Dad no longer sat by his bedside quarrelling with each other — they were all smiles, real smiles at last. But Tiffany kept fingering the humble little bottles, reading the labels in growing wonder. *Panthacea: For strength, for health, for life*. Dr Bijlani could be as sarcastic as he liked. The fact remained: Stuart was coming home.

Tiffany set down the ginger beer and grabbed the hand that he waved in her face.

'Arm wrestle!' Stuart cried.

'Ugh, aargh, no more, it's an unstoppable machine,' Tiffany gasped, pretending to collapse under the puny force her brother was exerting. He knew, of course, that she was acting, but cheered in triumph anyway.

'I rule!'

'Now you get to thump *me* on the back,' said Tiffany.

'At last. Revenge is mine!' Stuart made a fist. 'Take that! And that. And –'

'Tiffany, that's enough.' Mum made shoo-ing gestures. 'Stop crowding him, love, you'll tire him out. Doesn't your room need tidying?'

'We're only playing. He loves it, don't you, Stuart?'

'There'll be plenty of time for that soon enough,' said Mum. 'Room, please.'

Huffing her annoyance, Tiffany trudged upstairs.

Cecile peeped out from behind the chunk of plaster in her hands.

'What do I look like?'

'Awesome.' Tiffany wished she had a mirror so she

could see her own face. The marbling of red and white make-up on Cecile's ebony complexion had turned her into another being. 'You look just like a tortoiseshell!'

'A *tortoise*—?'

'That's a kind of cat,' Tiffany added hastily.

'You've got the tabby markings,' said Cecile. 'Like Jim. I can see the M shape on your forehead.'

From the moment she arrived, Tiffany had sensed that this pashki class was special. She had puzzled over those clay moulds they had made of their faces. Here was the answer. Mrs Powell had created a plaster cast from each mould, then made plaster moulds from the casts. Inside each she had glued pieces of felt in curious patterns. She showed them how to wet the felt with coloured paints. Then they simply pressed the moulds over their faces and, when they peeled them off, the skin of their foreheads and cheekbones bore striking temporary tattoos.

'Goodbye human face,' said Mrs Powell, 'hello cat. From now on, you start each lesson by putting on your face print.'

Mrs Powell's own cat face-paint was so subtle Tiffany hadn't noticed it at first: spidery grey trails that followed the wrinkles of her brow, gathered to an M below her hairline. The class murmured, admiring each other's markings. Susie had curves across her temples and cheekbones that drew out her inquisitive almond eyes. Dark and pale rings gave Yusuf a hunter-ish stare, similar to an Abyssinian, Tiffany thought. The pale paint on Daniel's skin made him seem to be wearing a grey mask, which was set off surprisingly well by his specs. And Ben's was a pattern of fiery ripples that looked almost tiger-ish. He was sitting apart and seemed too preoccupied to pay much attention to anyone else.

'This is so cool,' Cecile smiled. 'You've actually got a cat, haven't you, Tiff?'

She made the idea sound as exotic as flamingos in the garden.

'He's just a moggy. A lovely moggy,' Tiffany added, guiltily.

'I've never had any pets,' said Cecile. 'Well, a guinea pig when I was eight. But that never moved and then it died.'

'You should get one.'

'As if. There's not even room for people in my flat. It's me and my little sister in one room and my parents and baby brother in another. And bikes and laundry everywhere else. If I was a cat I'd be out of there so fast . . .' Cecile sucked her teeth. 'You know I've never seen a sheep?'

'Pardon?'

'I've never seen a sheep. Or a cow. Except at London Zoo. I've seen them on telly, yeah, but not cows and sheep in fields and stuff. That's what growing up in Hackney does for you. S'why I came here. I thought it was a nature trail thing. You know, catkins. This is even better though. I never thought I'd actually get to *be* like an animal.'

Mrs Powell began the lesson. Over the weeks their pashki sequences had grown more and more dance-like: springing in graceful arcs, stopping dead and spinning on one toe, pouring oneself like water to the floor and rebounding as if suddenly rubber. For Tiffany every second was an ecstasy of movement and it looked as if Ben, too, had learned many steps to per-fection. Everyone had made progress, even Olly, though he joked that he only kept coming because Mrs Powell would hunt down and kill anyone who tried to leave.

'Always remember your catras,' said Mrs Powell, circling them like a stalking lynx. 'Your exercise rou-tines prime you physically, and help to wake your Mau body up. But it is by invoking the catras that you help your Mau to grow. In most of you it is still just a spark. What we have to do is fan the flames. Yusuf, recite the catras for me.'

'Uh –' Yusuf glanced at Tiffany.

'Abysmal,' said Mrs Powell. 'Heavens, there are only six. My old teacher in Kashmir . . .' She trailed off, and stared for a moment out of the window, as if a stray grey thought had overtaken her. She recovered quickly. 'My old teacher made us learn Akhotep's catra chant off by heart. In the original ancient Egyptian. I know that it would bore you children to tears, and probably cause your heads to explode, so I have composed a much shorter version. In English. By the next time we meet, you *will* all have memorised it.'

She slipped into her dreamy reciting voice:

Ptep is my head, the balancing blue sky;
Mandira is my green all-sensing eye;
Kelotaukhon, copper maw, my mystery;
Golden chest of Parda strongly glows;
Lower crimson Oshtis feels and knows;
Nimble tail is Ailur, indigo.

The class chanted it back to her, hesitantly at first, then twice more. By the third repetition, Tiffany fancied that she was seeing each catra as she spoke it, like a neon lamp blinking on a blank screen inside her forehead, triggering warmth in the corresponding centres of her body.

They finished the lesson by practising Pur, the meditation pose. Tiffany despaired of ever getting this right. The Sphinx crouch was easy, but that was only part of it. You did actually have to purr. The trick was to hum as low as you could possibly go. Then, somehow, you had to shift it even lower, so it was just a throb in your throat. Everyone found it impossible, but Mrs Powell insisted that it wasn't.

'Pur is important,' she said. 'Cats purr when they are happy, but they also purr when they are sick or injured. A cat will purr just before it is put to sleep by a vet.'

Tiffany didn't want to think about such horrible things.

'Like OM in yoga,' said Mrs Powell, 'Pur aids relaxation. It acts as a pain killer and can keep fear at bay. It may even help cats recover from injury. Some say it is the secret of the cat's legendary nine lives. So come along, concentrate. Purr with me.'

She made the inhuman rumble that seemed to come from everywhere and nowhere, and for the next eight minutes Tiffany sat trying to copy her and getting a sore throat. On the way out, as a consolation, she helped herself to two of the chocolate brownies Olly had brought for them to share. Good old Olly. He might not have the grace of a puma yet, but he understood about cat treats.

When Dad called up the stairs to ask if she was coming to the hospital for Stuart's physiotherapy, Tiffany, enjoying a Saturday lie-in, naturally said no. A moment later the front door shut. She listened to the silence in disbelief. No one had bothered to mention that they were *all* going with Stuart. Mum and Dad had left her alone in the house.

'*Owwr-rree.*' Rufus galloped into her room. He butted her protruding bare feet, as if to say *At least you're still here.*

'Yes. Same old me.' She crumpled his ears. What to do, then? There was drinking pineapple juice straight out of the carton and stuffing herself on toast. Then she phoned round her sprinkling of friends, but only Natasha was in and her family had the plague, or so it sounded from the sneezing. After an hour of mindless TV she ran out of ideas. She stomped upstairs and logged on to the internet. Mum's Favourites folder was open. Idly curious, Tiffany read more of the articles about Panthacea and its inventor, Dr J. Philip Cobb.

Cobb himself (she read) *is a walking advertisement for his products. Even though his childhood accident in the wildlife park left him partially disabled, Panthacea has returned to him 70% use of his withered arm.*

'*But I still leave the heavy lifting to my staff,*' *he jokes. With the prospect of multi-million pound drug company contracts around the corner, and countless fellow sufferers standing to benefit from his research, this is one pill that Philip Cobb should have no trouble swallowing.*

Her heart leaped. If major companies wanted to buy up Panthacea, perhaps there really was something in it. You could fool a few desperate people, Tiffany knew, but not hard-headed businessmen. It looked like Stuart might get better. Really better. Maybe this time next year he'd be running round the school fields playing football. No, not football, he hated that . . . so maybe he'd be charging about with his friends, pretending to be superheroes. Maybe he would *have* some friends.

Mum had left a jar of Panthacea on the computer desk. Tiffany unscrewed the lid and peered inside at the pills. Chunky ovals, the colour of dark moss, they looked nothing special. The jar had a funny aroma. Knowing she shouldn't, she picked out a pill and touched her tongue to it. As Stuart had said, it was bitter, like aspirin, only thicker. Greener. On an impulse she popped the pill in her mouth.

'What are you doing, Tiffany?' she mumbled aloud, the tablet snuggling awkwardly in one cheek. The bitter taste spread through her mouth as the pill softened with saliva. She hurried to the bathroom and spat it out in the toilet. The lump floated in circles on the water, disintegrating. She watched it, queasy. What had possessed her to do that?

Screwing the lid back on she returned the jar to its exact same place. But, as she surfed onto a chat room to kill another hour, she found herself wishing she had swallowed that pill after all. She wasn't exactly Miss

Universe herself. With the last PE lesson of the year approaching, and Miss Fuller ominously promising the class 'a surprise', she needed all the help she could get.

'Ah, Rufus,' she crooned. 'Where's *my* medicine, eh?'

The ginger cat purred on her lap.

'If this is Miss Fuller's idea of a nice surprise,' Avril whispered, 'I pity her kids.'

'If she ever has any,' Tiffany whispered back. 'She'll have to catch a man first.'

'And shut him in the cellar,' sniggered Avril.

'Locked in a cage.'

Miss Fuller had set up the gym horse and spring-board. Her treat was a vaulting contest. Whoever sprang highest or furthest without suffering serious injury got to take home a live tarantula. Or something. Tiffany hadn't really been listening.

'No way are we surviving that.' Avril watched grim-ly as the first boy, Jason Wilks, rocketed over the horse.

'And that's just the lowest notch,' Tiffany muttered. 'Look, she's putting it up. Typical.'

Avril went paler. 'How high is it going to be when it's our turn?'

'She knew we'd go to the back of the line, didn't she?' said Tiffany. 'Evil, muppet-haired witch.'

'I'm going to be sick.'

'Should've thought of that earlier.'

Tiffany closed her eyes and reminded herself that, in forty minutes, Miss Fuller would be nothing but a bad memory. But the ignominy of being the class lump wouldn't pass so easily. Week after week she'd come here to be humiliated. How could she be good at pashki and so useless in school sports? Yusuf, she had discovered, was one of the year's top footballers, yet at Cat Kin she could run rings around him. Last lesson she had wowed everyone by Eth-walking the long, winding course Mrs Powell had set for them in Clissold Park. Tiffany had done it in under a minute, beating Ben's time by one second and everyone else by a mile. But in PE she was like a different person. A different species.

'Emma! Go,' shouted Miss Fuller. Tiffany heard bare feet run to the springboard, judder off it and land with a wettish smack on the mat. Emma grunted, as if she had fallen badly. Tiffany's knees almost buckled under the weight of the butterflies in her stomach. She heard Miss Fuller raise the gym horse still higher.

Then, in the blackness of her own eyelids, she saw cats' eyes. Mrs Powell had encouraged them to practise their catras until they appeared at will. An indigo eye swam into view (that was Ailur, Tiffany recalled), merging with a golden one, Parda. Why these should appear to her now, and what they meant when combined, she couldn't think. But their presence was comforting and she felt strength in her again.

'Excuse me? Tiffany? Thank you for coming, pet, but can you wake up now?'

Tiffany started at the sound of Miss Fuller's voice. She opened her eyes to find herself at the front of the line. Everyone was staring at her, grinning like a pack of wolves. In her confusion she had lost sight of the gym horse. She looked left, right, turned round and finally saw it. With no time left to be nervous, she ran at it and prayed.

The vault turned out to be easier than it looked. She bounced up and skimmed over the frayed green padding on the crown of the horse. There was the tiniest jolt as she touched down on the wooden floor, and that was that. She raised her hands above her head for good measure, the way gymnasts did on television, and walked to the back of the line, heart thudding with relief. She'd done it as well as any of them.

It took her a moment to notice how silent the gym had become.

'Tiffany . . .' Miss Fuller's voice sounded different. Almost human.

'What did she just do?' one of the boys whispered.

'That was the wrong way round,' said someone else.

'Tiffany . . .' Miss Fuller was peering at her like a

mole faced with an exam paper. 'Why did you do it that way?'

'Miss?' Tiffany had no idea what they were on about. She wondered if she'd cut herself and glanced at her arms and legs.

'The springboard's on *this* side,' said Jason, frowning in confusion.

'Did you *see* that?' cried Avril.

Tiffany stood bewildered as the gym dissolved into uproar. She looked back at the apparatus and understood. Somehow, being muddled, she had run at it from the wrong end, jumping with no springboard to launch her and no mats to cushion her landing. Yet the horse now towered on its highest notch, as tall as she was.

'Can you, er, do it properly next time, please?' Miss Fuller stammered at last.

7

Clawmarks

'I think you should get down from there,' Tiffany whispered for the second time. She was in the Hunter crouch, peeping through the bushes.

'The guy won't mind, will he?' said Ben. 'He's dead.'

He shifted his position on the back of the marble lion and peered between its rain-bitten ears. The two policemen were in the open now, talking to a young couple who were taking a walk through the graves.

'I meant, they might see you,' said Tiffany.

'They might *hear* us, if you keep talking.'

That hiss was Tiffany blowing through her teeth. Ben ignored her and tried to pick up the policemen's conversation. By concentrating on the green catra, Mandira, he could make their voices seem louder. The older officer, a thickset man in a too-tight uniform, asked the couple if they had seen anyone lurking in the cemetery. They hadn't.

'If you do,' said his partner, 'we advise you not to approach them. It's probably kids, but you never know.'

Tiffany glided from her hiding-spot like a draught. Once she was in her black pashki cat-suit and tabby face-print it was almost impossible to make her walk normally.

'I warned you back there,' she whispered. 'That lady in her garden saw you.'

'She saw both of us.'

'*I* was careful.'

'Please accept my humble apologies.'

Given the choice, Ben would rather have been paired with Yusuf, Daniel, or perhaps Attila the Hun. But over the weeks Yusuf had tended to hang out more with Olly, which was kind of inevitable since they both went to the same school, and Daniel had surprisingly latched onto them. Ben had started to wonder what was wrong with him, only to realise, as the long holiday wore on, that he was simply getting too good at pashki. The Cat Kin were spending more time outside, trying out new moves and routines in the parks and streets, and Mrs Powell had ordered Ben and Tiffany to practise together. They were too far ahead of everyone else. Ben could see the logic of this. It was just a shame that Tiffany was an expert at rubbing him up the wrong way.

The policemen drew nearer. Ben slid off the lion monument and alighted on the grass, for the moment still hidden. The ivy-robed trees cast the ground in green shade, the sun dripping through like rain into an old tent. Shadows of tree trunks wove among the graves, vaults and petrified angels. Ben Eth-walked after Tiffany to a denser patch of undergrowth. This must be how it felt to be a burglar. A cat burglar, ho ho.

But they hadn't been stealing. Or rather, they had only been stealing space. Territory, said Mrs Powell, was a vital part of a cat's being. A cat built up a store of special places where it owned (it believed) every breeze and grass blade. This was the fifth rudiment of pashki: Laying Claim. Mrs Powell sent them out to find unfamiliar territories and pass through them unnoticed, while getting to know them and absorbing their essence. 'And do *try*,' she added, 'not to get arrested.'

That was starting to look likely. The two officers had parted where the path forked and the thin policeman looked as if he might pass within arm's reach of their hiding-place.

'Keep still,' whispered Tiffany.

'It's lucky I have you to tell me what to do,' muttered Ben.

'*Quiet.*'

The policeman's radio crackled. He ignored it, but Tiffany, who was already tense, jumped. The leaves shook and the officer turned.

'You! Stop there!'

'Run?' whispered Ben.

'Yes.'

They scarpered. In his panic Ben forgot everything he'd learned. Robbed of the agility of pashki he blundered towards the nearest path, running as if through tar or a bad dream. He could hear the younger officer jabbering into his radio as he chased.

Was he jinxed or something? To be caught by a copper would be the final straw. Over the past few days he and Tiffany had crept through people's gardens, across walls and over garages, travelling whole streets without setting foot on a pavement, and had hardly drawn a glance. Ben found that pashki let him move, if not invisibly, then unobtrusively. He could cross someone's field of vision and they would simply ignore him. Only rarely had they been spotted. Once a man had bellowed from his bathroom window and they'd had to hide behind his chimney-stack. And just now a woman had yelled as they crossed her garden, forcing them to scramble over a lopsided wall and drop ten feet into the cemetery. That they did these things without thinking amazed and alarmed them both.

Mrs Powell had organised extra lessons for the summer holidays, and Mum had remarked, grumpily, that Ben seemed to be doing little else nowadays (though as far as she knew, it was just an ordinary self-defence class). His mum had a point. He'd stopped playing pinball altogether. But amongst the Cat Kin, Ben found he could relax. He could forget about John Stanford's threats, Mum's ever-blackening moods, Dad's disastrous attempt to help.

His favourite lessons were in Ten Hooks. One of the nine pashki rudiments, Ten Hooks was non-contact sparring, based on the way cats fought. Whenever he practised the dreamlike slashes, lunges and kicks, usu-ally with Tiffany, he could go as long as five minutes without dreading what was going to happen to his family.

It was when he thought of Mum, working extra hours in the organics shop or sitting alone in the flat that now felt like a prison, that the guilt came, clawing at his conscience. He should be at home comforting her, not wasting his time being taught tricks by a half-mad old woman.

For Mrs Powell got stranger by the minute. For three lessons now she'd been talking up something called *Mau claws*. She said that, just as the Mau body could extend beyond your head to create an effect like whiskers, it could also be forced out through your fingertips or toes, so you would actually seem to have claws for a second or two. This (she claimed) was extremely difficult and needed energy from all the catras in sequence, blue, green, gold, copper, red and indigo, to feed the Mau body to the point where it became almost a physical presence. To Ben it all sounded about as likely as bending spoons with telekinesis.

Running through the cemetery, he felt a tug on his arm.

'This way.' Tiffany darted down an alley of head-stones. Ben strove to keep up, trying to recapture the cat grace that had deserted him.

'I didn't think that cow would actually dial nine-nine-nine,' he panted. 'She must have a really boring life.'

'Urk.' Tiffany stopped so suddenly that Ben thumped into her. 'Up ahead.'

Alerted by his colleague, the fat policeman was running from the other direction.

'Split up!'

'Wait. I've got an idea,' said Tiffany. She veered off into a thicket of tall graves.

'That's a dead end,' hissed Ben. 'Not that I'm trying to be funny or anyth—'

'You don't remember! Last lesson she showed us how to Freeze.'

Ben shook his head. He wasn't trusting in that mumbo-jumbo now.

'We've got to try!' said Tiffany. 'Stand still. Focus on your Kelotaukhon catra. In your throat. It's copper.'

'I'm more worried about the coppers over there.'

'Oh, be quiet. We spread out. I'll stand here. Now Freeze.'

Ben stood near a statue and tried to be one himself. He heard his heart beat slower. Through half-closed eyes he saw the young officer run past. Moments ticked by. The two policemen slowly returned to the field of graves, looking confused. Ben saw the thin one stare straight at him, and he held his breath.

Kelotaukhon, copper maw, my mystery . . .

The gaze slipped off.

'They were right here,' the officer grumbled.

Eyes swept over him again.

'Maybe it's the vampires,' chuckled the elder. 'This place is meant to be full of them. Did you bring your silver handcuffs?'

'Hysterical.' His partner scowled. 'I'm not seeing things, Trev. They can't have gone anywhere else. I was right on their –' He pointed straight at Ben. 'Hey! There's one.'

Ben bit his tongue. Now he was cornered. Tombs reared on all sides and behind him was the sheer wall of the cemetery. Grinning, the constables advanced through the headstones. Ben glanced skywards in despair. Branches cut the clouds. A cherry tree grew near the wall.

He jumped for the lowest bough but it was too broad to give a proper grip. His feet scraped at the trunk while the feeling drained from his hands. All that time he'd spent in arcades when he should have been learning to climb trees. One policeman chuckled. They were almost on him.

Then his fingers found a knot or something in the branch. With a jerk of his elbows he was up in the leaves. Climbing as if hounds were after him, he saw the top of the boundary wall, leaped onto it and lowered himself over the other side, hanging from his fingers. Mossy brick pressed cold against his cheek. The policemen's voices drifted over the wall.

'Come out of the tree!'

'He's not in it, Trevor.'

'What? Where'd he go?'

'Search me. I'm not following him. People aren't meant to move like that.'

The older man let out his breath. 'Who'd work in Hackney? You answer a call and you find yourself chasing Spring-heeled Jack.'

The policemen went quiet.

'Trev?'

'What?'

'Does this place give you the heeby-jeebies?'

Another pause.

'Yeah,' said Trevor. 'Let's get out of here.'

When the silence told him they were far away, Ben lifted himself back onto the wall. He found Tiffany there, sitting on her heels.

'Hey, Ben! That was really good.'

Ben looked down and his stomach turned a somersault. That rickety cherry was the last tree any kid would try to climb. And you'd have to be stupid to jump from its branches across to this towering wall. Nevertheless, he appeared to have done both.

'Look there.' Tiffany spoke softly, pointing at the cherry tree's bough. Pale lines, like knifestrokes, marked the crusty bark. 'Do you think . . . ?'

'Let's go. I don't want to wait for them to come back.'

'But don't you see? You did it! You must have got your Mau claws to work.'

'Don't be silly.' Ben turned on her, suddenly angry without knowing why. 'Those scratches are where the bark flaked off. You don't believe everything Mrs Powell says, do you?'

'So what are you doing here on a fifteen-foot wall?'

Ben found that he had folded his arms, both hands

stuffed protectively into his armpits. Not that he was scared to look at them or anything.

'That's different,' he mumbled. 'Balancing and jumping you can practise. Those are *possible* things.'

'Really? I've done some pretty impossible jumps lately. So have you. We could probably enter the Olympics and –'

'Look, pashki's just a weird martial art. There are karate experts who can smash bricks, right?'

'I was reading my book with the lights off last night. Can they do that?'

Ben hesitated. He didn't want to admit that he'd been doing the same.

'Tiffany, humans aren't made to do these things. It's . . . freakish.'

'It's fantastic.' Tiffany lay down on the wall, watching the sky blow by.

'Okay then. About Mrs Prowl.'

'Our teacher's name is –'

'What does she want with us?'

Tiffany laughed.

'No, listen, just for once.' Ben was warming up. 'Why does she take the class? Not for the money. What we pay wouldn't even cover her rent.'

'So? She's keen for us to learn. She doesn't want pashki to be forgotten.'

'But don't you remember? She tricked us. We met

at the leisure centre, but we haven't been back there since. She's nothing to do with that place. I'd bet you that no one there has even heard of Felicity Powell.'

He thought he'd got her with that one. Tiffany continued to stare at clouds.

'I don't think that's suspicious,' she said at last. 'You have to understand how cats are. She could never be an instructor in a busy leisure centre. Cats are their own bosses. They need their space.'

'She is *not a cat*. And she lied to us!'

'Don't be paranoid.' Tiffany backward-rolled and stood, ignoring the steep drop either side. 'Anyway, you like pashki. You're streets ahead of everyone else. Except me.'

'I knew you were going to say that.'

Tiffany dropped her eyes, as if she hadn't meant to.

'I don't understand,' she said, 'what's suddenly made you upset.'

'Who's upset? I'm not upset.'

'Something is really bothering you.' Tiffany met his gaze again. 'It doesn't take cat senses to see it.'

She had a point. The idea that he had invisible claws was weird, but why should it make him angry? Maybe he was anxious more than angry. Maybe the word was *afraid*. It wasn't just pashki. Everything he trusted in, his parents, his home, was shifting like quicksand around him. And now he was doing these inexplicable things. He felt the terror of losing himself, like a figure in a fog.

'Do you want to talk about it?' Tiffany asked.

He wavered. He could tell her. It hardly mattered if she avoided him ever after. But tell her what? That he and Mum might be thrown out of their home before the end of the month? That he broke into a sweat whenever the phone rang? Or that he suffered nightmares in which rats seethed out of the toilet and changed into John Stanford, gnawing away the carpets, walls and floor before turning his grinning yellow teeth in Ben's direction?

He imagined telling her what it was like now that Mum never smiled. Now that she had given up her craftwork and only spoke to snap at him. How she'd punished him with two weeks of near-silence for getting Dad involved. Could he tell Tiffany about his last Sunday lunch with Dad, where he'd tried to ignore the bruises and missing teeth that were the work of Toby's fists, so that they hardly said a word to each other all day? The more he thought about it, the more impossible it seemed. He couldn't tell her any single thing. They were all tangled together in a lump. To answer her would mean spilling his guts.

'Of course, I'm not a qualified therapist.' She gave a little smile.

That grin. At once he understood. She was after

juicy gossip to feed her posh friends at ballet. To make them giggle with the story of a boy who broke down in tears. That was the only reason she was interested.

'Hey, just forget it,' he snapped. 'Go and find some other cripple to help.'

She drew in her breath sharply. It was as if he'd struck her. What had he said? Suddenly unable to meet her gaze, he picked moss off the wall for something to do. When he looked up a minute later, Tiffany had gone.

8
Fall on Your Feet

Tiffany sniffed the breeze. The nutty woodland air was spiced with hot spaniel and the usual London fume. She could hear barking, a ball game and the splash of swimmers in the mixed bathing pond nearby. Both footpaths were deserted. She crept under the trees. She had been looking forward to this day for more than a week.

'All clear, Mrs Powell.'

'I repeat,' Mrs Powell was saying, 'do *not* stray off the routes I have marked unless you want to end up in hospital. All of you must look for the cats' eyes painted on the boughs. These show the safe trees and the safest routes between them.'

'Phew,' said Olly. 'Roots I can manage. I thought you were going to make us walk along the branches.'

Susie folded the newspaper that she seemed to be always carrying.

'Olly, if ignorance is bliss you must be the happiest person on earth.'

Olly stared up into the tangled attics of the wood, his adam's apple bobbing in fright. Tiffany didn't blame him. Even she felt edgy. It was probably like this for people taking their first parachute jump.

'Follow me.'

Mrs Powell stepped onto the bole of an oak trunk, which grew at a slant out of the soil like a lazy wooden arm reaching for an alarm clock. As easily as if she were mounting stairs, she walked up the gentle slope to a fork in the branches that drooped across the dell. Tiffany was at her side in four springy steps.

'Come on,' Mrs Powell hissed to the others, when they hesitated. 'A dog could climb this.'

Yusuf came first, arms spread for balance. Kitted out in the close-fitting black sportswear that seemed to have become their unofficial uniform, he looked more feline than ever. Susie went next, humming a tune through the newspaper she now carried in her teeth rather than leave behind. Tiffany followed Mrs Powell along the left-hand bough to make room for them. It felt as safe as flat ground. She could have put her hands in her pockets, except that she didn't have any.

Perched over the dell she parted the leaves. The city of London looked near enough to touch. Office blocks floated in the exhaust haze like fairytale towers, the wheel of the London Eye no more than a charm bracelet dropped among them. With birdsong in her ears, it was easier to think she was studying a painting.

'It's like being out in the countryside,' breathed Cecile.

'You can still see the town, though,' said Susie, sounding oddly relieved.

Cecile's eyes shone. She sat astride the right-hand bough. 'How did you find this place?'

'How would you *lose* it?' Mrs Powell replied. 'Hampstead heath takes up half a page of the map.'

Sadness crept over Cecile's tortoiseshell face. 'Never been here before.'

'Woah!' Halfway up the sloping trunk, Olly swayed and waved an arm. Daniel grabbed it, steadying him.

'Stop looking down,' said Daniel. 'Look where you want to go.'

'That *is* where I want to go.'

'Headfirst?' Daniel took his hand away. 'Come on, it's a cinch. Climbing scaffolding's a lot harder and my dad does that every day. Carrying bricks.'

'You have strange hobbies in your family.'

'That's his job!'

'So pay me what he's getting and I'll climb this tree.'

'Oh, move it.' Daniel pinched the back of his calf.

Olly yelped and scrambled up the rest of the trunk like an acrobat. Daniel pursued, laughing. Last came Ben.

Tiffany watched him walk up the tree. Like her, he might have been out for a stroll. Pulling on a pair of leather gloves with the fingers cut away, he stared distractedly down into the hollow where a fallen tree lay, its soil-caked roots like a warrior's round shield. With the smallest turn of his head he could have looked at her, but he didn't. Since that afternoon in the graveyard, when he'd acted so strangely, they hadn't exchanged a single word.

What had she done to annoy him? As far as she could tell, nothing. She was no longer so angry about what he'd said (since he couldn't have known about Stuart), but if he was determined to ignore her, she was happy to ignore him back.

Once, over a Friday fish and chips in the school canteen, Avril had claimed that, if a boy starts being nasty to you for no reason, it means he secretly likes you. 'Not that any boy's ever been nasty to me,' Avril had sighed. It had never happened to Tiffany either.

Her ears pricked up.

'This lesson,' Mrs Powell was saying, 'will be your last for a few weeks. You'll be relieved to hear that I'm off on holiday tomorrow.'

Olly mimed a cheer.

'Where's that?' asked Yusuf.

'Around and about,' said Mrs Powell. 'Kerala, mainly.'

'South India,' Susie put in.

'Yes. I'm patron of a wildlife sanctuary there. I pop in from time to time. See how the inmates are getting on.'

'Cats?' said Yusuf. 'Big cats, like, tigers and so on?'

'Of course,' Mrs Powell smiled. 'I'll bring you photos.'

She hoisted herself into a higher fork where the whole group could see her.

'So it's to be a special lesson,' she said. 'Out here you can put together everything you have learned so far, and maybe more. I'm going to take you along the Wild Walk. A path I've mapped through the treetops. You may discover what you're capable of.'

A whisper of leaves was her only answer. Nervousness crackled in the air. Olly raised a hand.

'This Wild Walk,' he began. 'It isn't dangerous at all, is it? Only I promised my mum that I'd be home today by –'

Mrs Powell pointed towards the sycamore next door.

'There's our first port of call. Tiffany, get your claws ready and lead on. Ben, you be the eyes at the back. The rest of you wait for my word.'

It took Tiffany a moment to register what Mrs

Powell had said. Turning in surprise, she almost lost her balance and had to grab at a twig.

'Watch where you're going, Tiffany,' said Mrs Powell. 'You're not that good yet.'

Tiffany half-closed her eyes, mixing blue Ptep and green Mandira until she felt the tingle of whiskers. She imagined thin posts under her feet and stepped along the oak bough onto the sycamore's smoother bark. She heard Olly whisper, 'She didn't answer my –' and a grunt as Daniel elbowed him in the ribs.

So Mrs Powell knew. She had guessed about her Mau claws. Tiffany had only begun to feel them in the last couple of days. Irked that Ben had got there first, she had run through the catra exercises until her head ached, and her only reward was cramp. Then it happened. Waking up late on Tuesday she'd had a good stretch, dragging one arm across the poster above her bed. She turned to find three rips in Elijah Wood's face.

After that it grew easier. With just a little effort she could bring that tight feeling to her fingertips, as if tweezers were pinching the skin. Then, for a second, there was something there. Whether it was a static electrical charge or a real, ghostly thorn, she couldn't say. But by Wednesday's breakfast she found she could lower her finger over a Rice Krispie and, before she actually touched it, burst it to dust.

She had lined up five Krispies on her place-mat, popping them in turn, when Stuart asked what she was doing. She couldn't resist showing him a trick. Concentrating, she curled her right hand and jabbed it at the nearest cereal box. Clouds of Ready Brek billowed over the table as her fingers punctured through. Her parents weren't amused. 'Haven't you grown out of playing with your food?' Mum demanded, making her re-house the cereal in a Tupperware box. Stuart was now bubbling with questions about how she did it.

He'd been so much better recently. Though he hadn't yet made the miraculous recovery they all hoped for, on his best days he could have passed for a normal kid. After all (Dad scathingly pointed out), lots of boys with full use of their muscles spent more time slouched in front of the telly than Stuart did. He took four Panthacea pills a day and no longer complained about the bitter taste. He could walk from room to room using crutches and had even started going swimming, with the help of armbands. At first Tiffany had gone too, until she'd splashed him and got a telling-off from Mum. That was a bit rich, seeing that Stuart had started it.

Tiptoeing along the sycamore's almost horizontal upper trunk, Tiffany began to see the treetops in a new way. The roadmap of branches really had become roads, winding in every direction, including straight up and straight down. She could have taken any of them. To her left she saw a tiny yellow eye painted halfway up an oak. This looked tricky. Creeping along a thinner limb, she focused hard on her fingertips before hopping across the gap. The bark clung to her hands like clay to a car tyre, giving her time to scramble onto a bough.

Olly moaned, 'You're kidding!'

'Tiffany,' said Mrs Powell, 'that was good, but do pay attention. There is a much easier way of reaching that tree. Not everyone has claws yet.'

'Sorry, Mrs Powell.' Tiffany tried not to smile.

'Yeah,' said Yusuf. 'Nine out of ten for skill. Two out of ten for good thinking.'

Tiffany stuck out her tongue at him. She'd never felt so chuffed. There was a twenty-foot drop below her and she cared nothing, absolutely nothing about it.

She practised making scratch-marks on the wood while Mrs Powell led the others round the easy way. Yusuf was looking more confident and Susie was singing to herself. Then with a start she found Ben right beside her, dusting off his T-shirt. He must have taken the same tricky route as her.

'Hmm. Quite easy really,' he mumbled, and stalked off after the others.

Huh? She crouched still, her thoughts and feelings a mishmash. What had that been about? Was he trying to make some sort of point? Or just wind her up for spiteful reasons of his own? Taking a short cut across a raft of thin branches she snatched back her place at the front of the group.

'What *is* that you're humming, Susie?' she asked. The tune was getting stale.

'Oh. Was I?' Susie blushed. 'Just something I'm playing with the school orchestra. *Peter and the Wolf*. It's my clarinet part.'

'I thought it sounded familiar,' murmured Mrs Powell.

Step by step they picked their way through the sturdier boughs. Thicker and thicker meshed the branches until it was hard to spot the eyes painted on them. Elderly moss-clad trees stretched at strange angles, like giants roused from sleep.

'Flow,' Mrs Powell commanded, watching Daniel and Cecile wobble along a chestnut's limb. 'Think with your body not your brain. Use your Felasticon.'

'Um.' From the way Cecile licked her lips, Tiffany guessed that she had forgotten what Felasticon was. Impatiently Mrs Powell explained it again.

Tiffany hadn't forgotten, though the seventh rudiment was still new to her. Now was a good time to try it. Summoning her Ptep and Ailur catras, she stretched for a branch that should have been out of reach, caught it and swung herself up. Felasticon. The reason cats moved like cats. Human spines, Mrs Powell said, were mere strings of beads, the bones linked by ligaments. But the bones in a cat's spine were joined by muscles. The whole thing could flex like living elastic, at once a powerhouse, shock-absorber and rubbery rudder. Human beings couldn't, of course, develop backbones like this, no matter how much pashki they did. But the Felasticon stretch produced a similar effect.

One by one the Cat Kin dropped from branch to branch. Mrs Powell waited below on a massive log that bridged a ditch. Susie jumped onto Yusuf's back.

'I'm tired of all these stupid leaves and things. Carry me!'

'Sure,' said Yusuf. 'Leopards can lift their own weight into a tree, can't they?'

'Are you suggesting I weigh as much as you do?' demanded Susie.

'With all the chips you eat, definitely.'

'Put her down, Yusuf,' said Mrs Powell. 'You're a cat, not a pony. We'll take a breather here and then make our way back.'

They found places to sprawl along the log. After several minutes (though it could have been longer; Tiffany thought she might even have dozed off) Mrs Powell rounded them up and led them into the octopus limbs of a conifer.

Revived by her nap, Tiffany scrambled through the

wood's vaulted roof. She was just reminding herself to slow down and let the others keep up when she felt a throb of unease, like a red light, in her stomach. Something was going on behind her. She hurried back along the branch.

'What's the problem?' Daniel was saying. 'It's an easy one. It's no sweat.'

'Enough,' snapped Mrs Powell. 'Let him take his time.'

Olly stood bent-kneed midway along a bough. He wasn't moving. At the edges of his face-print his skin was deathly white. Everything cat-like about him had drained away. He looked like a plump teenage boy with a terror of heights, stuck twenty feet above the ground.

'Why doesn't he move?' whispered Cecile. 'He's managed thinner branches than this.'

'I reckon it's vertigo.' Daniel wiped his glasses, which had steamed up. 'My dad—'

'Oliver.' Mrs Powell's voice rang out. 'There's nothing to worry about. I want you to close your eyes.'

Olly swayed. He flung out his arms and whimpered.

'Close your eyes,' repeated Mrs Powell, 'and picture blue. A blue cat's eye. See it, Olly. The blue eye.'

Ptep is my head, the balancing blue sky . . .

His eyes stayed open, darting to and fro as if the

leaves were closing in on him. His breath sounded like someone sobbing. Tiffany could smell the sweat glistening on his forehead. She wanted to shout at him, *Don't be scared. Don't be scared.* Because fear was the problem. She had discovered for herself that pashki didn't work properly if you were afraid. A cat's sense of fear was stronger than a human's. It could become so violent that it smothered everything else. And then you were in trouble.

Little by little his breathing settled. Tiffany thought he might move. He didn't. Minutes passed. Mrs Powell climbed into a smaller holly tree, a few yards adrift of Olly, though it was hard to see what she could do if he actually fell.

'He's not going to make it on his own,' whispered Yusuf. Too loudly. Olly began to shake. He tried to kneel on the bough, then changed his mind.

'No, Yusuf,' Mrs Powell hissed. Yusuf had climbed down to where Olly's branch sprouted from the oak and was now standing on it, stretching out his hand.

'Come on, Ol.' He sidled closer. 'Give me your arm. You'll be okay.'

'Yusuf.' Mrs Powell was barely audible above the shivering leaves. 'Leave him. Don't be a fool.'

'Do as she says,' gulped Susie.

'I've got him.' Yusuf seized Olly's hand. Olly wouldn't, or couldn't, turn to face him. He had frozen. Mrs Powell crouched below on her branch, as tense, Tiffany could feel, as a bowstring at full draw.

'Step away from him *now*.'

Something in her voice made Yusuf react. He tried to take back his hand but Olly gripped like a vice.

'No –'

The next few seconds were hard to follow, even though Tiffany saw them in slow motion. Yusuf pulled to get free. Olly fought to hold on. Yusuf reeled and, with a shout, shoved him away. Olly stepped backwards onto nothing.

Mrs Powell leaped, a blur, hooking her left hand onto the bough. With her right she snatched at Olly as he fell. She caught the neck of his grey T-shirt, her fingers going through the cotton, and Olly stopped with a jerk, his shirt stretching like gum but amazingly not tearing. Mrs Powell clung on, her other hand clamped to the bark, the tendons standing out in ridges.

'Quick as you can, please,' she said through gritted teeth.

Ben was there before she'd stopped speaking. Bracing his feet in a fork of the holly tree he grabbed Olly's legs to take some of his weight. Daniel clambered to his side and seized Olly's arm. The three of them together eased him down. Olly cried out as he swung against the pointy leaves.

'Hey. Anyone? I need some help here!'

'Yusuf!' Susie screamed. Her newspaper fell fluttering to the ground like a shot pheasant.

In the confusion Tiffany hadn't seen Yusuf fall. Now he clung to a stubby branch that jutted like a broken bone from another trunk. His legs kicked empty air as he struggled to pull himself up. Every time he managed to get his chest across the branch, he slipped down. His olive skin had flushed dark and he was gasping.

'Hold on, Yusuf,' cried Mrs Powell. 'Tiffany, I need you. Come and help with Oliver.'

Tiffany got ready to move. Then a creak came from Yusuf's branch. In horror she saw it had no leaves. Yusuf was hanging from dead wood. It groaned as he scrabbled for a better hold.

'Tiffany!' Mrs Powell called. 'Quick! I can't be in two places at once.'

She dithered. Could Mrs Powell get here before the branch broke? There was no time to wonder. Someone had to help Yusuf now.

'I'm on it!' The answer came in a flash. She couldn't get to Yusuf along the dead limb – it would snap. But a second, slender branch passed almost directly over him. It might bear the weight of one.

'Yusuf,' she called. 'See that branch above you? You're going to grab it.'

His eyes rolled towards her, all bloodshot whites. 'No way. It's too high up.'

'Not yet.'

Tiffany scrambled down the tree trunk and placed a foot on the branch. The tip of it trembled like a fishing-rod at the bite. Come to that, it wasn't much thicker than a fishing-rod. Hardly daring to watch, she took a few steps with her eyes closed. She opened them when the branch bowed under her weight. If she stepped much further it would bend and tip her off.

'Tiffany!' Yusuf gasped. 'I think this thing's gonna break!'

'Listen.' She spoke quickly. 'On the count of three, I want you to reach up and take hold of this branch.'

He groped. 'I can't reach it!'

'On the count of three!' she shouted. 'Ready. One. Two.' She braced herself. 'Three!'

She bounded one big stride along the slender branch and landed on it hard. It bent right down to the dead limb where Yusuf hung. In that instant Tiffany sprang back up, stretching out. *Felasticon.* Her finger-tips found the oak's rugged hide just before its trunk knocked the breath from her body. She hung there, dizzy, a rainbow of catras strobing in her head, until the world swam back into focus.

Getting a proper grip on a squirrel's hole she looked over her shoulder. Yusuf had done it. The supple branch, with her weight gone, had pulled him up as he grabbed it. Reaching the safety of a three-way fork he slumped, panting, on a pillow of ivy. Never had she seen anyone look so relieved, unless it was Olly, now down on the ground picking holly leaves out of his shirt. High in the oak, Tiffany found a comfy place to sit. She found she was grinning like an idiot.

'That,' said Mrs Powell, 'is *not* what I told you to do.'

'Right,' someone muttered.

'Let's hear it for . . . for disobedience,' Yusuf panted. 'Ten out of ten, Tiffs.'

'No,' Mrs Powell shot back. 'Disobedience is what got you into that mess, Yusuf. If you'd done as I said neither you nor Oliver would have fallen.' Her tone became softer. 'Still. That's what happens when you train people to be cats. As Akhotep points out, cats heed no words.' She paused. 'So there's no real point in saying, well done, Tiffany.'

Mrs Powell rubbed a hand absently over her mouth. They rested again before moving on at a gentler pace. Olly stayed at ground level, Yusuf keeping him company.

Tiffany was walking on air. Daniel wouldn't shut up about what she'd done, telling it over and over, complete with sound effects. Cecile said she was officially the Cat Princess, and Susie was speechless. Though she tried not to bask in it too much, Tiffany became aware of a swagger in her step as she moved from branch to branch.

Her Mau whiskers vibrated. Ben was crackling through the twigs of a nearby tree.

'Hey,' she said. 'That's not on the route, is it?'

'What if it isn't?'

'Only the ones with painted eyes, remember,' said Tiffany. 'Come on. We don't want any more accidents.'

'Oh, *we* don't, do we?'

The scorn in his voice practically shook her from her perch.

'What's got into you, Ben?'

'I bet you thought that was clever.'

'What was?'

Ben crouched on a crooked beam, seeming to bristle. Why? Tiffany looked round. Mrs Powell was busy helping Cecile cross an awkward gap.

'It was worth the risk, was it?' said Ben. 'To make yourself look good. There's a time and a place for showing off.'

'I wasn't showing off!' She crossed into the forbidden tree. 'I was helping Yusuf.'

'Mrs Powell told you to help *us*. We could have dropped Olly.'

'But you didn't,' Tiffany replied. 'And my plan worked.'

'By a fluke, yeah.' Ben flicked a wing-shaped seed off a twig. It helicoptered down to the undergrowth.

'I'd no time to think,' said Tiffany. 'Anyway, even if Yusuf had fallen, he'd have fallen on his feet. Cats always do.'

Ben shook his head. 'You are unbelievable. So sure everything will turn out all right. Let me tell you now, it doesn't. You fall too far, you don't get up again.'

'And you're the expert.'

'I haven't grown up wrapped in cotton wool, no.'

That hurt. For a second Tiffany wanted to scream at him.

'I can't help it if I'm actually good at something, can I?' she hissed.

'Is that so.' Ben stepped onto the end of his branch, so that it dipped like a rollercoaster rail. 'You've got a point to prove? Come on then, prove it.' His eyes were slits, utterly feline. 'Last one back to the dell is dog food.'

The branch shuddered like a diving-board as he leaped, plunging into the waterfall leaves of a willow. Before the green ripples had died he was scrambling up the steepest bough, calf muscles creasing with the strain.

Tiffany was convinced she would do the sensible thing. To follow him would be stupid. For one thing, it would play into his hands, and for another, Mrs Powell would skin her alive. Not to mention the perils of straying off the route. It was the silliest, most childish thing imaginable. So it came as a real shock to find herself sprinting along the sycamore's arm and springing after him.

Later she would ask herself why. Coming first at things didn't interest her, or so she believed. Racing against a moody boy who didn't even like cats was hardly worth risking her life. She would look back and think that, if it weren't for this one rash impulse, things might have turned out differently. But for now, it was as if some inner demon had taken control.

Ben was clambering upwards, probably a good tactic for moving quickly through the wood. Tiffany wished she'd thought of the fingerless gloves – her own sore palms were traced with bark patterns. Ignoring the shout from behind her ('*Tiffany! Ben! Stop this instant!*') she jumped for the bearded willow, grabbed an armful of tendrils and swung like Tarzan through its horseshoe frame. She let go. There was a moment of terror as she sailed through emptiness. Then her inner cat kicked in, twisting her in mid-air so that she touched down on the willow's outer limb. She looked up in time to see Ben hurtling, black against the sky, into the crowning branches of a . . . there was no time to tell what kind of tree it was.

Okay, so he was pretty fast. She could do better.

Though he had the altitude, down here the treescape offered more opportunities. A tree bearing bobbly green fruits fanned its branches like the spokes of an umbrella. She bounded from spoke to spoke, catapulting herself off the last branch. In a blink she was inside a cathedral of a horse chestnut, emerald light glimmering through leafy windows, its mighty boughs straining higher like a spire towards the sun. Up she dashed through the rafters as if ascending a spiral staircase, leaping out through a portal in the leaves.

Twigs crashed in her right ear. Ben had landed on the same branch as her. He had the cheek to flash a smile before springing off, one jump ahead. They were in a piny evergreen that stuck out rafts of foliage like rainclouds. The rafts shook and thundered, showering needles and cones, as first Ben and then Tiffany bounced from one to the next.

But, she saw, Ben had made a mistake. He had strayed too far to the right, where a gap in the woods made it impossible to continue. By cutting up the inside, around the trunk of the pine, she could nip into the next tree and take the lead. With a thrill of triumph she skidded down a nobbly branch and looked round for Ben. Her heart missed a beat.

He was flying through the air in a mind-boggling leap. She stopped still, aghast. More than twenty feet of nothing yawned between the pine and the nearest safe landing, an oak. He would never make it.

He made it.

Her horror turned to disbelief. Foliage buckled and burst with the force of Ben smashing through it. Had he sprouted wings, she'd have been less astonished. She pursued, but with a sinking heart. If he was ready to dare jumps like that, she was not going to win this race. Now he was one whole tree ahead. Her catras kindled, Ailur for agility and Parda for strength, and she poured herself onwards. Ben was already gone. Surely he couldn't have left her behind so quickly?

She spun on one toe. The oak tree looked empty. Her eyes were drawn by a flock of ducks rising like smoke from the shrub layer, as if something had disturbed them. Her insides lurched. Something was wrong. Trembling, suddenly unsure of being up so high, she struggled down to the ground and ran stumbling between the trees.

She pushed through bushes on to the shore of a large pond, where she found herself surrounded by a dozen women in swimsuits. One tall, athletic woman covered in tattoos was wading out of the shallows, dragging some heavy floating object behind her. She heaved it up onto the wooden jetty and stood there pink-faced, panting with exertion.

'Just what d'ya think you were doing?' she spat,

wiping her eyes. 'Think it's fun to bomb into the water out of the trees, yeah? You could have killed someone. And this is the *women's* bathing pond, as if you didn't know.'

Ben, his T-shirt and tracksuit leggings ripped and soaking wet, rolled over with a groan. His face was masked with mud and pond-weed, mingling with his cat-paint to turn him into some sort of water-goblin.

'Sorry. He's with me.' Running to his side, Tiffany helped Ben to stand.

'You can keep him. Little creep,' muttered some-one else.

When they had limped through the trees a safe dis-tance, Tiffany let him walk on his own. He crumpled onto his knees. For a second she worried that he was terribly injured. Then she saw he was laughing.

'Come on, get up.' She jabbed him with her foot. 'What's so funny?'

'You were wrong,' Ben spluttered, still catching his breath. 'I was right.'

'What do you mean? Right about what?'

'Cats don't . . .' Ben stopped to spit out a string of algae. 'Cats don't always fall on their feet.'

9

The Uninvited Guest

Sensible Jim had evaporated through the cat flap in the first heat of Mrs Powell's rage. Ben wished there was a pashki trick for following him. Mrs Powell stopped shouting. He waited. As expected, she was only taking another breath.

'Don't think I'd be sorry if you broke your necks,' she fumed. 'I couldn't care less, believe me. But if you kill yourselves with your games it is I who will go to jail. And I'm not spending the last years of my life locked in a cell.'

Ben couldn't look at Tiffany. He knew he would see tears on her cheeks.

'Sorry,' he mumbled. 'I don't know what got into me.'

'A feeble answer,' said Mrs Powell. 'You know full well what got into you. As do I. The point is, *you control it*.'

Tiffany whispered some wretched apology of her own. Mrs Powell glowered a while longer. Then she said:

'There once were two cats at Kilkenny. Each thought there was one cat too many. So they quarrelled and fit, they scratched and they bit, till instead of two cats, there weren't any.' She smiled thinly. 'You two haven't been getting along, is that it?'

Ben shuffled his feet.

'I know what got into you,' Mrs Powell repeated. 'Unfortunately, that makes it difficult to know who to blame.'

'It was mostly my fault,' said Ben. 'You mustn't blame Tiffany too much.'

'Very noble, I'm sure,' said Mrs Powell. 'The fact is, you're both at the stage when you'll begin to ignore me anyway. The Mau heeds nothing but its own voice.' She gave a humourless laugh. 'You ought to feel sorry for me. It's hard being a teacher when your ultimate goal is that your pupils will stop listening to you.'

Tiffany showed no sign of understanding this any better than Ben did. He wondered if he would faint on the studio floor. He ached all over, his skin itched with twig scratches and he felt as damp and rank as a compost heap. He longed to get home, soak in the bath and fall into bed.

'Still,' said Mrs Powell, 'you're alive. And possibly

wiser. Perhaps I can enjoy a worry-free holiday.'

She saw them out, peering intently into their faces as they crossed the threshold. Ben felt as if something had put its paw on his grave.

'Cheerio,' she said. 'I'll see you in a few weeks. Meanwhile,' her eyes glinted in the stairwell's pale light, 'stay out of trouble.'

Ben had suspected that one day he might be attacked in his own home. But not by Tiffany.

'*Mostly* your fault?' she cried. 'I like that. "Oh, Mrs Powell, you mustn't blame her!" Damn right she shouldn't. What did *I* do?'

'Well . . . you did follow me.'

'A good thing I did. Someone had to keep an eye on you.' Tiffany flushed a little. Ben had been surprised to hear her voice on the entry phone, asking if she could come in. She was calling round, she said, to see if he was okay after his fall yesterday. Now, having satisfied herself that he wasn't fatally injured, she was ripping into him.

'I told her it was me,' Ben protested. 'What more do you want?'

'But the way you said it made her think it was *my* fault!' said Tiffany. 'While you look good by offering to take the blame.'

She'd lost him already. 'Did I?'

'*Did I?*' she mimicked. 'Yeah, Ben. As if you didn't know. So now Mrs Powell's hacked off with me, while you're some kind of hero for owning up to something you didn't do, when you did, and – *ugh!*' She slapped her own head.

Smiling certainly wasn't a good idea. She glared at him but that only made it worse. Fighting the giggles, he backed away down the hall.

'You've got to admit,' he was cornered against the linen cupboard, 'it is pretty funny.'

For a second he thought he was a goner.

'Shut up.' A grin had caught her unawares. 'You probably just ruined my life.'

'One down, eight to go, eh?' Ben slipped past her into the kitchen and opened the fridge. Mum's friend Lorelei had dragged her out to dinner this evening, in a bid to take her mind off things, so it was sandwiches for Ben. He found a plate of them wrapped in cling film.

'Then again,' Ben couldn't resist saying, 'it kind of *was* your fault.'

'What?'

'Sandwich?' He held the plate out. She ignored it.

'What do you mean?' she asked, dangerously.

'Well,' said Ben, 'you do sometimes lord it over the rest of us. Always trying to prove you're the best. Which you probably are.'

'That is *so* made-up,' snapped Tiffany. 'I don't do that. I never expected to be any good at pashki. You're the competitive one. And the –'

'The what?'

'Well . . . a bit rude, since you ask. Acting like I'm not there.'

'You don't exactly chat much to me, either.'

'Well, if you'd been less . . . I don't know, wrapped up in yourself.'

'That's what I thought *you* were like.'

They stared at each other a moment. Slowly, Tiffany broke into a smile.

'We seem to be talking.'

'Yeah.' Ben felt suddenly shy. 'It doesn't hurt that much, does it?'

'No.' She laughed. 'Friends, then?'

Feeling his face go a shade redder, he fetched two plates from the cupboard.

'Want to share these?'

They went into the lounge, where a pair of his boxer shorts were drying on the radiator. He snatched them off, stuffing them under a cushion as he sat down. They munched happily at tinned tuna and cucumber.

'It's funny,' Tiffany spoke with her mouth full, 'I really thought you were angry with someone. Me, or Mrs Powell. I guess I imagined it.'

'No, you didn't.' said Ben. 'I mean, I am angry. But not at anyone you know.' He took a deep breath. 'Are you sure you want to hear this?'

She nodded. He looked at the wall beside her and told her everything. From the first appearance of John Stanford to the wrecked front door, to Dad's beating at the hands of the thug Toby. As Tiffany listened, Ben felt a weight lift off him. Soon he was talking not to the wall but to her face.

'Phew,' said Tiffany, when he finally trailed off. 'Can't you go to the police?'

He repressed a groan.

'We did try,' he said. 'Apparently, no crime has been committed. Stanford's too good at covering his tracks.'

'But the door . . . your dad . . .'

'This is Hackney,' said Ben, bitterly. 'The door could have been kicked in by any druggie. And my dad went looking for trouble and got it. Thanks to me. I should have kept my mouth shut.' He picked at his sandwich. 'Sorry. I bet this is a real downer for you.'

Tiffany flicked a crumb at him. 'Don't go back to being like that. You should talk about it. I know what it's like when . . . when no one will listen.'

'Yeah?'

'Yes.'

Now it was her turn to talk. She told him about her

brother. Of a terrible, creeping illness, of hospital wards and empty houses, of parents pushed near breaking point. By the time she finished, the living room was darkening and the remaining sandwiches had gone crisp. Ben didn't bother turning on the light. Both of them could see perfectly well.

'Sorry,' said Ben, after a while.

'S'alright. It's nothing you did.'

'I mean . . . I've been thick. I always thought you must have this perfect life, compared to me.'

'I look at lots of people and think that,' said Tiffany. 'But there's no such thing. Even if Stuart wasn't ill . . .' She looked sad, then brightened. 'Anyway. He's getting better. With this new medicine. So things probably are tougher for you.'

'Not that we're being competitive or anything,' said Ben.

They both laughed. Tiffany was okay, Ben decided. Maybe more than okay.

'Do your parents know?' she asked him, abruptly. 'About the Cat Kin, I mean?'

'As if!' said Ben. 'Well, Mum knows I take a class. It was her idea that I do self-defence. To her, pashki's just a kind of karate. That suits me. As for my dad . . . well, I don't really talk to him enough. So it's never come up.'

Tiffany gave the wryest of smiles. 'Sounds *ve-ry* familiar.'

'You keep it secret too?'

'Ha.' Her smile soured. 'Wouldn't matter if I didn't. Wouldn't matter if I recited Akhotep's catra chant at breakfast. One day, I swear, I'll climb the stairs in two strides and they won't even blink. All my mum and dad think about is –' She stopped.

'Stuart?'

Tiffany gazed at her feet. 'I'm not, you know, jealous of him or anything. I – I love him. And he's ill. He needs them more than I do.'

Ben took a breath and found his mind had gone blank. He couldn't think of a thing to say that wouldn't sound stupid.

'Of course,' Tiffany went on, her voice sounding husky, 'I never would tell them the real story. About pashki. But I do sometimes feel . . . it might be nice if they were a little bit curious, now and then. Don't you think?'

Ben decided to gather the plates.

'Shall, er . . . shall I put the TV on?'

Tiffany checked her watch. 'I ought to be going. Even my family might be wondering where I am by now.'

'Sure,' said Ben. He felt relieved and disappointed. 'I'll give you a call and we can do some more –'

'Yeah . . .' Tiffany looked distracted. 'What's that?'

Ben heard the footsteps in the lobby.

'You see?' he sighed. 'My mum doesn't even like staying out late anymore.'

He went to open the door. Tiffany got in his way.

'Don't.'

'Huh?'

'That's not your mum,' she whispered.

A keyring jingled, faint.

'Of course it's her.' Ben hated the fact that he was whispering too. 'No one else has a key to this place.'

'I don't know how I know. I just do.'

The hairs rose on his neck and he had a sudden, stabbing pain in his gut. He had no idea who stood on the other side of that door, but she was right, it wasn't Mum. A key scratched in the lock.

'Hide.'

He opened the linen cupboard and scrambled to the top rack. There was just enough space to curl up. Tiffany dived into a lower shelf. Ben pulled the closet shut just as the front door opened.

Through a crack he saw a blond man in a suit. For a moment John Stanford stood there listening, then made for the bathroom. Ben heard him running the taps, opening and closing the medicine cabinet, shaking bottles of shampoo. He flushed the loo.

Stanford. He was here. Here in their home. He had a *key* to their home.

Ben's blood, already cold, went arctic. This wasn't

an ordinary landlord's key. They'd replaced the original lock when the door got smashed. Stanford must have come here, in secret, to have his own key specially made. When? How many times, for heaven's sake, had he been in here without them knowing?

'Is that . . . him?' Tiffany whispered.

Ben couldn't speak. His mind was in freefall.

Stanford crossed his thin field of vision, entering the kitchen. Praying the cupboard door wouldn't squeak, Ben eased it open a centimetre. Stanford was banging drawers. He opened the fridge, took the top off the milk bottle and tossed it in the bin. He found the bottle of whisky on the windowsill, chose a glass off the draining board and poured himself a huge measure, swigging it as if it were orange juice.

'What's he *doing*?' asked Tiffany.

Ben didn't dare *shush* her so he poked her with a folded section of Christmas tree. Stanford had another whisky, finishing the bottle, then rifled in the kitchen cupboard. He fished out the bag of sugar. Ben watched in sick astonishment as Stanford dug into it with a dessert spoon and helped himself to a generous mouthful.

'I'm going to get him.' The words just broke out. 'I'm going to rip him to pieces.'

'Sssh, Ben.'

'When he comes out of there I'm jumping on him.'

'No, Ben. He's twice your size.'

'We could take him together. We're faster, we can do things . . .'

'Mau claws or not, he'd be too strong.' Tiffany's voice was almost inaudible. 'Ben, listen. You know pashki doesn't work properly if you're afraid. And I am.'

Ben was too. Mortally so. He wanted to bury himself under the spare blankets. But John Stanford in his home, unchallenged . . . he couldn't stomach it. He steeled himself. Stanford sauntered back into the hall, wiping his mouth and dusting crumbs of sugar off the lapel of his sharp suit. Ben tensed. He had to do it. Now.

A terrifying racket turned his limbs to jelly. Wild dogs barking, gnashing their prey. He shrank back into the darkness. He heard a beep.

'Hello?'

The barking had stopped. Ben peeped out of the cupboard. John Stanford was holding a phone to his ear. That noise must have been his ring tone.

'What, tonight?' Stanford's face wrinkled. He glanced out of the window. 'Yes, I am in the area, but . . . All right, if you insist. See you in twenty minutes.'

He touched his jacket pocket.

'Make that forty. I've left the plans at home.'

Not for the first time, Ben clocked something odd

about Stanford's voice, in the way he pronounced certain words.

'Yes, you're busy, everyone's busy. I'll be as quick as I can. The traffic tonight would give Buddha a migraine.'

Stanford mouthed something at the phone and turned it off. There was a watercolour painting on the wall, one of Mum's. He nudged it askew before going out, slamming the door. His footsteps crossed the lobby.

Ben burst from the cupboard. Tiffany rolled out tangled in a bedsheet.

'What was all that about?'

'The scum!' Ben balled his fists. 'I'll kill him.'

'Shouldn't you –'

'Call the police? Talk sense.' He thumped the wall. Think, think. Why had Stanford come? Thank heaven Mum had been out. Stanford had a key. He could return again, and again, and again . . .

Ben stopped dead.

'I've got to follow him!'

'Why?'

'He's meeting somebody. He said something about plans, you heard.' Ben was gabbling now. 'It's to do with this place, I know it is. And you can bet it's not kosher.'

'So?'

'Tiffany, if I can prove he's doing something illegal,' cried Ben, 'those lame coppers might finally lift a finger! I can't let him get away.'

He tore across the lobby and opened the main door just in time to see Stanford's silver saloon pulling away from the kerb.

'He's gone,' said Tiffany. 'You can't chase him without a car.'

'That's what you think.'

Ben sprinted to the corner. Lonely trees grew beside the main street, their leaves styled into overhanging quiffs by the constant passing of tall vehicles.

'We're not going to catch him,' panted Tiffany.

'No,' said Ben. 'We're going to catch a bus.'

Amazingly, there was one around when they needed it. Stiff and awkward in their everyday clothes they climbed to a branch that grew over the road, just as a shiny red 73 came chugging round the bend.

'This is a seriously bad idea.'

'My family's in serious trouble,' Ben replied.

'It's impossible to move properly in jeans. And I'm wrecking these shoes.'

'Maybe I can ask Mr Stanford to wait so you can go back and change.'

'Maybe you can stop being so sarcast–'

'*Jump!*' Ben interrupted.

He landed with a thud on the bus's curved roof. Tiffany dropped behind him. They threw themselves flat as another low branch whipped past. The bus crunched over a speed hump and Tiffany was nearly bounced off.

'I don't see why we can't pay our fare like normal people.'

'I've got no cash,' said Ben.

'I'd rather risk a fine than my neck.'

Ben grinned. 'Don't tell me you haven't always wanted to do this.'

Windows of first-floor flats flickered by as the bus picked up speed. A woman at a kitchen sink emptied a teapot over her clean washing-up as she turned in astonishment to watch them pass. Early streetlamps blinked on.

'Anyway,' Ben added, 'we need to be mobile.'

'Mobile?'

Ben's hunting eyes found their target. The silver-grey car was shouldering its way through a junction about a hundred yards ahead. Their bus caught up with another as they neared a set of traffic lights. The lights switched to amber.

'Quick!' Like an athlete off the blocks Ben ran along the roof. He leaped onto the top of the next bus as it accelerated through the changing lights, leaving the other standing at red.

'Oh,' said Tiffany, 'mobile.' She gave him a sour look and rolled away from the roof's edge. She had barely made the jump in time.

Ben struggled to keep Stanford's car in view. It was a long way ahead, jostling with vans and taxis, a grey mouse in a maze. The traffic thickened like syrup. More and more buses filtered into their road until they were stuck in a crawling train of them.

'Hurry *up*.' Ben slapped the bus as if it were a lazy horse. Then he realised how daft he was being. Beckoning Tiffany, he took a running leap onto the next red roof in the queue, then the next, using each one as a stepping stone. By the time they reached the leading bus, Stanford was clearly visible, swerving right at a crossroads without indicating. Their new ride pulled away and Ben whooped in triumph. Then a thought struck him.

'What number bus are we on now?'

'How should I know?' Tiffany demanded.

'We need one that's going his way!' He caught the bus's reflection in a shop window as they approached the crossroads. It was a 38. That meant it would go straight on. In the corner of his eye he saw a bus turning.

'Get the Four-seven-six!' he yelled. Its rear-end swung out and they flung themselves onto it. Ben fought a wave of dizziness.

'This is the last time I'm going out with you,' said Tiffany.

Shouts rose from behind them as more and more pedestrians caught sight of the two crazy kids clinging to the bus's roof. Riding down a one-way street, Ben saw the silver car take a left.

'Here's our stop.'

They hopped onto the next bus shelter and scrambled down to the pavement, ignoring the dumbstruck looks from waiting passengers. Stanford had driven into a road lined with dignified Victorian terraces. A short way down it they found his car, parked at an angle outside a three-storey town house.

'What now?' asked Tiffany, breathless. 'Do we go in?'

Ben shook his head. 'He said he was on his way somewhere. He's just picking something up. I want to know where he's going.'

'We can't bus-surf around London all night.'

'No.' Ben tried the boot of the car. It opened.

'Tell me you're joking.'

'I'm not asking you to come, Tiffany. It's not your problem.'

'It is, if you get in there,' she said. 'Don't be an idiot.'

The tremor in her voice was enough to make him reconsider. Then a lit window of the house went dark. Time to decide. To his dismay he found himself climbing into the boot.

'Ben, *please!*'

'Go home and wait,' he said. His heart was hammering. 'If you don't get a call from me in the next two hours, phone the police.'

Tiffany ground her teeth. 'Oh, you fool. Right. Shove up.'

'What?'

Tiffany crawled in beside him. There was barely enough room for them both and he got her feet in his face. He curled up smaller and squirmed to find a more comfortable position.

'Now who's being stupid?' he muttered. 'Nobody knows where we are.'

'Then we'll just have to take care of ourselves, won't we?' said Tiffany.

Ben eased the hatch of the boot down, being careful not to close it all the way. Under him something rustled in the darkness, maybe a plastic bag.

He heard Stanford come out of the house and open the driver's door. Then Stanford muttered to himself. His footsteps drew nearer and Ben knew, with horrible certainty, that he had walked round to the back of the car. A heavy hand shut the boot hatch with a firm and final clunk.

The car roared into life and began to move. Muffled

music reverberated through the chassis. Then they were speeding off in an unknown direction, locked in the boot of John Stanford's car.

10

The Funny Farm

'And now . . . the end is near . . . And so I face . . . the final curtain.'

Two muffled voices seeped into the cramped darkness, one smooth as brushed velvet and accompanied by a band, the other singing along almost half a tone off-key. The car veered, tyres squeaked, and the second voice broke off to curse at another driver. Ben banged his head on a wheel-arch.

'It's locked.' Tiffany was struggling with the boot mechanism. 'Ben, we're stuck in here. He locked us in. We're —'

'Stop saying that, okay? And move your foot, it's in my face. *Ow*, not there!'

'Sorry.'

'We'll be all right,' said Ben, trying to keep the fear out of his voice. 'He'll open the boot sooner or later and then we'll leap out and disappear.'

'I did what I had to do . . .' sang the voices, 'and saw it through . . . without exemption.'

'Why?' breathed Tiffany. 'Why do you think he'll open the boot? There's nothing in here.'

Ben tried to straighten his crooked neck. 'Doesn't feel that way.'

'Please be serious! Nothing that he knows about, I mean. We could be trapped for hours. Days. We've got no water or anything. Ben, we could suffocate in here! We could –'

'Ssshh!'

The stereo had gone silent. A lone voice quavered, 'I did it myyyy wayyyy' . . . and trailed off. The car slowed and swung to the left.

'What's happening?' Ben couldn't help himself.

'We're stopping.'

'I guessed *that* part.'

'Oh no,' whispered Tiffany. 'He's got out of the car.'

The door clunked. Amidst the swish of passing vehicles Ben caught the sound of Stanford muttering.

'He's coming round to the back!' he hissed. 'He must have heard us!'

Leaping out of the boot suddenly seemed like the worst plan ever. But that hardly mattered since it wasn't going to happen. Ben found his legs had gone to sleep. If the boot opened now, Stanford would find them lying here, helpless as sardines. Ben tried to shrink into the floor of the boot, seeking a hidden spot, anything. Something dug into his back. He was lying on a polythene bag with knobbly objects inside. In desperation he pulled it free, just in case the bag was big enough to cover them like a blanket. It wasn't.

The boot opened. Cool air and car headlights swept in. A foolish instinct made Ben shut his eyes, as if this could make him invisible.

'Excuse me, sir.'

A deep, unfamiliar voice.

'What?' Stanford barked in annoyance. Ben opened one eye. Stanford was turned away from them, holding the boot ajar with one hand. He hadn't yet looked inside.

'You can't park here, sir.' Ben glimpsed the luminous sleeve of a traffic policeman. 'It's a zebra crossing. I must ask you to move.'

'There's something wrong with my car, you –' With a visible effort Stanford wrestled himself under control. 'I mean, I'm terribly sorry, officer. I was checking a fault in the boot. I heard noises. Probably didn't shut it properly.'

At this Ben snapped out of his daze. He wouldn't have another chance. He twisted the plastic bag into a rope.

'Sympathising as I do, sir, you'll have to deal with it

elsewhere.' The policeman indicated the angry hoards of traffic that were massing behind the silver saloon. Ben hooked the twisted carrier bag around the boot door's locking mechanism just as Stanford, with a petulant sigh, slammed it shut. Ben checked the door just in time to stop it bouncing back up.

A jolt, a screech of tyres, and they were moving again. They had been thrown around three sharp corners by the time Ben trusted himself to speak.

'That was close.'

'You idiot. Why didn't you shout to the policeman? He would have helped.'

'I didn't hear you shouting very loud.'

'Your foot was in my mouth!'

'Well, it doesn't matter. Look . . . I can open the door now. So we're safe.'

'I've been safer, thanks.'

'Like I said, I want to know where he's going.'

Eventually the car drew to a lazy halt. Ben felt the chassis rise as Stanford got out. He held his breath until he could no longer hear footsteps.

'He's gone.'

'Can we get out now, please?' begged Tiffany.

Ben lifted the door. The evening smouldered orange with street lamps. They were in a deserted alley bordering a patch of waste ground. Far off he saw a gang of youths bouncing on a discarded mattress.

Shadows of trees moved like eels in oil against a towering wall to his left. He had a strange feeling. At points on the journey he'd been convinced that he knew where they were going. Insistent tugs in the pit of his stomach while the car veered through the winding streets, as if he had swallowed a glowing, pulsing red magnet . . . *Oshtis feels and knows*. But the sensation kept slipping away. Now he strained to recognise the view before him. Finally it clicked.

'The old factory . . .'

'What?'

'We're back where we started,' said Ben. For some reason this made him more uneasy than ever. Over there was his own apartment block, a ghostly outline, and looming above them . . .

'That building,' he whispered. 'You can see it from our flat. It's been deserted for years.'

'Is that where Mr Stanford went?'

'Might be.'

A great black chimney, like a wizard's tower, loomed against the paler sky.

'You said it was a factory?'

'A long time ago, yeah.'

'I think my dad mentioned it once,' said Tiffany. 'He grew up in this borough. He said they used to make dog biscuits here and it stank for miles.'

Whatever this place had been, once upon a time, it

was dead and silent now. Or appeared to be. Ben clambered out of the car. The carrier bag that he had used to jam the lock fell to the ground. Tiffany picked it up.

'Hey.' She reached inside. 'Oh my – Ben! I don't believe this.'

Something had drained the colour from her face. She pulled out a brown jar, a cardboard packet and some printed leaflets. Each bore the same bold word.

Panthacea

And under this, in yellow: *For strength, for health, for life*.

Ben didn't get it.

'This is the medicine!' She shook it at him. 'It's what my little brother takes for his muscular dystrophy. What was it doing in the back of this car?'

'Search me,' said Ben. 'Do you reckon Stanford's ill with it, too?'

'Of course not. You don't know anything. He'd hardly be able to walk around.'

'Well . . .' Ben was at a loss.

The dusky light cast two tiny images of the factory in Tiffany's eyes.

'*He* can't have anything to do with Panthacea, can he?'

'Uh . . . maybe he has a friend who . . .'

'I want to know.' Tiffany shut the bag in the boot. 'We have to follow him.'

Suddenly Ben didn't feel so keen.

'It's getting late,' he said. 'You said your parents would be wondering where you are.'

'Well, they *might*,' said Tiffany. 'But I can't leave it like this.'

'They're only pills.'

'Pills my little brother takes every day.' Keeping low, she stalked towards the building.

'We can come back in daylight.'

'Darkness is daylight for us.'

'Tiffany,' Ben hissed. 'I'm sorry I dragged you into this but . . . you don't know this guy like I do! He's a nutter. He is one badly dangerous headcase.'

'That's what I mean,' said Tiffany. 'If he's connected with Panthacea, even slightly . . .'

They flattened themselves beside an ancient fire escape, the only visible entrance. There was a shackle on it, unlocked.

Ben made one last effort. 'You know what they say about curiosity and the cat, don't you?'

Ignoring him, Tiffany shunted the door open and tiptoed into the blackness. Ben knew he had no choice but to go with her. Tiffany opened a second door. A glow picked out the edges of a yawning space. On silent feet they crept into a gloomy hall, drawn by a murmur of voices off to the right.

*

At the heart of this dead cavern, where it seemed that only rats scuttled unseen through decades of dust, something was alive. Beyond stout pillars, inlaid with surprisingly ornate brickwork punctuated by rusted signs, two figures faced each other across a pool of light. Dust-ghosts twirled in these harsh yellow beams, rising to the arc lamps that glared from their wall-mountings. Ben willed his whole being into the soles of his feet, bidding them to pad upon the air above the floor, in the silence of Eth walking. Luckily the factory was webbed about with shadows; it was easy to slip among them as they stalked towards the light.

' . . . so what can I do for you, John?' The gangly figure in the brown camel-skin coat looked at his watch, which he wore nurse-fashion on the inside of his wrist.

'You asked me here.' It wasn't hard to catch the irritation in John Stanford's voice.

'Did I? In that case come into my office.'

The thin man beckoned with his right hand. His left, Ben noticed, was tucked protectively under his coat, as if his arm was hurt. The two men moved into an area enclosed by cardboard boxes, where a desk, a computer and a cabinet stood forlornly like a furniture shop display.

Seating himself on the desk, the man fixed his pale

eyes on Stanford. Ben was reminded of the sick snake he'd once seen in a pet shop. 'You have the architect's drawings?'

'Here.' Stanford fished in his pocket. The thin man dropped the folded papers to one side without a second glance.

'I'll study them at leisure.' He smiled mirthlessly. 'So, how's the work going?'

'If that's all you wanted to ask me, Doctor Cobb,' replied Stanford, 'you could have mentioned it on the telephone –'

'*What* did he say?' Tiffany hissed in Ben's ear.

'Ssh! They'll hear us.'

'He called that man Doctor Cobb. Philip Cobb is the name of the scientist who makes my brother's medicine –' Tiffany bit her own fist as if that was the only way she could silence herself.

'Since you ask,' Stanford was now saying, 'it's fine. Horton and Forrester have agreed the contract. The building can be under way shortly.'

'Shortly? And the hold-up is?'

'If you think your science is complicated,' said Stanford, 'you should try dabbling in real estate. It takes a week for a solicitor to stir his own tea.' He sniffed noisily. 'It's nothing to concern you. Just acquiring the last bit of land from the so-called owners. They've been a pain but that's about to stop.'

'Is it?' said Doctor Cobb. 'I wanted the laboratory finished and in production by next summer. That's looking less likely, wouldn't you agree?'

'We have this place in the meantime.'

'Oh yes, it's perfect, an abandoned dog-biscuit factory,' said Cobb. 'Just the sort of image I want plastered across my homepage. And as for the toilet facilities . . . I'd rather hold it in.'

Stanford appeared to bristle, a smell of danger wafting this way. Before he could speak, however, Cobb sprang from the desk like a spider.

'No, no, stop there, stop *right* there.'

Ben seized Tiffany's arm and got ready to flee. It took him a moment to realise that Philip Cobb's attention was directed elsewhere. They were not, after all, alone in this desolate building. Cobb ran to a pair of workmen who were struggling to operate an ancient goods lift. The lift had ropes rather than cables and a bulky iron cage that looked as if it belonged in a museum. The men were barged aside with surprising force.

'Do that and you'll regret it,' Cobb snapped. 'For heaven's sake, it's not rocket science. Granted, it's similar to rocket science, but it's not.'

He singled out one of the labourers, a kid who looked barely seventeen.

'The lift is empty, you dunce. So you need to

unload the counterweight before you take the brake off.' He pointed up to a stack of weights that dangled at the top of the lift gantry. 'If it's not properly balanced it'll come crashing down, wreck the mechanism and very likely you as well. So if you don't want to end your days on my dissecting table,' Cobb slapped a peeling cardboard notice, 'learn to read.'

He trudged back to the office area. Stanford was grinning.

'So how is *your* work going?'

'Couldn't be better,' Cobb said, acidly. 'Anyway, we'll get there. We're just about meeting demand . . . even if we do have to trek between three different processing plants to make one batch. But that'll change with the new laboratory.'

'You'll have it ready by this time next year.'

'I don't doubt it.' All at once Philip Cobb became jolly. 'I say. Care for the grand tour? You can finally get to see the good work your money's doing.'

'It's about time. I'd be charmed.'

Stanford strode after Cobb, skirting round the goods lift which the two drones were still trying to figure out. Ben hung back, looked around for Tiffany and saw her slinking off in pursuit.

'No!' he hissed. 'We're leaving. Now.'

She ignored him, ducking behind a bail of metal poles. He caught up with her just in time to see Cobb pull aside the vinyl drape that divided the factory across the middle.

'Over here we have the extraction hall.'

Lines of portable lamps dazzled more than they illuminated. Wires and tubes snaked like roots across the concrete floor, weaving between chunky objects arranged in a grid. Ben wondered what they might be. Stanford seemed equally puzzled. The objects were somewhat larger than travelling trunks and glinted strangely in the lamplight. A flicker of movement from the nearest one made Stanford flinch. In that moment Ben saw it was a cage. A cage with something inside it.

He became aware of a foul stink.

'Meet the inmates,' said Philip Cobb.

The thing in the cage was a leopard. Stanford stepped backwards and bumped into another cage, containing a second leopard. Next to that lay a tawny cat with tufted ears. Over there was something black, perhaps a panther. Everywhere – cages. Stanford's jaw was hanging open. Ben heard a stifled gasp beside him.

'Where did I get them all?' said Cobb, gesturing with a left hand that looked unnaturally small for his body. 'Here and there. Private collections. Imports. The odd zoo closure. One or two I've had for years.'

Stanford peered at the leopard from a safe distance. It was crouched, as if to spring. But this was because the cage was too small for it to stand properly. Its rounded ears brushed the top bars. Ben wondered why, if it couldn't stand up, it didn't simply lie down. It blinked two burning eyes, turning its head mechanically within the cage's narrow space, left and right, left and right, like something clockwork.

'What,' Stanford asked, licking his lips, 'are they for?'

'But of course!' Cobb rubbed his hands, as if enjoying a delicious joke. 'You don't know. I envy you business-types. None of you cares a hoot about how anything works, so long as the profits come in. You won't be bored by an explanation, I hope?'

'Mein Vater war ein Architekt und meine Mutter war ein Doktor,' growled Stanford. 'And English is only my third language, Doctor Cobb. Make it as intellectual as you like.'

'Oh.' Cobb seemed taken aback. 'Right then, look at this fellow. I call him Grizzle 'cos he's got a mean temper.'

The leopard gave a snarl like a chainsaw.

'Move round here where he can't see you,' said Cobb. 'Look there, in his side.'

Ben squinted from his hiding place, trying to see. Running under the leopard's ribs was a clear plastic tube, held in place by a scabby gauze dressing. As he watched, a dribble of dark fluid ran down the tube towards a vat outside the cage. Another tube coiled away from the vat to who-knew-where.

'What is that stuff?' asked Stanford.

'Bile,' said Cobb. 'Milked from the liver.'

'Why?'

'It's our raw material,' said Cobb. 'That's what Pan-thacea is, mostly. The bile from big cats. The Chinese have known for centuries about its medicinal properties. I've taken it a step further. A virtual cure for wasting diseases – made from one hundred per-cent natural ingredients.'

Ben heard a sob. In panic he grabbed Tiffany around the mouth, hardly aware of what he was doing until she began to squirm and gasp for air. He relaxed his hold a little, enough to let her breathe, but she was shaking as if some terrible noise would burst from her at any moment.

Philip Cobb wiped his good hand through his hair. Ben couldn't stop staring at the leopard. Now he understood why it didn't lie down. If it did, the tube sticking from its side would be forced further in.

'Of course,' said Cobb, 'the cages have to be just the right size. If we gave the animals room to turn, they'd lick at the tubes and pull them out.'

'Doesn't it . . .' Stanford frowned curiously. 'Doesn't it hurt?'

'They're used to it. Ah, it's feeding time.'

A pair of dark-haired young women had appeared in the hall, pushing trolleys that overflowed with hunks of meat. Cobb said a few words to them in some foreign language and the women began dropping meat through the bars of the cages, using pincer sticks at arm's length. The hall echoed with snuffles, grunts and growls as at least two dozen big cats ripped into their rations. The panther writhed as it tried to whip around in its cage, straining after a bit of meat that had fallen out of reach.

'We ship the bile down to my other little lab in Kent,' Cobb bawled above the din, 'which is where the pills are pressed. That's the place you can see on our website. A country house with woodland views. You'll have to come and visit sometime.'

'Charmed.' Stanford stopped to gaze at a gigantic tiger that gnawed the bars of its cage, licking off meat-blood with a tongue you could have used to sand wood.

'That's Shiva,' said Cobb. 'We go way back. One of my first acquisitions.'

He approached the cage and, to Ben's deep discomfort, produced a key. The tiger stopped its feeding frenzy. Cobb stepped within six feet, letting the key twinkle. The tiger stared. Cobb took another step. Five feet away. Three.

Shiva's paw crashed into the cage door. Hooks the size of knives raked the bars as if playing a hideous harp. A roar came from Shiva's throat, like an earthquake deep underground. Cobb didn't move.

'Shiva's been with us four or five years. Did you hear of a charity called Tigers for Tomorrow? No? They went bust, trying to breed Indian tigers for release into the wild. They were desperate to find homes for their few success stories, such as Shiva here, who was almost old enough to be released. They were grateful when I stepped in.'

Stanford lit a cigar and took a drag.

'But they didn't know you were . . . ?'

'They weren't in a position to ask,' said Cobb. He shot Stanford a searching glance. 'You're not a vegetarian or something, are you?'

'Hardly.' Stanford chuckled. As they passed a cage containing a smaller, weaker-looking tiger, he flicked a lump of cigar ash down onto its head.

'Don't,' snapped Cobb. 'If you wouldn't mind. That bile is precious. I can't have it contaminated.'

They pushed through the industrial curtain into the relative stillness of the first hall. Ben scrambled from shadow to shadow, trying to find the way back to the exit, dragging Tiffany after him. She was stumbling like someone recently blinded. Cobb strode into his makeshift office, shut the key away in the desk and unfolded the papers that Stanford had brought with him. He smiled dreamily at the drawings.

'Doctor Cobb,' said Stanford, 'you've impressed

me. When I bought us this godforsaken place I thought only of a temporary warehouse. I never imagined you could get up and running with so little.'

'Thank you.'

'Now that I see it for myself, however, I'm a little concerned . . . Those beasts. It's not exactly legal, is it?'

'I can show you my licence to keep exotic animals,' said Cobb.

'Keep, yes. But aren't there people who might . . .' Stanford sucked on his cigar. 'What I'm saying is, you wouldn't throw this place open to the public, would you?'

'If the public wants to come and look around, I shan't stop it,' said Cobb. 'However, it has not asked yet. John, no one cares.'

Stanford breathed out a grey cloud. 'Good.'

11
Locked Out

The wind on her face felt cold. Had it started raining? She jerked to a halt. A truck blew past inches in front of her, horn blaring.

'Easy.' Ben let go of her shirt. 'We're away. They didn't see us.'

Everywhere seemed half-real. She didn't recognise this street. Far behind them the factory blacked out the moon. They must have been running for minutes.

Ben was speaking to her.

'I said, there's no way you could have known.' He gripped her shoulders so she had to look at him. 'You mustn't blame – hey. You're crying.'

Was she? That explained the coldness on her cheeks. And the shaking inside her, as violent as Rufus coughing up hairballs . . . these were not coughs, but sobs.

'Those,' she gasped. She had no breath. 'Those. Poor.' She sank to the pavement. 'Those. Poor. How could . . .'

'You kids all right?' A taxi driver slowed to roll down his window. Ben must have waved him on, for he was gone when she looked up. She mopped at her tears and gulped air.

'What?' she mumbled, when Ben spoke again.

'I can walk you home,' he repeated, 'if you want.'

She shook her head, not because of anything he'd said, but to try and rid it of what she had seen.

'What are we going to do? I can't believe anyone could be so . . . Those poor cats. What are we going to do?'

'Report it to someone,' sighed Ben.

She could tell how much good he thought that would do. But surely someone *had* to care about this? The police, the RSPCA, Greenpeace, *somebody* . . .

'It depends on them believing us,' Ben said, gloomily. 'Enough to break into that factory and look inside. When its burglar alarm kept ringing a few months ago, my mum couldn't even get the police to come round and turn it off.'

Tiffany hardly listened. This was making as much sense as a nightmare.

'How can they be doing this here?' she wailed. 'It's not just sick, it's crazy. Why bring all those animals into London? I'd have thought they'd choose a place in the middle of nowhere.'

'This is the middle of nowhere.' Ben sounded bitter. 'If you don't want the police poking their noses in, you're a lot safer in a city than you are in Cumbria. It's like hiding in the jungle. So much other stuff is happening, you fade into the background. That's their plan.'

'But Ben . . .' Tears welled up again. She cupped a hand to her side, where an imagined pain was growing by the moment: a plastic tube, a festering wound. 'What are we going to do?'

'We'll think of something,' said Ben. 'We will.' He looked at his watch. 'It's late, Tiffany, we should be getting home.'

Like a sleepwalker she traipsed into the lounge, resigned to the ear-bashing she was sure to receive. Mum and Dad were watching television in ominous silence. She dropped into an armchair and waited for the grilling to begin.

After a while Mum said, 'Do you know if Stuart's managing okay up there?'

'Uh,' said Tiffany.

'That is, getting ready for bed,' said Dad. 'Rather than reaching level four of Alien War Pigs or whatever it's called.'

'Perhaps you'd better check on him in a minute, Peter.'

Tiffany eyed her parents, puzzled. They weren't exactly falling over themselves to scold her for coming in so late.

'Are you feeling okay, love?' Mum asked, after a while.

'Mmm.'

The television newsreader rambled on. She became transfixed by his outrageous tie.

'You've lain low today, Tiffs,' said Dad.

'There was a ballet programme on earlier,' said Mum. 'I tried calling you but you had your headphones on, I think.'

Then it struck her. Neither of them had noticed she wasn't in the house. She'd been out all evening, spent some of it locked in a maniac's car, and all the time they'd assumed she was upstairs. Without a word she got up and left the room.

'Tiffany?' Mum called after her. 'Don't be a stranger.'

She climbed the stairs. The bathroom light was on.

'Hi!' said Stuart. He spat out a mouthful of toothpaste. 'Where have you been?'

'Nowhere.' It was an effort to speak. 'Just with a friend.'

'A boyfriend?' Stuart grinned.

Normally she would have tickled him for that. Instead she turned away. Then she saw something that made her stomach heave. Stuart, glass of water in hand, was lifting a pill to his mouth.

'No!'

'Huh?' Stuart dropped the pill and it rolled behind the loo.

'You can't. Er . . .' She had to think. 'I've told you not to drink the water from the bathroom taps. It's from the tank. It could make you ill.'

'Cow plops. I always drink it. So do you!' Stuart tipped another tablet from the jar and swallowed it. Tiffany clutched at the bathroom door, woozy.

'You won't be taking that stuff much longer, will you?'

Stuart laughed. 'It's all right, I don't mind the taste anymore. I quite like it, actually. Panthacea doesn't make me fat like those other medicines.'

'Listen, Stuart . . .'

'Guess what. Today I managed to walk all the way to the high street *and* round the shops. I only needed the chair on the way back. And I haven't had a cough for ages.' He skipped out of the bathroom, steadier on his feet than he had been in months. 'Watch out, Tiffany. Soon I'll be strong enough to punch through card- board like you can. How do you do that, by the way? Show me again.' He trailed her across the landing into her room. 'Showme-showme-showme!'

'Oh, go to bed!' she yelled.

Stuart gazed at her with hurt eyes.

'Spoilsport,' he muttered, trudging out.

Tiffany went to bed and lay awake.

The flat was silent, but it was the kind of silence that told him Mum was home. Ben found her in the kitchen, sipping coffee. He had to resist the urge to hug her. He'd never needed to see anyone so badly.

'Hi, Mum.'

'Is that it?'

Her expression stopped him short. No wonder. It was, after all, pretty late. And as for the shock at coming home to find him gone . . .

'Mum, I'm really sorry. I –'

'You what? You went out?'

He nodded.

'I know,' she said. 'I know because I arrived home to an empty flat with the door wide open.' She sniffed. 'Mind you, at the time I didn't think you'd gone out. I thought someone had kidnapped you.'

Ben bit his lip. Dashing after Stanford he hadn't thought to shut the door behind him. 'Sorry. I – I had to leave in a hurry.'

'No doubt, Benjamin. You had important things to do.'

'I did! We –' What on earth could he tell her?

'Like getting hammered on whisky and cider at the bus-stop,' Mum's voice rose, 'with those scummy kids you hang out with.'

'*What?*'

'Don't you dare –' Mum grabbed the whisky bottle off the sideboard and waved it in his face. 'This was half full. I'm not so cracked in the head yet that I can't remember things. There's only you and me living here, you idiot. Who else is going to drink it, the mice?'

'But it wasn't me . . .' He had to tell her. It was his only way out of this. But no. He would face her anger. Better to get flayed than to tell Mum that John Stanford had been inside their home, and could come back whenever he felt like it. Ben had no idea what that news might do to her. 'I – I knocked it over and the lid wasn't screwed on. I had to mop it up.'

It was the feeblest lie he'd ever tried.

'I can smell it on your breath from here,' Mum shouted. Another lie, Ben thought, numbly. They bred like flies.

'My one night of freedom,' Mum went on, 'when I'm meant to be getting myself together again, and you have to wreck it. Do you ever think of me for just one moment?'

'Mum, listen, you don't under–'

'I mean, who'd have kids? They start noisy and

smelly, they're cute for ten seconds and then they turn into ungrateful, thieving monsters.' She took a step closer and screamed in his face. '*Where have you been?*'

Something broke inside him. 'If you could shut up for five seconds, you'd know by now!'

She slapped him. The left side of his face went stinging hot. The moment after that he would never clearly recall.

He blinked, stunned from the blow, and saw Mum sprawled on the floor on the other side of the kitchen. What was she doing down there? He walked towards her, only to see her cower into the corner. She was shielding her face. A scarlet bruise was rising on her left cheekbone and three red lines ran down to her chin. Ben stared at his right hand, still hooked in a claw shape.

'Mum,' he whispered. 'Are you hurt?'

Not taking her eyes off him, Mum groped for the sideboard and pulled herself upright.

'Out.'

'Mum,' Ben pleaded. 'I didn't mean to. I don't know what got into me. I never –'

'Out!' she cried. 'Get out! How dare you? How dare you hit your mother?'

Ben clutched at his head. This was not happening.

'You're not sleeping under this roof!' Mum advanced, breathing hard. He retreated before her, confused, terrified.

'No, Mum.'

'Get to your father's!' she bellowed. 'Go on, run to him. A right pair you make. A right pair of thugs. I wouldn't take it from him and I'm damned if I'm taking it from you. Get out of my home!'

Moments later he was standing on the pavement, transfixed by the light shining from their kitchen window, the last glimmer of life in the empty block. The wind had turned chilly. He folded his arms, wishing Mum had given him time to put on a coat or at least a sweater. Maybe if he stood here long enough the world would pop back to the way it was meant to be, like a crushed rubber ball. At length the light went out. He shivered some more. Nothing else changed.

Her words continued to ricochet round his head, striking sparks in the great black cloud of his confusion. *A right pair you make ... I wouldn't take it from him.* What did that mean? Could he pretend he didn't know? Come to that, how could he let four years pass and never once ask Dad exactly why he and Mum weren't together anymore? Maybe it was because he hadn't needed to. The little scar by Mum's eye never came from walking into any door.

He turned his back on Defoe Court and began to drift along the street like the blown scraps of litter, hardly knowing or caring where he was going.

12

Monsters in the Attic

And now, just when she thought things couldn't get any worse, Ben had disappeared. Tiffany had been round to his flat twice in the past three days, only to be told by a voice on the entry phone (presumably his mother) that he wasn't in. At last she found his mobile number scrawled on the cinema ticket she'd been using as a bookmark. She dialled, sure no one would answer. Someone cautiously said, 'Yeah?'

'Ben?'

'Oh. Hi, Tiffany. How's it going?'

'What do you mean, how's it going? It's all going to hell in a cat carrier. As if you didn't know. Have you been avoiding me?'

'No. Nothing like that.' Ben sounded tired. 'I'm staying at my Dad's. Family stuff. You don't want to know.'

She got the impression that he meant it this time.

'Ben, we need to talk. You said we could do something about those poor cats.'

'Like what?'

'Like anything!' She almost shouted it. 'We can't let it happen. All those leopards and tigers and things, in those cages with tubes stuck in them. They can't turn round, they can't lie down, they can't even sleep.' Her voice cracked. 'Ben, please. We're their only chance.'

She waited.

'What do you think I am?' said Ben. 'You think I don't care? That stuff they're doing makes me sick. They should get life in prison.'

'So let's do it!' said Tiffany. 'We'll tell the police together. All they have to do is look inside that factory.'

'The factory that everyone knows is empty.'

'Just one *look*,' she cried. 'That's all it takes. We could make something up. Say there are drug dealers squatting there. That's the truth, anyway.'

'Maybe,' said Ben. 'But Tiffany, we've got to be careful. My Mum tried calling the police before, about a Stanford thing. It didn't do any good.'

'This is different.'

'But what if Stanford knows someone in the police force? What if he can get away with anything because his friends cover it up? The only thing we'd do is give away who we are and where we live. You *don't* want Stanford knowing where you live.'

'I'll take the risk. If it means stopping Doctor Cobb.'

'Think about it,' urged Ben. 'Look, I'll . . . I'll call you back later. We'll work out a story, maybe. Don't do anything stupid yet.'

'When shall I do something stupid?' she replied.

There was a seething kind of silence.

'Look, just wait, okay?' Ben hissed. 'This isn't my only major problem right now.'

'Why? What's more important than this?'

'I'll tell you another time,' said Ben. The line went dead.

She sat with the phone in her lap for several minutes. She couldn't believe it. Ben had chickened out. There was no other explanation. That was why he'd been avoiding her. She was halfway through re-dialling his number when she stopped and threw the phone at her pillow. She was wasting her time. The person she really needed to talk to wasn't even in the country.

No Ben, no Mrs Powell. What about the other members of the Cat Kin? She had Cecile's number, and Susie's. She wavered, then tried the second one.

'Hello, you!' said Susie, sounding surprised. Apart from furtive chats at school in corridors or the dining room, they had hardly spoken to one another outside of the class.

'Hi.' Tiffany bit her lip.

'Hello?' said Susie again. Tiffany found she'd been staring mutely into space.

'Susie,' she said. 'I've got a problem. Maybe you can, uh, give me some advice.'

'Oh, me too!' said Susie, as if a problem was the latest gadget. 'My father and big brother want us all to holiday in Wales next year, can you believe that? White water rafting, and they know perfectly well that I can't even swim, or at least not very well, only four lengths in a warm pool. And in *Wales*. As if it won't be rainy enough here. I'll make Dad change his mind so we can go home to Hong Kong instead. I can't bear the countryside, can you? A big old waste of space. And I really don't know about white water rafting. It sounds very stupid and risky, quite danger-ous and rather boring too. *In a minute!*'

Tiffany wrenched the phone away, half-deafened.

'Sorry, Tiffany, that was my mother calling me to do silly chores. Anyway, Wales sounds awful, doesn't it? Do your family drag you on daft holidays too? Lis-ten, great talking but got to dash, mother's going to pop.'

'Bye,' said Tiffany. She stood dazed for a moment. She had forgotten how some people went temporarily insane when they had a phone to their ear. She reflected, and decided not to ring Cecile. It wasn't fair to drag friends into this. There was only one sensible thing to do. Call the police.

The station's operator put her on hold for ten nerve-wracking minutes. Her breath was loud in her ear. What if Ben was right? No, that couldn't be.

'Stoke Newington police.'

'Um. I want to report a crime.'

'Go ahead, love.'

'There's this old factory off Albion Road,' she said. 'They're keeping tigers and leopards in there. In tiny cages. They've all got tubes stuck in them and this scientist is using them to make medicines. He takes the bile from their livers –' She bit her tongue. It sounded ludicrous even to her.

'Say again, love. I'm listening.'

'It's true,' she protested. 'Look, I'm not sure what's going on. But it's something very bad, and it's inside that derelict factory. Can you check it, please?'

'Something bad,' echoed the officer, slowly, as if he were writing those very words on his pad. 'Can you fill me in on some details? What did you say your name was?'

The phone fell from her hand and lay on the carpet, burbling faintly, before going dumb. Tiffany ground her teeth. She would not pick it up again until she had a story they would believe. An hour later, it was still lying there.

Ben wondered about calling her back. He wanted to explain. Tell her what had happened with his mother. Tiffany should know. She needed to know.

'Benny!' Dad called from the living room. 'I've made a pot of tea. You want to come through and watch the boxing with me? I'll tell you by round two who's going to win.'

'Just a second,' Ben mumbled. His father had been unbearably merry ever since Ben had shown up on Wednesday morning, dazed after a night walking the streets. Not that Dad knew the real reason. He thought Mum was letting him have more 'access' at last.

Alone in the tiny spare room of his father's flat, Ben hugged his knees and watched the pigeons scratch on the windowsill. His memory was stuck in one groove, as if by replaying it over and over he could erase it, make it not have happened. His hand had struck at Mum quicker than thought, as electric current leaps from a wire. The force of it had thrown her across the kitchen. Invisible claws had scored her face. It was no enemy, no hired thug who had done this to his mother. It was him.

He clutched his right hand by the wrist, as if it were a snake he had to strangle.

'How could you?' he whispered. 'How could you do that?'

'Ben?' Dad knocked on the door. 'They're coming into the ring.'

'In a minute!' he snapped.

All those hours of practising pashki and he'd never thought what it was doing to him.

I don't know what got into me.

The cat-self he had awakened, his Mau body, had reflexes too fast for him to control. If he was hit, he would hit back, no matter who got hurt. And this thing was strong too, strong enough to knock a grown woman off her feet. He shrank inside, just as he had when he was five and had accidentally set the waste paper basket on fire, thinking the whole flat, the whole world, would burn down. This was the same feeling. He hadn't meant this to happen. What had he done?

'Tiffany! Check this out.'

She glanced up from her magazine in time to see Stuart popping two large pills in his mouth and swallowing them in one gulp. His eyes bulged like a frog's.

'Cool, eh? Bet you can't do that.'

'Stuart!' Mum scolded. 'One at a time, love. You'll choke.'

'No chance,' he grinned. 'I'm the world's greatest pill-swallower now. I could do four if I wanted.'

'They're not toys, you idiot!'

'Tiffany! None of that,' said Dad. He rolled up a couple of towels and stuffed them into a kit bag. 'Cathy, where are my swimming goggles?'

'Unless you gave them to me to be ironed, dry-cleaned or baked, Peter, I can only assume they're where you last put them,' said Mum.

'A simple I-don't-know would have done.' Dad went whistling up the stairs.

'I'm sorry, Stuart,' said Tiffany. 'But you know it's bad to take too much of any medicine. Especially,' she made sure she caught Mum's eye, 'one we don't know much about.'

'I take two at lunchtime. It says so on the label.'

'Mum, don't you think so?' Tiffany pleaded. 'He's practically well now. Shouldn't he come off that stuff soon?'

'Why?' smiled Mum, filling a watering can at the sink. 'Anyhow, I don't know what you mean by *well*. You're going to get a lot better still, aren't you, Stu?'

'Yeah!' said Stuart. He poked Tiffany, teasing. 'You're just jealous 'cos you know I'll be stronger than you when we're both grown up.'

'Give me a break.' Tiffany felt like smashing the Panthacea jar on the floor. That would get their attention. 'All I'm saying is, he can't just keep taking pills.'

'And why's that?'

'I dunno, Mum, you tell me. You're the one who always goes on about nature being the best doctor.'

'But Panthacea *is* natural, darling,' said Mum. 'Look here, it says on the label. Where are you going?'

Tiffany was going upstairs in a hurry. Probably to be sick. She stared down the loo until the nausea passed. Someone knocked at the door.

'Tiffany?' It was Dad. 'Did you want to come swimming with me and Stuart? We're off in a minute.'

She had to drink from the tap before answering, her mouth was so dry.

'No,' she said. 'I'd just get in the way again, wouldn't I?'

'Not a chance,' said Dad. 'Go on, it'll be fun.'

'I don't feel like it today. I might help Mum in the garden.'

'Okey-dokey. Don't let her get too muddy or the restaurant won't let us in.'

'Right.'

When she was ready to go back downstairs, Stuart and Dad were on their way out.

'Peter, my burgundy silk blouse,' said Mum, catching them on the doorstep.

'What about it?'

'Have you seen it? I want to wear it for the meal tonight.'

'Well, unless you gave it to me to wash the car

with,' said Dad, giving Mum a kiss on the cheek, 'I expect it's where you last put it. See you girls later!'

The blouse never showed up, so Mum compromised with a black evening dress and sparkly jewelry. She still looked pretty stunning and all the waiters fussed round her. Cathy Maine hadn't dressed up like that for months, perhaps years, and it was, Tiffany supposed, a great evening. But only one detail of it stayed with her: watching Stuart wash down yet another of those tablets.

She lay in bed next morning, listening to the black-birds imitate car alarms, noticing the extra notes they made, too high for ordinary human ears to hear. It was absurd: she had these new abilities, yet she couldn't stop her little brother taking a drug that was brewed from unimaginable suffering.

And should she? For the fact remained that, evil or not, Panthacea was helping him get better. Stuart would have a childhood at last. He would run, swim without floats, hold a book without getting exhausted. He could catch a cold and they need not live in fear that it might be his last.

Her brother, on one side. On the other, a room full of wild animals. Surely it was no contest? Tiffany dug her nails into her palms. No, she would not accept that. Stuart, she felt sure, would not accept it. He was the only young boy she knew who would rescue spiders from the bath rather than drown them. He even pitied the fleas she occasionally combed from Rufus's coat, crushing their armoured bodies between her fingernails. Stuart cared. No matter how magical Cobb's potion might be, the mere thought of the pain it had caused would be enough to bring him crashing down to earth.

And that wasn't all. Her brother might even be in danger. Those pills seemed to be doing him good at the moment, but she would never trust anything that had been touched by that dreadful skeletal scientist. Cobb did *not* care. Awful side-effects might kick in any day.

A thought struck her. It was Monday. Dad was in the City crunching numbers, and although Mum would be working from home she rarely surfaced from the study. Stuart, by the sound of it, had the telly on.

In the bathroom Tiffany found the current batch of Panthacea, a package of three jars. She found the fourth jar, half-full, in the kitchen. She went back upstairs and stared at the hatch in the landing ceiling. It was so high that Dad was the only one in the family who could reach it and lower the heavy wooden ladder.

Tiffany closed her eyes and let the catras boil through her like bubbles of light. She leaped. Her right hand found the lip of the hatch, the Mau claws letting her hang for one instant while she flicked the latch and pushed the trapdoor open. She dropped back onto the landing with the lightest thump. From the study came the tap-tap of Mum sending emails. Breathing deeply yet silently, Tiffany gathered up the pill jars and crouched under the open hatch. She focused on two catras, blue and indigo, and launched herself upwards.

Felasticon. Her whole body stretched as it threaded through the hatchway, and she had to duck to avoid banging her head on the roof's rafters. She landed on the balls of her feet at the very edge of the trapdoor, heels jutting out into space. Not bad for the class PE wimp.

All their junk had been stowed up here in the attic: boxes of old-fashioned vinyl records, winter clothes, her once-cherished doll's house. She prowled across the rafters, taking care not to let any creak. At the very edge of the eaves she found a box crammed with a spaghetti of wires and dusty bulbs. She buried the pill jars deep inside.

Mum was still typing away in the study. Biting her lip with the strain, Tiffany managed to close the trapdoor softly behind her as she lowered herself down, dropping the last few feet. She'd done it. The Panthacea was hidden where they'd never dream of looking, a place Tiffany could never have gone by herself. And if they ordered some more, expensive as it was, she would hide that batch too.

She returned to her room and picked up a magazine. It was done. She leafed through the pages without reading them. For some reason she didn't feel any better.

13
Declawed

The music pounded in Ben's ears loud enough to bruise his brain, but at least that stopped him thinking. Encased in the din from his earphones, he sleepwalked round Clissold Park and almost didn't see the two figures practising balances under the chestnut trees. Before he could take evasive action, Yusuf waved. Ben pulled off the earphones.

'Pardon?'

'I said, Hey, Ben!'

'Hi.'

'Look, Olly, the maestro's here. Want to join us?' Yusuf sat on the grass and hooked one foot behind his head. 'We were just – ugh! – running over some basic stuff.'

Though he'd tried to avoid them, Ben now felt glad to see them. It seemed like years since he had talked to anyone without either arguing or having to keep something a secret. With these two, neither felt very likely. In happier circumstances, Olly would be guaranteed to make him laugh at least twice, with his clownish comments and a tone of voice that could turn the twelve times table into a comedy sketch. And there was something disarming about Yusuf, both in his brazen un-English vowels and the way he just got on with things, to the point of risking his life in the woods. Yusuf himself joked that he got this attitude from his father, who had once been Captain Mansour in an armoured division of Iraq's Republican Guard (at least, Ben assumed it was a joke). For the moment, Ben was just grateful that he had found his friends.

'Thanks, I'll . . . sit this one out,' said Ben. His ears were still ringing and it was hard to think of a suitable lie. 'Don't want to wreck my jeans. I ripped one pair already doing Chasing the Bird.'

'Good excuse,' grinned Olly. He winked at Yusuf. 'I told you. Ben's out of our league. To him we are but lemmings who fall out of trees.'

Ben flushed. 'It's not like that. It's —' It was just that his last pashki-related memory was of knocking Mum across the kitchen. If he so much as tried the simplest Eth walk right now, he knew, he would see her face. The idea of practising a routine at the moment was unthinkable.

'No sweat,' said Yusuf. 'We know it's true.' He straightened up, stretching luxuriously. 'Wait up. We do have something to show you. Ol, shall we let him in on our plan?'

Apparently this meant going to Olly's house, a bus ride into a smarter patch of North London. This time Ben paid the fare.

Squeezing into Olly's bedroom, which was large but a total bombsite, the three of them picked their way through a jungle of empty boxes, paint tins, laundry piles, rolls of paper, broken CD cases and two easels.

'Check these out,' said Yusuf. He grabbed a pile of A3 sheets from the computer desk and spread them across the available floor space. Ben peered at them out of politeness. Someone had been busy. Every sheet bore a laser-printed design, each one different: neon paw-prints, the silhouette of a cat's head, a sea-green eye on a black background, several logos with fancy lettering, saying *Cat Kin, Pasht* or *Mau*. One especially striking design showed a spray of thin, curved lines that looked familiar somehow. Ben was impressed in spite of himself.

'These are great, Olly. Did you do them?'

'Yeah. Yusuf says some of the concepts are his, but he's a big fat liar.'

'You're a brilliant artist.'

Olly went pink.

'Anyway, you get the drift?' said Yusuf. 'Judo teams have their own uniforms, so I don't see why we shouldn't. This way we can make Cat Kin more of a club.'

'And *here* is the prototype,' said Olly. From under his bed he pulled a black T-shirt and a pair of stretch running trousers. The shirt was printed with the curious pattern of radiating lines. 'Yusuf's idea, if you believe that for one nanosecond.'

'It's good.' Ben frowned, still trying to place the image.

'It is good. In fact it's the cat's whiskers,' said Yusuf.

Of course. Those lines were like the spray of hairs from a cat's snout and eyebrows, making one imagine an invisible cat face, with only the whiskers glowing in the dark.

'Mm.' Ben pretended an enthusiasm he couldn't feel. All this talk of Cat Kin only made him think again of what he'd done. The fear that Mum would never forgive him was like a constant pain. He could imagine how those caged animals felt, with the torment of the tubes in their flanks . . .

No. Best not to go there.

'He's a hard man to impress, isn't he?' said Olly to Yusuf.

'Sorry,' said Ben. 'It's a great idea. I've just got a lot on my mind.'

'Nothing as important as *this*, I bet,' said Olly, feeding a CD into his computer. 'You know that new game, Cygnus X-1? Voila! Pirated two weeks before release. I had to kill for it, too.'

'Dunno,' said Ben. 'I should be getting home.'

'Are you crazy?' Yusuf slapped his head playfully. 'This is an advance copy. Not even Prince Harry has this one yet.'

It wasn't fair to be miserable around these two. The joy of the summer holidays was still pumping through their veins and the world would be paradise for a couple more weeks yet. They deserved to be rid of him.

'Look, I've got to go,' said Ben.

'Okay.' Olly and Yusuf exchanged a puzzled glance.

Riding the bus back to Dad's in the afternoon sunshine, Ben knew he could wait no longer. He had to see Mum and sort things out. He jumped off two stops early and ran across the park. As he wove between pushchairs and dog-walkers he tried to rehearse what he would say. 'Sorry,' was as far as he could get. Perhaps it was enough.

Approaching Defoe Court he glanced at the clouds. It sounded like a storm was coming. Another rumble followed the first, this one tinnier, as if it weren't real thunder but the kind made by stagehands using sheets of metal. He quickened his stride. Something about the view was different. A tall pylon-thing was rising behind the rows of houses. A crane. A third boom reached his ears and this one definitely wasn't thunder. By the time he reached his street he was sprinting.

Boom.

He saw walls, strangely familiar but topped by ragged summits. He saw windows, empty of glass, and through them holes of sky. He saw bricks heaped like snowdrifts. A giant metal pear hung by a hawser from the tip of the crane. As he watched, the pear swung, languid as a handbag, into the fourth storey of the block. The wall coughed dust and shifted out of line. Another thump from the wrecking ball and the brickwork buckled, showering in chunks to the ground.

Boom.

The pavement seemed to move under him like the deck of a boat. Where was he? He should have been standing outside his flat. Somehow he had taken a wrong turning and ended up at a building site. Instead of a block of apartments there was a semi-ruin.

Then his brain woke up and pointed out that they were demolishing his home.

'Mum!' Mechanical roars drowned him out. 'Mum! Where are you?'

He ran into a chain-link fence that sprang before

him like a spider's web. The crane's caterpillar treads had ploughed up the tiny gardens. Somewhere in the mud lay Mum's cherished basil, rosemary and sage.

Between skips and parked trucks he saw the dust-smeared windows. It looked like the flat was empty. Of course it would be. They couldn't knock down a building with someone still inside it. Could they?

'Mum!' he yelled, so loud it hurt.

'Oi!' A man in a hard hat waved at him. 'Clear off. Ain't you kids got no sense of danger?'

She had gone. But all his stuff would be in there. His clothes, his books, his computer, his favourite duvet cover. Would Mum have bothered to save any of it?

He backed away, hypnotised by the swing of the wrecking ball. His eyes slid down the crane's neck to the orange cab, emblazoned with the name *Horton and Forrester*. The driver sat tweaking levers as if playing a computer game. Ben watched a fissure open up in the wall and found himself staring into his bedroom. He peeled his hands from the fence and fled.

Something bulky flumped through the letterbox. Stuart heaved himself off the sofa and hurried into the hall. Tiffany heard his grumble of disappointment and relaxed.

'Not come yet?' she asked.

'Just some of Dad's stupid CDs.' He flopped onto

the sofa with a dry cough. 'If it doesn't come soon I'll end up back in hospital.'

'You don't seem bad today,' Tiffany said, as brightly as she could.

'I soon will be,' said Stuart, 'once the last lot wears off.' He lowered his voice. 'Know what I think? I think Mum accidentally threw the jars away when she cleaned out the bathroom. Not that she'll own up to it.'

'Maybe you're right.'

Tiffany turned up the television. This had been the most uncomfortable fortnight of her life. When Stuart first complained he couldn't find his medicine, the first thing Mum did was ask Tiffany. And after searching the whole house she did everything but accuse her outright. Finally Dad took Tiffany aside and asked her to think, carefully, if she might have put Stuart's pills anywhere . . . at which point Tiffany had to shout that they blamed her for everything and that she wasn't her brother's drug-dealer. That shut them up. It helped that Stuart was on her side. 'Of course Tiffany can't have lost them,' he told his parents. 'She never loses anything. Not even her swimming goggles, *Dad*.'

Once every room and dustbin had been ransacked, her parents gave up and ordered a fresh course of Panthacea from the Only Nature's Own website. The price had risen to seventy pounds a pack. Tiffany squirmed in silence. She'd just managed to put more money into Doctor Cobb's pocket. And soon she'd have another batch to hide. *You can hide a hundred batches*, sneered a nasty inner voice. *Those cats will still be caged*.

On Sunday Tiffany woke late and headed hungrily downstairs. Mum was ironing.

'Hi!' Tiffany poured oat crunchies and drowned them in milk. She glanced at Mum to see why she hadn't answered. On the ironing board was something purple.

'Isn't that your nice silk blouse?' said Tiffany. 'The one you were looking for?'

'Yes.'

'You found it, then.' Tiffany was puzzled by Mum's stony face. 'Where was it?'

Dad appeared in the doorway. He held three little boxes and a jar.

'I found it,' he said. 'In the attic.'

The bowl slipped from her hand. Milk and china smashed across the floor. She groped for the nearest sink cloth.

'Leave that.' Dad put the Panthacea on the sideboard and came close, lifting her chin so she had to look him in the face. 'I'm not going to ask *if* you did it,' he said, 'that's clear enough. I'm not going to ask *how* you did it, though I confess you've got me puzzled. What I want to know, Tiffany, is why?'

She tried to turn her head aside. The look in Dad's eyes was unbearable, it was one she had never seen before. He held her fast. 'Talk to me, girl. Why did you hide your brother's medicine?'

'What were you thinking?' Mum burst out.

'Are you trying to get back at him for some silly –' Dad couldn't even finish the sentence. 'Because if you are –'

The time had come. She had to tell. But, but . . . if she told them the truth they might never believe her, and if they did believe her it would be worse. Stuart would know what he had been swallowing these past months. The terrible way the pills were made. Her throat closed till she could barely breathe.

'Young lady, you're not leaving this room till you've explained yourself,' said Mum. But Tiffany had tuned out. She couldn't take her eyes off Stuart, who had entered the kitchen holding a book to his chest.

'Tiffany?' said Stuart. 'You were only playing a joke, weren't you?'

She stared at the floor. The patterns on the tiles blurred with tears.

'Don't you want me to get well, then?' Stuart asked. 'Do you only like me when I'm ill, or something?'

She pushed Dad's hand away with a violence that made him gasp in surprise. She ran past Stuart, down the hall and out into the street.

'Should we have let her do that?' murmured Dad, agonisingly clear to her feline hearing. 'Better to ground her.'

'And give her what she wants? It's attention seeking, Peter. Jealousy's a terrible thing.' A sigh. 'And I thought she adored Stuart.'

Slouched behind the wheel of the car, Ben lowered the sun visor as the sun sank to blind him. He floored the accelerator but, unsurprisingly, the car didn't move. The Volkswagen was parked on top of another car, with another stacked upon its own roof, just one more wreck in a mountain of them. Ben knew Hamish's Car Dump from when he and his rougher mates from the high-street arcade used to mess around on dull weekends. How he had ended up here today, alone in this metal elephant's graveyard, he wasn't sure. Perhaps it was the last place he could feel at home.

Just once, he had plucked up the courage to go back to the flat. It wasn't there. Even the rubble had been carted away. Yet home still called to him piteously. He had heard that people who lose a limb can still suffer pain in it. He believed that now.

After watching the walls fall he had fled to Dad's flat. There he found Mum, sitting on the sofa with a whisky glass trembling in her hand. Bit by bit the story came out. It seemed that John Stanford had lost patience. Suddenly there were builders outside. There were lawyers in her home, bearing deeds that explained it was her home no longer. Lucy Gallagher had no time to wonder how Stanford had conjured this. She packed what she could fit into her car and the demolition crew closed in. Most of what she'd decided to save, it turned out, was Ben's stuff.

Dad was being a rock. He was managing to smile and joke. Mum kept repeating that she'd been a fool, now she'd lost everything, every penny. Dad refused to listen. He talked of court battles, of compensation running into millions of pounds. There was no question of it: Stanford had broken the law. Now they'd take him to the cleaners. Mum nodded. She didn't believe it. Nor did Ben.

Sitting down to dinner that evening had been weird. Ben couldn't help noticing that Mum and Dad were back together. At least, they were sitting at the same table. But no one ate or spoke much and Dad was clearly struggling to keep up the flow of good cheer. They hadn't got back together. Mum was only here because she had nowhere else to go. Dad would sleep on the sofa. They weren't a family. They were three shipwrecked strangers clinging to the same chunk of driftwood.

The springs in the old car seat were like a bed of nails. Ben got out and climbed to the ground. A taste of rust hung in the air. He saw a metal bar jutting from a chassis and worked it loose.

Stanford had destroyed them. Stanford and his sick friend Cobb. Their lives had been nothing, hedgehogs dazed and blinking in the fast lane of the M1. Now it was over.

Ben swung the bar like a tennis racket. It connected with the Volkswagen's near headlight and he had to cover his face as glass sprayed over him. He shook the fragments out of his hair and smashed the other headlight too.

Hefting the bar he took a roundhouse swipe at a windscreen, turning it to crushed ice. Yelling, he walloped a door until it crumpled like foil. Hands black with rust, he beat at the cars until he had no strength. The bar dropped and he fell to his knees.

Bit by bit his senses returned. Smashing up a scrap yard was not the answer. It was a waste of anger. He got shakily to his feet.

An idea had been lurking in his mind for some time, but he had avoided it, like a suspicious package. While in the grip of a strange power he had hurt someone he loved. Well then, if he had no choice but to hurt people, he could at least choose the right ones. He had a weapon. He had spent the past few months learning how to use it. Now was not the time to cast it away.

Ben drew deep breaths and bent in the Arch On

Guard stance. His legs were stiff; it was a fortnight since he'd done any pashki. After a few warm-up poses, which twanged his tendons like the first PE lesson of term, he knelt to run through his catras. At first he saw only darkness. After an age a blue glow flickered on his retinas. He tried the others, green Mandira, golden Parda. All he saw were faint blotches, as if he had stared too long at a light. What was the matter?

He was out of practice. That was all. Best to start from scratch, with the pashki rudiments. He picked a clear path through the junkyard and Eth walked along it, imagining thin posts under each foot. Halfway, he wobbled. Something tripped him and he went sprawling.

He lay for a long time, a fan belt snagged around his ankle. Out of practice? It was worse than that. A simple Eth walk had defeated him. The pashki movements were clear in his head, but his muscles were on strike. He strained one last time to summon up a catra and saw nothing but the black of his own eyelids. It was as if his Mau body had withered away like a disused limb.

A sound roused him. His mobile phone. He plucked it from his pocket and saw the name on the screen. Tiffany. It continued to play the James Bond theme at him. At the fourth repetition it fell silent.

With a cry of disgust, at himself, at everything, Ben hurled the phone into the mountain of scrap metal.

14

Mother Cat's Secret

'Ben . . .' A soft click. *'Doesn't answer. Please leave a message at the tone.'*

Tiffany hung up. That was it. If she ever got the chance to speak to him again, she wouldn't. The one person she thought she could rely on had let her down.

She checked her phone messages just in case her parents (or Ben) had tried to call. They hadn't. A proper mum or dad might have wondered where she'd got to by now, but no. Hardly surprising. She turned the phone off.

Seeing Theobald Mansions she walked faster. After a whole day dithering and killing time in clothes shops, she knew who she had to see. *Please*, Tiffany wished, *please be back from India.*

She reached the entrance of the run-down block

and pressed the entry buzzer, leaning close to the speaker for an answer. She buzzed again and waited a long time. Nothing. Mrs Powell wasn't there. Tiffany turned from the doorway with a sniff, ready to burst into tears. She stopped. She breathed in again. A familiar scent hung in the air. She couldn't have described the sensation in human words, but she knew it was Mrs Powell as surely as if she'd seen a photograph. She'd stood on this spot in the last twelve hours.

Tiffany stepped back from the entrance and looked up at the top-floor flat. Her heart rejoiced to see the balcony window ajar. Perhaps Mrs Powell had only popped out for cat food. Tiffany sat on the step for half an hour before the other, fouler smells from the lobby got the better of her. This was no place to linger. She considered the open window, five floors up. It would be silly to try and climb up there. She'd promised not to do anything silly.

The next thing she knew, she was running next door to the leisure centre. Partly for the convenience, and partly so she could practise slipping past the attendant unnoticed, she'd got into the habit of storing her pashki kit in one of the lockers. She donned it quickly in a deserted corner of the changing room, daubed her face-print with blue and grey paints and pressed the tabby patterns onto her skin. Thus camouflaged, night-black from neck to ankle, she slunk out of the fire exit into the lowering twilight.

The flats in Theobald Mansions had square, concrete balconies, like giant window boxes. Tiffany looked at them and they became, in her mind, a ladder.

A short, sharp run took her across the forecourt. She sprang for the lowest balcony and after a moment's wriggling panic pulled herself up. Balancing on the balustrade she worked out her route. She'd have to jump to the balcony diagonally above, one-along and one-up, and carry on like that, in zig-zags, all the way to the top.

Which meant truly heart-stopping leaps. She was risking her life quite unnecessarily, yet there was no question of turning back. Her nerves were alive with the same fire that had caused near disaster on Hampstead Heath: the bloody-minded determination of cats to finish whatever foolish adventure they started.

A jump, a moment's delirium, and she was clinging to another ledge and not lying broken on the ground. That was good. She quivered on her perch, gathered her strength. The exact same leap again. Third floor. There was a rhythm to it. On the fourth landing she slipped, but brushed it off as lightly as if she'd tripped on a step.

It was with a cheeky pirouette that she vaulted over the side of Mrs Powell's balcony. Stairs, who needed them? She reached through the open window, unlatched the French windows and parted the curtains. Her eyes adjusted to a gloomy room she'd never entered before. There was a bookcase, a telly and an ancient record-player. Jim's scent hung in the air and his hairs coated the sofa like hoar-frost. She hoped Mrs Powell wouldn't mind her coming in like this.

'I heed no words nor walls,' Tiffany said aloud. She picked a pamphlet off the coffee table, attracted by pictures of tigers. It was a glossy newsletter about a place called the Periyar Reserve in Kerala. That must be the wildlife park Mrs Powell had been visiting. Tiffany lapped up the snapshots of Indian rainforests, of flame-coloured beasts lurking through the leaves, forgetting her troubles in a fleeting daydream. Mrs Powell had said she was a patron of the park, so Tiffany hunted for mentions of her name, but found none. She put the pamphlet down and the hairs on her scalp stiffened as one.

On the coffee table, previously covered, was a copy of *New Scientist* magazine, open at a centrefold. Tiffany didn't have to read a word to recognise the man in the full-page photograph. Clad now in a white coat, with a jar in his shrivelled left hand, was Dr J. Philip Cobb.

She couldn't hold the magazine steady. She also seemed to have forgotten how to read. Stumbling through the article, as if she were fleeing a vampire in a dream, she caught only snatches: sensational wonder-supplement, groundbreaking research, Panthacea, Only Nature's Own, soon to be expanding. Multi-million pound new laboratory. It wasn't the article itself that had made her brain crash. It was the fact that she'd found it here.

The sofa creaked as she sat heavily. Her thoughts, which had frozen like packed ice, began to move again. Soon they were in avalanche. Why had Mrs Powell been reading an article on Doctor Cobb? What had Cobb said to Stanford?

'Where did I get them all? Private collections. Imports. One or two I've had for years . . .'

It made horrible sense. If Cobb needed to import more big cats, as he surely would, who better to ask than someone who really understood them? Mrs Powell lived within sight of the derelict factory. And she had access to a steady supply of exactly the creatures Cobb desired. Tiffany jumped up from the sofa, feeling as if the walls were closing in on her. Could Mrs Powell really be in league with that monster? It was impossible. It was unspeakable. It . . .

It meant she had to get out. Now.

She burst on to the balcony, panting for breath. One look over the side told her it was hopeless. If she hadn't been afraid before, she was now. Climbing down the way she had come up would be suicide. She ran back inside. It would have to be the stairs. The room had darkened, as if her cat eyesight now ran on fading batteries. A hard tug opened the door (the rug had wedged under it) and she was in the hallway. The flat's front door – was it left or right?

Before she could choose, her legs were swept from under her by a scything low kick and an unseen figure pinned her to the carpet, pressing a knee in the small of her back.

Tiffany squirmed and cried out. To her amazement the weight lifted off.

'Tiffany Maine! What in the name of Anubis are you doing here?'

Tiffany scrambled away before twisting round to face the dark figure. 'N– nothing. I was just leaving.'

Mrs Powell held up a hand. 'You know I've no patience for this sort of thing. Just skip the fibs and get to the facts.' She turned on a light and tightened the cord on her dressing-gown. Underneath it she was wearing pyjamas. Her hair was a mess but her lined face had a healthy olive tan. 'Well?'

It would be safer to stay silent. Then she'd merely be told to leave, never to return. But Tiffany had to know.

'Did you . . .' she whispered. 'Are you . . . are you part of it, then?'

'Part of what?' Mrs Powell shot back.

'Only Nature's Own,' Tiffany said. 'Dr Philip Cobb. Panthacea. Are you in on it? Please tell me,' she swallowed, 'please tell me you're not.'

Mrs Powell looked her in the eye.

'I'm not,' she said. 'Anything else, while you're here?'

The relief that flooded her was so great, she could have wept. 'You're not helping him? You're really nothing to do with that man?'

'You know of him.' It was half-question, half-statement. 'And Panthacea?'

'A lot, yes.' Tiffany began explaining about Stuart and his illness, then stopped.

'Go on.'

'I'm sorry,' said Tiffany. 'You said we should stay out of trouble.'

It was a physical effort to tell the story. She related what had happened when she and Ben followed John Stanford. Where they had gone, what they had seen. 'I had to talk to someone,' she finished. 'You were the only person I thought might help. But then I saw that article about Doctor Cobb on your table, and I . . .'

'You assumed I knew him personally,' said Mrs Powell. 'The logic of young people. So if I were to find a poster of Elijah Wood in your bedroom, that would mean he's your boyfriend, would it?'

Tiffany blushed. Well, she could dream.

Mrs Powell smiled tenderly. 'Come on, girl.' She led Tiffany into the small but spotless kitchen and put the kettle on. Jim appeared with a chirrup of recognition, rubbing his silver coat around Tiffany's calves and rumbling like a bulldozer.

'Give him this.' Mrs Powell handed her a pale yellow fragment. Tiffany fed the Parmesan cheese to the cat, who squirmed in ecstasy as he gnashed it down. Mrs Powell poured tea for the two of them and a little, diluted with milk, into a saucer, and sat at the kitchen table.

'Now then,' she said. 'One more time. Cobb is holed up in the old factory?'

'Yes,' said Tiffany. 'That's where he works. I don't know if he sleeps there or goes home.'

'If it really is him, you'll find that he *doesn't* sleep. Or hardly at all. Not enough to go to the trouble of owning a bed,' said Mrs Powell.

'How do you know about him? Who is he?'

'I've been trailing him for many years,' said Mrs Powell. 'He has tried schemes like this before, although nothing so vile. Last time I and a few friends managed to get him stopped. But he disappeared. Then two years ago I heard that he'd ended up back in London. I bought this flat so I could watch and wait, and prepare. And it turns out I was right. Too right. He's made his move too soon.'

'What do you mean?'

Mrs Powell set her tea upon the table. Her stern face softened and for a moment Tiffany saw it as a great pool of sadness.

'You wanted me to tell you that I was nothing to do with Doctor Cobb,' said Mrs Powell. 'But, Tiffany, I'm afraid I can't do that. Because I am everything to do with him.'

Tiffany's cup rattled in its saucer.

'You see, that piece of human filth . . . that pus-caked hairball . . .' Mrs Powell heaved a long breath, 'is my son.'

'You have to imagine me aged twenty-two,' said Mrs Powell, tidying her grey hair with her fingers. 'Hard to do, yes?'

Tiffany could make no sound. Mrs Powell went on.

'We were a footloose couple, Terence and I. Not the type to settle down in a cosy home together. Nor did I ever become Mrs Cobb. I walked by myself, and all places were alike to me.'

The phrase rang a bell with Tiffany. Rudyard Kipling, of course.

'I had James,' said Mrs Powell, 'while we were backpacking round the world. Yes, his proper name is James. We simply took him along, extra luggage. He lived in airports and hostels and, at the age of four, had not seen England. He loved every minute.

'The longest we stayed anywhere was eight months, in Sri Lanka. I'd always been fascinated by cats, so I found work at the Yala Colombo leopard breeding programme. Terry put up with his girlfriend being a bit loopy. Didn't understand the whole cat thing. Bear in mind this was years before I'd heard of pashki. Though it's true that what happened next almost certainly threw me on to that path.

'It was my fault. I never pretended otherwise. I was a feckless young miss. Wouldn't wear shoes or socks and kept shredding my feet on bits of glass. Drank the tap water everywhere and got sick at both ends. And I let James play where he liked, with whatever local children were around. Let him grow up independent, like me. It used to drive Terence round the bend.'

Mrs Powell's voice was dry. She refilled her cup and drained it.

'One day I was in the leopard enclosure, helping sedate an animal that had a suppurating ear. James wasn't with us, I was never that stupid. He was outside the fence playing with a coconut husk. I'd forgotten that three baby leopards were roaming at the other end of the compound.

'Poor little Jamie. He stuck his arm through the wire to touch them. Oddly enough, the kitten he chose to stroke didn't seem to mind in the slightest. It was its mother who minded.

'She was at the wire in a flash and had Jamie's arm in her jaws. A second longer and she would have torn it off. But I heard him cry out –' Mrs Powell paused and shut her eyes before resuming. 'Such a cry. I ran over. I jabbed the mother leopard in the face with my ward-stick, half blinding her. Something I still feel sorry about. She was just another mother, protecting her child.

'The doctor didn't know if James would make it. His arm looked like it had been mashed in a machine. When at last he was stable, Terence took him back to England and told me not to follow. The surgeons in London saved the arm, but it never grew properly after that.'

'And did you never see him again?' Tiffany asked, softly.

'Of course I did. You don't tell a mother not to follow her sick son. I waited as long as I could, which was four days, then got a direct flight with all the savings I had left. I visited him every day in hospital.'

Tiffany's skin broke out in goose bumps as she thought of Stuart.

'I watched him get better. That is, until,' Mrs Powell smiled bitterly, 'Terence got a court order preventing me from seeing James unsupervised. They said

I was an unfit parent. And I believed them. I let myself be shut out of his life. He wasn't even James by then. Terence was using his middle name. He said he'd always preferred Philip to James. I ask you! No one prefers Philip.'

'Mrs Powell,' said Tiffany, 'I read something. On Doctor Cobb's website it mentions his accident. It says his mother died.'

'That's what he tells people,' said Mrs Powell. 'It might as well be true. His father made sure James — sorry, *Philip* — knew who to blame for his injury. For all I know, he ended up thinking I'd fed him to a leopard deliberately. He grew up hating and fearing me as much as he feared and loathed cats.'

'If he's so afraid,' said Tiffany, 'how can he bear to have a factory full of them?'

'They can't hurt him now,' said Mrs Powell. 'He uses them, he tortures them, and they make him rich and famous. Do you not know the word for it? It's *revenge.*'

The kitchen windows had become ghostly mirrors, as if the darkness outside was wrapped close to imprison the light within. Tiffany and her pale reflection stared at each other. Minutes had passed since Mrs Powell stopped speaking. How late was it? She ought to ring home.

'So. What now?' she heard herself ask.

'I go tonight,' said Mrs Powell. 'There is no point waiting.'

'But what will you do?'

Mrs Powell paused on her way out of the kitchen.

'Why, stop him of course.'

15

Into the Prison

It took Tiffany a moment to recognise the shape that detached itself from the other shadows in the hall. Mrs Powell had changed into a close-fitting outfit quite different from the one she wore to teach. The pattern reminded her of Jim's dappled silver coat, but in night-blues and greys. The biggest change was her face-print. Stripes streamed off the central M like lines of magnetic force. This was no mere camouflage; it was war-paint, framing eyes green and cold as a dusky winter sky.

'The hot water's on the blink again,' she remarked. 'You'll have to use the Swarfega soap by the sink to wash your face. You can go in my bedroom to get changed. Where have you put your street clothes?'

'Er . . . they're in the leisure centre,' said Tiffany. 'It'll be closed now. But I thought . . .'

'Best leave the face paint on then,' said Mrs Powell, 'and go home as you are. If anyone sees you, they'll assume you've walked out of an amateur production of *Cats*.'

'I'm coming too, aren't I?' Tiffany burst out.

'You most certainly are not,' said Mrs Powell. 'I will have enough on my mind without you to look after.'

Tiffany bristled.

'I know everything you're about to say,' said Mrs Powell. 'You don't need looking after. You can take care of yourself. You're not going to be told what to do. Etcetera. It's my fault. I've trained you too well.'

She placed a hand on Tiffany's shoulder. Tiffany thought she could feel a faint tingling, like the webs of static on a television screen.

'But not well enough, I'm afraid. Not yet. One day.'

'One day what?'

'You. Ben. And the other Cat Kin. You don't think I was teaching you as a hobby, do you? I knew Philip Cobb was out there. And others like him.' She closed her eyes and Tiffany wondered at how aged she looked, with her iron grey hair and crow's feet wrinkles criss-crossing her tabby makeup. 'If Philip does not meet with an accident, he'll be around long after I'm too old to do anything about him. Sometimes I feel I'm waging a private war. I need soldiers. I hoped some of you might be ready to join me when my son reappeared. But his scheme is already in full flood, and my army is still nothing more than – no offence, my dear – nothing more than a sack of kittens.'

Mrs Powell pulled on grey suede boots. She took a carton of milk from the fridge and drank straight from it like a teenager.

'Pop round tomorrow and I'll tell you how it went. You can let yourself out.'

She faded down the hall on velvet feet. Tiffany hesitated, then followed just as stealthily to peer round the studio door. Mrs Powell stood by the open window.

'I know you're there.' She didn't turn. 'I mean what I say. It's too early to expose you to such danger.'

Tiffany said nothing.

'I'm not being held responsible.' Mrs Powell faced her at last.

Tiffany put on her most determined expression. Mrs Powell sighed.

'The problem is, I can't stop you following me. And I really don't need to be distracted by your elephant feet clumping along behind. So, as long as I'm stuck with you . . .' She jerked her head towards the window.

Tiffany climbed a ladder of rusted couplings where a drainpipe had once been fixed. Standing on the very edge of the guttering, Mrs Powell peered over the rooftops.

'Under my very nose. As if he were mocking me.'

Like a beached oil tanker the factory blackened out the Hackney skyline. Tiffany's mouth was too dry to speak. Already she was having second thoughts.

'His glorious new laboratory is under way, I see,' said Mrs Powell. 'There's a crane. And a lorry. Good. A building site on his doorstep should give us extra cover.'

She was off, bounding along the slates as if they were springy turf. Tiffany settled into the effortless grace of Eth and tried to keep up. The roofscape felt like an alien desert, all angular mountains and eerie flat plains.

Apartments even seedier than Theobald Mansions led like a thread into the distance, tangling in the knitting of old and new buildings that made up Stoke Newington. The rooftops were roads that led everywhere.

Mrs Powell slowed. 'Big gap. Are you up to it?'

Four floors down, in an alley that looked like a chasm, a pair of young men were noisily arguing. Tiffany nodded. Mrs Powell sprang across, stopped as neatly as a dart in a bullseye, and beckoned. Taking a moment to focus, Tiffany cleared the jump.

'Well done,' said Mrs Powell. 'Next time, try and land more cleanly.'

As the roofs slanted more steeply, Tiffany lagged

behind. Around them, like steam, rose the mutter of evening traffic, mixed with the thump-thump-thump of drivers who felt their musical tastes had to be shared. Bats twirled over the street glow like ashes from a bonfire, pricking her ears with machine-gun squeaks.

Mrs Powell let her catch up.

'We are close. Think before you take your next step.'

The factory loomed beyond a wire fence. Tiffany leant on someone's satellite dish to rest, and then found, to her alarm, that she was alone. Unexpectedly Mrs Powell sprang from a nearby tree, somersaulted the wire and landed softly on the other side.

'Tiffany?'

Balanced on the tree's overhanging bough, Tiffany understood that she had one last chance to turn back. It was a nasty drop to the concrete. Nastier things waited beyond. But her biggest fear was disappointing her teacher.

'Ugh.' She hit the ground awkwardly. Rubbing her ankle eased the pain.

'Brave girl.' Mrs Powell hustled Tiffany behind a lorry, sniffing the air. The factory towered over them, a silent tomb.

'There was something –' Mrs Powell's voice came out of the darkness, 'something I said to you. When I told you and Ben off for running amok in the woods.'

Tiffany waited.

'I said I couldn't care less if you broke your necks,' said Mrs Powell. 'I just want to clear that up. It wasn't the truth. I do care. I care very much indeed.'

'I know,' said Tiffany.

Mrs Powell's eyes mirrored the moon. As if on some invisible signal, she shimmered across dunes of building sand to flatten herself against the black wall. Tiffany followed, becoming her shadow.

'At least you had the good sense not to drag Ben along,' said Mrs Powell.

'Actually I begged him to help. But he doesn't care.'

'Oh?' Mrs Powell frowned. 'Perhaps it's for the best. He's not ready for this kind of thing. Neither are you, of course.'

'At least *I'm* trying.'

'Sshh.' Mrs Powell listened, then whispered, 'Don't blame Ben. It's harder for him.'

'So he used to keep saying.'

'Few are so lucky as you,' said Mrs Powell. 'Your Mau body is strong, like mine, yet willing to be tamed. But Ben's . . .'

'Yes?'

'I felt that Ben's Mau was different. Volatile, violent, like a Scottish wildcat. Ready to squirm from your grasp if it's not handled right. It can be a frightening thing to live with.'

'Oh. Does he know?'

'I didn't tell him. I didn't want to scare off such a promising pupil. But I think he knows by now.' Mrs Powell bit her lip. 'I may have made a mistake. I should have spent more time on him. I always put it off.'

Tiffany grew aware of the crane leaning over them, a gangling skeleton, and shivered.

'But he didn't even seem to *want* to help me.'

'As long as you're here,' said Mrs Powell, 'you can help *me*. How did you get into this place?'

'There's an old fire exit. On the other side. But I think they lock it.'

'Ground floor?'

'Yes.'

'No good,' said Mrs Powell. 'One should always look down on danger.'

She studied the factory windows. The lowest were a bus's height above the ground and were boarded up with chipboard planks. A band of bricks divided them from the upper storey, and one of these panes had already been smashed by a thoughtful hooligan.

'That's our way in.'

Mrs Powell sprang onto the nearest boarded window and climbed it. Reaching the band of bricks she drove herself upwards with a double kick and seized the sill of the window above.

Tiffany crawled up the flaking planks behind her,

fearing she could never copy that leap to cross the unscaleable few feet of brickwork. To her relief, a gloved hand stretched down. She marvelled at her teacher's strength as she was hauled bodily onto the sill. Mrs Powell tugged the last jagged fragments from the window frame while Tiffany huddled out of the wind, which was blowing colder and harsher by the minute. Feebly she tried to joke.

'I suppose it's too late to change our minds.'

'For me, thirty years too late.' Glass tinkled as Mrs Powell slipped through the hole.

'Curiosity killed the cat, they say.' Mrs Powell's voice was quieter than the draughts that stroked the rusty metal walkway. Far below burned harsh white light, casting peculiar shadows on the girders of the roof that hemmed them in on either side. 'But curiosity *saved* the cat many more times than it killed her.'

The smell was dust and rotten plaster. Tiffany wondered if anyone had walked this gallery in her lifetime.

'I expect you've seen it in your cinema films,' said Mrs Powell. 'Professional assassins learn a place inside out before striking. They check for blind spots, escape routes, potential cover. They do it without even thinking.'

Tiffany grasped her meaning. When Rufus had arrived at her house, joyfully freed from a Perspex box at Battersea, he had investigated every inch of their house and garden, sniffing, poking, peering. Only when the last door had been opened and the last cupboard sat inside did he finally turn into the laid-back puss she knew now.

'As I explained, it's called Laying Claim,' said Mrs Powell. 'That makes you useful now, Tiffany. You've been here before. Start telling me things I need to know.'

Tiffany felt a stab of exam-panic.

'I wasn't really paying attention last time,' she stammered. 'It was all too much of a shock. I don't remember anything important.'

'You may not think so,' said Mrs Powell. 'But the cat in you has seen, heard and smelt everything. You will have the memories.'

Did she? Reluctantly (since this building could not have spooked her more if it had been built from human skulls) Tiffany let her mind dwell on the factory. It was a surprise to find a crude mental map of its interior.

'There are two main halls,' she whispered, 'with a heavy curtain-thing dividing them. The cats are caged in the second hall.' The picture grew clearer. 'The next floor up is a sort of balcony that runs round the building. Like the spectator gallery at a swimming pool. And there's another one above that, a maintenance walkway or something. Which is where we are.'

She leaned over the rail and got a shock. The factory floor was empty no longer. The vast space was filled with yellow plastic crates, piled in blocks and pyramids, some as high as the fork-lift truck parked among them. It made the first hall into a maze of lanes that converged upon Cobb's makeshift office.

'Mrs Powell!' she burst out. 'That's it! Over there, in his desk!'

'What about his desk? Don't babble.'

'That's where Doctor Cobb keeps the key. To the cages. I watched him put it in the drawer!' In her excitement Tiffany almost forgot how afraid she was.

Mrs Powell fixed her with a look. 'Do you know that the key will be in there now?'

'N–no,' she admitted. 'He had it in his pocket at first. But he put it in there like . . .' She clutched her head, remembering, 'like it was something he did all the time.'

Mrs Powell was still, as if struggling with a decision. At last she said, 'Follow me.'

A stairwell took them down to the lower gallery. Beams of dust-filled light rose like walls at the gallery's edge, boiling from the powerful arc lamps slung beneath. Mrs Powell twitched her head to catch sounds.

'We're not alone,' she whispered. 'Cobb is here. And others. No doubt he's taken measures against being disturbed.'

Along the gallery antique machines crouched under ghostly dust-blankets. Junk was strewn underfoot, chains, ropes, old sacks. Nothing moved.

'You must be my eyes,' said Mrs Powell. 'You can cover the whole floor from this balcony. I want to know if anyone comes within fifty feet of me.'

'How will I warn you?'

'With this.' Mrs Powell held a whistle.

'Won't they hear —?' Tiffany smiled suddenly. 'Of course! A dog whistle.'

'Must you call it that? Cats can hear octaves higher than dogs. Give it one blast if you spot danger.' Mrs Powell bit her knuckle. 'Some of those cats might hear it too. The smaller ones, like the ocelots. I don't know how they'd react. Still, it's a risk we'll take.'

She paused, one boot on the gallery rail.

'And you,' she said, 'listen for my signal.' A shrill note wailed at the back of her throat. 'That means get out of here. Don't wait.'

'But —'

'*Don't wait*. If trouble happens, there's nothing you can do that I can't do better. It's bad enough that I've brought you here at all. Now, *not another sound*.'

She dropped off the balcony. Rather than fall, she seized the cable that ran to the lighting array. In two seconds she had slid to the floor, through the lamplight that would dazzle any watching eyes.

She's done this stuff before, Tiffany reminded herself.

Mrs Powell crept between the yellow crates, like a laboratory animal running a maze. As she neared Cobb's office Tiffany scouted round the gallery for a better view. She bit her tongue when a gaunt figure in a brown coat pushed through the central curtain. She blew the cat whistle. Mrs Powell crouched by the wheel of the fork-lift.

Doctor Cobb made for his office. For the first time Tiffany could see his left arm properly. It was as if someone had stuck a child's limb on an adult's body. He used the shrivelled fingers to scratch his nose and the arm seemed to dangle, like the wing of a feather-less chick. She felt a strange mix of revulsion and pity. Then dread. Cobb was in the very place Mrs Powell was trying to reach.

He slumped in the swivel chair and chafed his eyes with his fingertips. Leaning back, he yawned. Almost at once he sat up and angrily shook himself. Tiffany couldn't breathe. If he turned to his right and took five paces, he would see Mrs Powell. Dismally cheery came a jingle.

'Doctor Cobb,' said Cobb into his mobile phone. 'Ah. A real thrill to hear from you. What can I . . .' A pause. 'What, tonight?' He grimaced. 'That's not necessary . . . I've already got guards in place . . . No, you're right, but . . .' Cobb stared towards the roof.

'Sometimes, John, I worry that you don't have complete confidence in me. I mean, I've shown every faith in *you* . . . Surely you can take my word on some things, without sending goons to check for yourself?' Another pause. 'I do beg your pardon. Employees, then. What? I'm sorry, you're breaking up. The reception in here is terrible. I think the pillars diffract the signal. I'll call you back.'

Now, Tiffany thought desperately, watching Cobb pace off into the shadows, mouthing soft obscenities at the dead phone. She heard a door squeak open. Luckily there was nothing wrong with Mrs Powell's hearing either. In a dozen fleet strides she had reached the office. The first thing she did was angle the desk lamp so that it shone upon the filing cabinet – to make it the brightest object, Tiffany guessed, and herself harder to notice.

The desk had three drawers. Mrs Powell's hands plunged into the first. Tiffany watched and hoped. Then –

'*Fool*,' she hissed at herself. Mrs Powell was depending on her. Where was Cobb? She had to find a spot where she could watch for his return. She hurried from pillar to pillar. A little further and she would have the perfect angle, letting her see clear across the first hall to the factory's main doors.

' . . . these ropes look older than you, Dave. Better tell the Prof they need replacing.'

The gruff voice made her skid to a halt. She had almost tripped over two workmen whose heads and shoulders poked up through the floor of the walkway. Clad in grey overalls, they stood inside the shaft of the goods lift, busying themselves with a tangled winch mechanism. Tiffany froze on one leg. After an eternity of thirty seconds the men tramped down the service ladder, happily grouching to each other about having to come here on a Sunday evening. She breezed over their heads.

Past the next pillar was a sinister-looking machine, like a giant mincer, shrouded in sheets. Squeezing in beside it she pulled the sheets over her and peeped through the balcony railings.

She was just in time to see that she was too late. Mrs Powell was shutting the last of the desk drawers in frustration – the key wasn't in any of them – and Doctor Cobb was on his way back. Tiffany raised her whistle. But, but . . . Mrs Powell had to be able to hear those crisp footsteps. Yet she wasn't trying to hide.

'Don't,' Tiffany whispered, hopelessly.

Even as Cobb turned the corner and stopped dead, shading his eyes from the anglepoise lamp, Mrs Powell turned to face him. The air clenched, like the straining heat before a thunderstorm. Cobb hugged his withered arm to his chest.

'Hello, James,' said Mrs Powell.

Cobb twitched, like an arachnophobe who finds his clothes crawling with tarantulas. He recoiled from her and yanked open the filing cabinet, pulled out a black object and pointed it at Mrs Powell.

'I warned you!' he gasped.

Tiffany focused on the object that he held, and a faintness came over her. It was a gun.

16
Fight or Flight

A mosquito whine hit Tiffany's eardrums. Mrs Powell's emergency call. The one that meant *Get out of here.* Cobb showed no sign of having noticed. In dismay Tiffany shrank deeper into the dust sheet. She couldn't run. Not yet.

Mrs Powell shook her head sadly.

'Is this any way to greet your mother?'

Cobb held the gun steady. He seemed to have mastered his shock.

'So we share fifty per cent of our genetic make-up,' he replied. 'Sorry if that doesn't make me go all gooey. Why do you persist in *following me around*?'

'Because I have no choice,' said Mrs Powell. 'As long as you persecute my fellow creatures, James, you will look over your shoulder and you will see me.'

'My name is Philip.' He cocked the pistol expertly

with one hand. 'Still obsessed with the pussycats, I see. Have you looked at yourself in a mirror?' He chuckled. 'You old witch. You think I do this out of spite? For your information, I'm easing the suffering of thousands.'

Tiffany detected a restless mewling from the other end of the factory. The cats too had heard the cry.

'You're not easing any suffering,' said Mrs Powell. 'You are simply shifting it on to creatures you hate even more than you hate human beings.'

'It's a mark of greatness,' said Cobb, 'to loathe cats. Elizabeth the First detested them. So did Napoleon. And Mussolini.'

'Tyrants,' said Mrs Powell. 'Interesting, isn't it? So many tyrants fear cats. Because cats refuse to fear them. They fight, or they flee. But they never cower.'

'Some of us have better reasons than that.'

'I know it, Philip.' Mrs Powell took a step towards him, holding up her hands. 'And I'm sorry. You'll never know how sorry. That was my fault. And I have paid for it.'

'I hardly think so.'

'Will you never accept that it was an accident?' Mrs Powell moved closer. 'James, Philip, whether or not it means anything to you, you are my son, and I did love you.'

'Stand still.'

'What your father told you simply isn't true. How did we become enemies, Philip? I was going to bring you up, take care of you, teach you so many things —'

'Don't touch me!' He pulled away, for she had laid a hand upon his shoulder. He stuck the muzzle of the gun in her face and she withdrew.

'I'm sorry.' Mrs Powell hung her head. 'You're right. I shouldn't have come.' She fidgeted with her belt.

Tiffany caught her breath. She knew what Mrs Powell had done. When she'd touched Cobb, her other hand had brushed across his coat. Had she picked his pocket? Had she just put something away in her belt? It could only be the key to the cages. Light shone through Tiffany's despair. She hadn't dreamed Mrs Powell could be so cunning.

'No, I'm glad you came,' said Cobb. 'You were the last person in the world who might have upset my enterprise. Now I can put you where all dangerous animals should be kept.' He gestured with the gun. 'Move.'

'Why? What's over there?'

'Spare cages, Mummy. You're joining your friends in captivity. You'll enjoy that. No doubt you eat the same food.'

'Your jokes used to be better than this.'

'I am really tired,' said Cobb, 'of talking to you. Start walking. *Slowly*.'

Mrs Powell obeyed. Cobb steered her towards the

curtain. Tiffany crossed her fingers. Was this the plan? To get put in a cage and let herself out later? It had to be. Tiffany could have cheered at such courage and cleverness.

'Through the partition,' Cobb ordered. Mrs Powell pushed the curtain aside and stepped through. The drape swung shut before Cobb could follow. For a moment it blocked his view.

'Stop!' he shouted. 'Stay where you are!' He forced his way through the curtain, waving the gun. 'Stop right –'

The gun boomed.

Mrs Powell, a few steps ahead of him, staggered as if she had been hit with a cricket bat and fell to the floor. A red stain spread on the concrete like an inkblot.

Tiffany choked. A howl of anguish had caught in her chest. Mrs Powell lay still. Tiffany gripped the balcony railings. *Please get up. Please move. Please don't be dead.*

Cobb stood like a statue, staring at his hand as if it did not belong to him. The gun had clattered to the ground beside the body. The spreading blood touched it and began to mould itself around the barrel. Shouts and running feet echoed across the hall.

'Doctor Cobb! Sir? Are you all right? What's happened?'

'Er –' Cobb snapped out of his trance. For the

moment, he was hidden by the curtain on one side and by crates on the other. 'It's nothing. I'm fine, Frank. I . . . I was testing my emergency firearm. I do it once a week. Sorry if I alarmed you.'

'Right you are, sir.' Tiffany caught a glimpse of a bearded security man and his green-suited partner, strolling back to their posts and lighting fresh cigarettes.

Cobb couldn't take his eyes off the body. Neither could Tiffany. She mopped at her tears and face-paint smeared her fingers. A voice in her head was moaning *Get out, get out of here*. But what did anything matter now? She knelt on the gallery sobbing. The sound of voices gradually roused her. Someone else had come into the factory.

'They're only doing it 'cos it's you, Mr S,' said a gravelly voice.

'And I appreciate it,' said a smooth, faintly accented one. 'But we can't leave our scientist friend unsupervised for too long, can we? Not with so much at stake. Insurance, Toby, insurance.'

'Right.'

John Stanford walked into the light. Behind him strode an enormous man, taller than Tiffany's dad and built like a moose across the shoulders. His shaven skull was crossed with white scars. Following this giant at a respectful distance were three other brutes, almost as big. Their stony faces made it plain that by rights they should be in the pub.

'John!' Cobb called from behind the curtain. 'Good evening. Can I have a word?'

'A pleasure.' Stanford turned to his bodyguard. 'Toby, take the lads to the loading bay to get settled.'

'The loading bay?'

'That's correct. I've laid on some perks to make up for calling them out tonight. You'll find lager and pizzas in my car.'

Toby grinned like a pumpkin. 'You're one of the good 'uns, Mr S. Come on, boys.'

He led the trio off. Stanford whistled as he picked his way through the crates.

'Doctor Cobb,' he called. 'Start spreading the news. The site is cleared, the deeds have been signed, the champagne is on ice.' He drew the drape aside with a hiss of steel curtain rings. 'And the builder says . . . *who . . . the hell . . . is that?*'

The fidgeting of caged cats prevented it from going totally silent.

'No one to worry about,' said Cobb at last.

'No one to—?' Stanford lowered his voice so that even Tiffany had to strain to hear. 'I have sacrificed my Sunday evening to come over here, to find what appears to be an aging circus performer who has fallen from her trapeze. Cobb, you can consider me worried. *Who is that?*'

'Her name was Felicity Powell, and at one time she was my mother.'

Stanford loosened his collar.

'She's dead?'

Cobb said nothing. Stanford saw the gun on the floor. He drew himself up.

'Goodbye, Doctor Cobb.'

'John, wait . . .'

'I'm sorry.' Stanford was striding away. 'You're on your own. I never invested at this level of risk.'

'Wait!' Cobb shouted. 'Let me explain, John. It's not really murder.'

'Self-defence? You shot an old lady? Not even my lawyers will touch that one.'

'It's not murder,' said Cobb, 'if no one notices. And no one will.'

Stanford hesitated. 'This had better be good.'

'This woman,' Cobb said, 'was alone. Pathologically so. You follow? No friends, no family. No job. Not even a bank account. All her life she was like that. Alone. She was the cat who walked by herself.'

'Say again?'

'Kipling,' Cobb elaborated. 'Never mind. My point is, no one will miss her. Not a single human being will care that she's gone.'

High in the gallery, Tiffany hung on the railings as if they were prison bars. *Not true*, she wanted to cry out. *That's not true.* Her tears rained silently to the floor far below.

'This is a minor upset,' Cobb smiled. 'Our plans are unaffected. We get rid of the body and it's as if she never existed.'

Stanford's forehead knotted with doubt.

'So much money, effort and time you've put in,' wheedled Cobb. 'For the opportunity of a lifetime. Don't throw it all away.'

Stanford looked ready to explode with rage. Finally he muttered, 'Has anyone else seen the body?'

'Not a soul.'

'Let's keep it that way.' Stanford swept out his phone. Tiffany couldn't catch what he murmured into it, but when he hung up he looked a fraction more cheerful. 'My man will see that we're not disturbed. Right, Cobb. Get rid of her.'

Philip Cobb eyed the body.

'I can't.'

'Can't what?'

'I can't touch it. You'll have to do it.'

'I am not hearing this!' cried Stanford. 'It's your mess. You clear it up!'

'No, John, listen.' Cobb's eyes had gone very wide and white. 'You don't understand. I physically cannot touch that . . . that *thing.*'

'Then you go to jail.'

'John, please! I'll make it up to you.'

'Twenty per cent more,' said Stanford immediately. 'On top of the original deal.'

'Ten per cent.'

'*Twenty.*'

'Fine,' sighed Cobb.

'Nice doing business with you. Give me your coat.'

'What?'

'I'm not getting blood on this suit. Give it to me.'

Cobb tore off his coat and threw it at him. Stanford wrapped it around Mrs Powell and picked her up.

'Not in my car,' he said. 'It's too risky. Those construction machines outside . . . We could bury her deep. Concrete it over. She might be found one day, but not in our lifetimes.'

'Put it in the meat locker,' said Cobb. 'It's refrigerated. Stop it rotting.'

'Your people use that. She can't stay there.'

'She won't,' Cobb replied. 'I just thought. It's about time the big cats had a change of diet.'

Suddenly he laughed in such an unnerving manner that Stanford backed away from him.

'By the time they're finished with her,' Cobb giggled, 'there'll be nothing left for anyone to find.'

So great was Tiffany's horror when she heard Cobb's plan that she may even have passed out for a minute or two. Her next clear memory was of shivering in the shadows, huddled, as if she had woken at the dead of night in a bath of cold water. Then it hit her with full force that she was in a place of death, of unspeakable evil, and that she was utterly alone. She longed for Mum and Dad to come and take her home. Why wouldn't they come? What was keeping them? A jolt. She sat up. No use dozing off and dreaming here.

A quick scan of the gallery revealed that little stood between her and escape. These upper levels were not patrolled. All she had to do was find the way she had come in and trust that her pashki wouldn't fail her. She was gathering herself to run when she hesitated. The thought of simply slinking away was more than she could bear. Somehow it felt worse than staying put. To come here, watch Mrs Powell get shot, and leave again, defeated . . . it would be too pathetic for words.

An idea, though she fought to beat it down, grew stronger. Maybe there was something she could do. It was too late to save Mrs Powell . . . but there was the key. Felicity had risked her life to get the key to the cages – the key that was now hidden somewhere on her. Tiffany could retrieve it, return another time, and finish the task they had set out to do.

Now it was too late to un-think that thought. Though it terrified her, she knew she'd have to follow it through. Whatever else happened on this dreadful night, she couldn't let Mrs Powell's die in vain.

John Stanford had disappeared. Cobb, on his hands and knees, was scrubbing the bloodstained floor with soapy water. Returning to the goods lift shaft, Tiffany climbed down the service ladder. Finding the meat locker would be easy – her nose was already steering her. She tried not to dwell upon what she would do once inside. She would have to search Mrs Powell's body for the key. What if her eyes were still open?

Crawling on all fours, she slipped under the partition into the second hall. Rows of cages made grim lanes in all directions. She remembered the workers pushing their trolleys of meat. They had come from over there. A few sniffs confirmed it, though the stench from the cages made her gag. Even through the odour of filth she could smell the cats' hopelessness in the air.

'We will save you, one day,' she whispered, as she passed a large cat too matted and scabrous to identify. 'Me and my friends. We will come back and save you.'

A lynx's long ears twitched and it turned in her direction. She hurried by, willing her feet to be feathers. It would be terrible if the cats themselves were to give her away. Hiding behind a gurgling coil of black plastic, she caught the gleam of a metal door against the brickwork of the far wall. She despaired when she saw who stood by it.

' . . . no one goes in, is that clear?' Stanford was saying. 'Not even you.'

Toby nodded, unquestioning as a guard dog. Why oh why did Stanford have to bring even more security men with him? Maybe he didn't trust Doctor Cobb himself. It was guards guarding guards guarding . . . Tiffany retreated amongst the cages. How to get past that brute . . . Without knowing precisely what she was trying to achieve, she took out Mrs Powell's whistle and blew four blasts.

Eeeeeeeep Eeeeeeeep Eeeeeeeep Eeeeeeeep

Bars rattled as the smaller cats reacted. Their immediate neighbours began to growl. A wave of alarm swept through the cages, until every cat that still had the strength was snarling and spitting, convinced there was some threat they couldn't see.

'Doctor Cobb!' A security officer spoke into his walkie-talkie. 'Something's up with the animals.'

The noise rose to a rumble. It was as if the factory's ancient machinery was grinding into life. John Stanford edged along the wall.

'Cobb?' he called. 'What's happening? Why are they doing that?'

He scurried back to the metal door.

'Change of plan, Toby,' he said. 'You're coming with me. We'll wait in the other hall until our professor sorts out his livestock.'

Tiffany clenched her fist in triumph. The meat locker was unguarded. As soon as Stanford and Toby were gone she ran to the door and tugged at the bolt, too frantic to heed the sudden, blood-red throbbing of Oshtis in her stomach: she still wasn't alone.

A hand clamped her left arm. She stared into the bearded face of Cobb's chief of security.

'You! How did you gain access?'

Panic gripped her. She struggled but he held her fast.

'Doctor Cobb! We've found our intruder. That's what set them off.'

That name yelled in her ear drove her wild. She writhed and kicked. The security man twisted her arm behind her back. Crying in pain, she cursed her stupidity. Rufus would never let himself be manhandled like this. Rufus would—

'*Arrgh!*'

The man yelped as she jabbed Mau claws into his leg. He let go of her arm and she spun, sweeping it across his chest. He gaped at the rip that split his green jacket open in flaps, holding his thigh like a child who has just discovered bees. Tiffany was already running. A radio crackled and the security man yelled blue murder.

'Prowler! Prowler in the cat pound. Secure the exits. She's got a knife!'

Tiffany wove between the cages, driven by a force beyond fear. It cried only *Get out, get away, survive*. She burst through the curtain to find two green-suited guards standing in that very spot. If these men were surprised that the intruder was a schoolgirl in fancy dress, they didn't show it – they grabbed. They were too close to sidestep. Like a gymnast Tiffany bent double at the waist and cartwheeled out of reach. She righted herself in time to see one of Stanford's terrifying thugs bearing down on her. There was only time to curl into a ball and roll at his running feet. It felt like being hit by a truck, but the roar as the man went flying told her that she had come off best.

Bouncing back up, bruised but in one piece, she ran through a labyrinth of yellow crates. Her courage wilted as yells and running feet converged on her. The ankle she had twisted was beginning to ache.

I'm not going to escape, she thought. Almost immediately another voice retorted, clipped and businesslike. *No, you will escape. Because you have to.*

And then she knew how. Somewhere nearby was the electric cable that Mrs Powell had slid down. She could climb it in seconds. By the time anyone could follow her to the upper levels, she'd be long gone. She raced between the crates, left, right, straight on. Her cat senses pinpointed her pursuers, almost as if she had a radar screen in her head. Not that way. Turn left. Go up here. Wait for him to pass.

Then a broad alley turned into a blind one. Crates hemmed her in on three sides. She doubled back to find Philip Cobb standing there, holding a rifle.

'I'm guessing you're a friend of my mother's,' he said dryly. 'What a very stupid decision.'

Steadying the barrel with his shrunken left arm, Cobb hoisted the gun to his shoulder. Tiffany screamed. And leaped. Twice her own height straight up, back-flipping onto the top of the crates. The pile shifted and she fell off it backwards, flipping again in mid-air to land on her feet, a tottering yellow wall now between her and Cobb. It was all over before the echo of her own cry had faded. Then she was sprinting across the open floor, wringing from her Mau body every last atom of speed, and only a cheetah could have caught her now.

The cable drooped from the lighting array. One of Stanford's brutes was barreling towards her but he was too slow. She grabbed hold of the wire, closing her eyes against the blazing lights, and had a ridiculous flashback: trying to climb ropes in Miss Fuller's PE class. But that was a whole life away. Swinging like a sailor in a storm she powered up hand over hand.

Then she heard a bang. And felt as if someone had kicked her in the side. Her hands slipped on the cable and she looked down. Her hip was a burning lump of pain. Had she been shot? Had he actually *shot* her?

All at once she was deadly tired. A mist darkened the pillars that leered over her. Before her vision clouded completely, she glimpsed a dart with red nylon feathers dangling from her side. A tranquilliser.

The cable slithered through her fingers and she fell to the concrete.

17
Lost

Ben tapped the right-hand button. The flipper juggled the ball on its snout like a dolphin. One lightning-fast stab and the dolphin became a tennis pro, volleying the ball up the multiplier chute into the Rats' Nest. Red trails of light poured down the board and his score went rocketing up.

'Not fair!' Raymond Gallagher cried. 'You can't beat me on my own machine.'

'Watch me,' grinned Ben. He seized the corner of the table and lifted, tilting the board to stop the ball on the very lip of the dropoff.

'Mu-u-um!' Dad's voice became like a small child's. 'He's cheating! Tell him he can't do that!'

Lucy Gallagher turned the television up another notch.

'Of course you can, it's in the rules,' Ben replied.

He hammered away at the flipper switches until his fingers were sore. His final score went straight to the number-one slot.

'All right, *sonny*.' Dad cracked his knuckles and barged him aside. 'If that's the way you want it. This is war.'

'Yeah, bring it on!'

'I will. Go to your room!'

'What?'

'You heard me, Ben. Go to your room. Ha! That means I win automatically.'

'No way!' Ben laughed, digging his fingers into Dad's ribcage and tickling. 'You can't use Dad powers! Dad powers aren't allowed.'

'Show me where it says that in the rules of Ratcatcher. I wrote them, and I can rewrite them, so there. Now go to your room.'

'No!'

'Go to your room times a million and no returns!'

The game deteriorated into all-in wrestling. Ben was picked up and dumped on the sofa next to Mum. She made a big show of moving to the armchair.

'Boys with their toys.' Yet there was a smile she couldn't quite hide. Ben saw Dad's twinkling glance and his heart gave a sudden, unexpected kick.

'I don't know what you delinquents are expecting for your dinner,' Mum said. 'Unless you want me to hack ice out of the freezer. Which is all you seem to keep in there, Ray.'

Dad consulted his watch.

'Ray? Did you hear?'

The entry phone buzzed and Dad hurried to answer the door. A minute later he reappeared with a large, fragrant carrier bag.

'Chicken tikka massala for you, Ben? Dhansak, yes . . . and a rogan josh with lemon rice. Your favourite, Lucy?'

'Ray!' Mum protested. 'Takeaways? Can I remind you we're on the bread line?'

'Bread, yep, couple of naan, we got them. What's the problem?'

'But we can't afford to . . . I mean, I can't afford . . . You shouldn't expect me to . . .' Mum shook her head more and more weakly as the paper bag scented the room. 'Ah, forget it. Let's have curry.'

It was months since Ben had enjoyed a meal this much. He used poppadums as shovels, guzzled lime pickle until his eyes streamed, stopped eating only when he could no longer sit up straight. But the food wasn't the reason he enjoyed it. It was because Mum and Dad were talking. Their chat was nothing special (an old friend who'd moved to New Zealand, tonight's TV) yet it felt like the most important thing he'd ever heard.

Afterwards Mum fetched her purse to pay her share of the meal. Dad waved it away. So Mum insisted on doing the washing-up. And Ben, to his own amazement and everyone else's, offered to help.

'You'd better change that tea towel,' said Mum after a while. 'I'm not sure Dad ever has.'

Ben got a clean one from the sink cupboard.

'Thanks for this.' Mum smiled, tentatively.

Ben realised he'd been wiping one spoon for over a minute.

'Mum, I'm —'

'Ben, you know I —' they began together. He decided to plunge ahead.

'I'm sorry for . . . for the other night.'

Mum relaxed so much her elbows sank into the soap suds.

'I know you are. You didn't mean it. And neither did I. Oh, Ben . . .' She hugged him, dripping dishwater down his back. 'No one should have to suffer what you have. I said such horrible things. However bad it's been for me . . .'

'I know, but,' Ben swallowed. 'I am sorry. I am. That wasn't me. And I won't . . . ever again . . .'

He hugged her back. It was going to be all right. They'd come out of this together. And if Mum could forgive him, she could forgive Dad. She was probably about to say that now. That she forgave Dad. And everything would be back to normal. The normal of four years ago. He held on and waited. He found himself listening to the buzz of the refrigerator.

'Ben,' she said.

She knew what he was waiting for. And she wasn't going to say it. Not tonight, anyway. They disentangled their arms.

'I promised a friend I'd call,' said Ben, edging away. 'Mind if I –?'

'No. Go ahead.'

He left her to wipe down the draining board. Sitting on the sofa he stared at the phone. The notepad was covered with crossings-out. All day he'd been trying to remember Tiffany's number. He'd only ever programmed it into his mobile – much more convenient, unless you were stupid enough to throw your phone into a junkyard and lose it. It began 07939 . . .

He had let her down, and it galled him. Maybe there really was no way for them to help those poor cats, but they could at least have talked about it. Tiffany had needed someone and he had shut her out. Even if he did remember her number, he wouldn't blame her if she never picked up.

On the other hand, she might have tried to call on his lost mobile, or gone to look for him at the home that was no longer there. It was a shock to realise that she had no way of contacting him. He *had* to remember that number. It went 07939 . . . 583 . . . no, 538. Then a four . . .

'Hey, Ben. Shift. I need the sofa.'

Dad held an armful of blankets and a pillow.

If she was dreaming, it was a dream without pictures or light. Voices swam through the black depths.

. . . not getting it into your head. This finishes us. We are sunk.

I don't know, John. Others might see it differently.

Maybe you're right about the old woman. That no one will miss her. But this girl . . . People will be looking for her!

I've been checking the news all day. There's nothing about any lost child.

Yet. It's only been twenty-four hours.

The voices dissolved into a noise like pounding waves. With each wave came throbs of pain. The roar ebbed.

. . . need another shot soon, I think.

This is kidnapping. We're in over our heads.

Not over mine. It's an opportunity, John. What we have here is nothing less than a human cat.

Congratulations. You have lost me.

A felimorph, like my dear departed mother. If you thought Panthacea was an exciting discovery, wait till I've studied this little specimen.

But she's a schoolgirl, for heaven's sake . . .

To us, John, she could be worth millions. Ah, there we are.

The rushing noise was coming back.

Cobb. She cannot stay here.

What kind of dream was this?

It had taken Ben over an hour searching in Hamish's Car Dump to find both pieces of his broken phone, and it took Dad even longer to coax the thing back to life with a soldering iron and much cursing. Tiffany's number at last flickered weakly on the screen and Ben, playing safe, wrote it down before dialling it on the land line.

It went straight into voicemail. She must have her phone turned off. He left some clumsy message about being sorry, said that he hoped they could speak sometime soon, and hung up. She'd probably never ring back.

A background burble of television reminded him it was almost time for *Eastenders*. He was pleased to find Mum and Dad sitting side by side on the sofa. Taking the easy chair he browsed through the TV guide while the local news burbled in the background.

'There's a James Bond double-bill on later,' he hinted.

'Huh. In cases like this it's nearly always the father whodunnit,' Dad remarked, frowning at the sombre-faced newsreader on the screen.

'That's a mean thing to say.' Mum shifted in her seat.

'Well, it is. Guy goes on TV acting all anxious, while all the time he knows the body's at the bottom of a canal somewhere. Mind you,' Dad added hastily, 'it is usually the step-fathers. Not the real ones.'

'What are you talking about?' Ben scanned the satellite listings.

Mum shushed him and turned up the volume on the news.

' . . . her parents believe that a family argument may have caused her to walk out,' a reporter was saying to the camera. 'The chief hope is that she will get in touch either by calling home or by ringing the confidential helpline at the foot of your screens.'

A freephone number flashed up.

'Earlier today Peter Maine made an emotional appeal for her safe return.'

A tall man came on screen, wearing an ill-matching open-neck shirt and trousers, as if he had dressed without noticing. Beside him stood a woman whose face might have been beautiful had it not been lined with lost sleep. The man spoke into a microphone.

'Truffle, we're not angry at you, sweetheart.' His voice was steady, as if he were concentrating on keeping it that way. 'We just want to know you're OK.'

Ben put down the TV guide.

'If you're out there and listening to this, please call. You don't have to speak to us, ring the other number if you want. Just say you're safe. We both love you, Tiffany. Please come home.'

Ben's fingers sank into the arms of his chair. He couldn't move. The television filled with a photograph. Tiffany, a year or two younger, in school uniform, smiling.

'Police are appealing for witnesses who may have seen Tiffany on Sunday afternoon.'

'S'cuse me.' Ben stumbled over Dad's feet on his way out of the lounge and dived into his new bedroom, slamming the door shut. A crippling weakness overtook him and he sank to his knees at the foot of the bed, shaking as if from a fever.

18
A Purer Source

At first there was nothingness, blacker than sleep. Then she was a bubble rising sluggishly through syrup. Shapes above her bulbed and stretched like freshly blown glass and the drowsy syrup smothered her, she was trapped, a fly in amber—

Tiffany retched and coughed herself conscious. She gulped foul-smelling air. Her throat felt as if she had been eating thistles. It was thirst, she realised, a thirst so fierce she hardly knew it as such. She groaned and heard a dry rattle.

Where was she? Her memory was smashed. Out of the wreckage came one terrible thought: she was in hospital. She'd had an accident, or she'd been struck down by some disease even worse than Stuart's. She wished hospital beds weren't so hard. Her back was cobbled with bruises and her hip was a knifing pain.

The grey haze around her sharpened into bars. She lay in a cage, the size of a coffin, at the edge of an office made of cardboard boxes.

The truth landed on her like lead. Only her thirst, the most terrible thing of all, kept it from crushing her.

' . . . so much for your theory that no-one cares.'

'Have you conclusive proof that it's the same girl?'

'Come *on*, Cobb. A kid shows up here, you stick her in a cage, and thirty-six hours later parents are appealing on the lunchtime news about their missing daughter. Is that *scientific* enough for you?'

Cold clutched at Tiffany's heart. Parents. Oh God. Mum and Dad. How long had she been missing? Thirty-six hours . . . ? They'd been on the news? What would they . . . ? Water. She had to have water.

'As you wish. Your theory stands for now.' Cobb, restlessly circling his desk, passed into Tiffany's line of sight. 'Even so, I wager you her parents know nothing about her. They don't know what she can do. And they can't link her with us.'

'The police will try to find her.'

'The police couldn't find their own gluteus maximus with both hands.' Chuckling, Cobb glanced at the cage. 'Hush now. She's waking up.'

He came nearer, peering in at Tiffany as if she were a rare, possibly hazardous insect.

'Good afternoon,' he said. 'How do you feel?'

'W . . .' Tiffany tried to speak. Her mouth was like rubber. 'Ter.'

'I'm sorry?'

She tried again, with all her strength. '*Water*.'

'Pardon? Ah, of course. John, fetch me that bottle, will you?' Cobb took it, ignoring the other man's muttering, and poked it through the bars. Tiffany drank in a frenzy, choking and coughing, until she was swallowing only air. The dreadful dryness had hardly shifted, but at least she could now move her tongue.

'You'll feel poorly at first,' said Cobb. 'You've been sedated.'

Tiffany tried to get up and bumped her head on the cage. A wave of dizziness forced her down again.

'How about food?' Cobb enquired.

As her thirst ebbed, the hunger pangs came. She had read about these but had never thought they would really be *pains*. Being this hungry was like bleeding inside. She managed a nod.

'Good-good.'

Something smacked wetly on the floor of her cage. Tiffany stared at it. It was a lump of meat. Raw meat. Nausea overcame her and she shut her eyes.

'It's fresh,' she heard him say.

'You imbecile.' That was Stanford. 'Stop playing games.'

'In a spirit of experimentation . . .'

'I don't care what you call it. You'll make her puke everywhere and then someone will have to clean it up, and I tell you in advance that it won't be me.'

Cobb smiled thinly. 'You know best, John, I'm sure. Give her whatever food you feel is appropriate.'

'Me?' Stanford boggled. Cobb was already walking back to his desk. Stanford scowled at Tiffany as if she were a dent in his new car. She gazed up at him.

'Please,' she whispered. 'Help me.'

'Shut up.'

'He's mad,' she pleaded. 'You know he's mad. You've got to help me get out of here.'

Stanford turned away. 'Toby?'

'Mr S?'

'Nip to the loading bay for me, will you? Get a pack of those sandwiches from the security men's van.'

'Right-o.' Toby seemed miffed at the task. 'What d'you want in 'em?'

'Anything. I don't care. Use your imagination!'

Toby mooched off.

'And a carton of juice or something!' Stanford called after him.

'Yes sir. Three bags full.'

Tiffany waited, fighting with faintness, until a triangular plastic pack was crushed through the bars. She ripped it open and crammed the limp white bread with fish paste and watery lettuce into her mouth. Twenty seconds later, when she had finished, she sucked at the carton of Ribena until it crumpled. Only then, in disgust, did she flick the lump of meat out of her cage.

She looked around for John Stanford. It was absurd, but she almost longed for his return. Anyone was better than Philip Cobb.

Could she shout for help? There were many others in the factory, security men, technicians, mysterious operatives. Surely they weren't all heartless beasts. Then she thought of the cats in their cages. No one working here could be unaware of them. Yet their suffering went on. Maybe they *were* all as evil as Cobb. At any rate, they did nothing to stop him, and wasn't that the same thing?

Cobb was paying more attention to his computer than to her. She had to escape. Oh, but how? She felt so weak. Hungry, thirsty, bruised and dizzy, and on top of all that she was dying for the loo . . .

'Hey,' she called. 'Hey! Doctor Cobb! I need to go.'

'I can't let you go,' Cobb murmured.

'To the toilet,' she insisted. 'Please.'

'You should have gone before you left.'

'I've been here two days, you said!'

Cobb stopped clicking the mouse.

'You there, Terry, no, Toby. Take her to the lavatory. And stand guard.'

'What am I today?' Toby groused, as Cobb unlocked the cage and pulled Tiffany out. 'Sandwiches, toilets. Why don't you hire a bleedin'—'

'— person with their tongue cut out?' Cobb spat, so violently that Toby stepped back in alarm. 'Listen to me, you lobotomised yeti. If you ever question again one syllable of what I say, I will let Shiva feed on your face. *Have I made myself clear?*'

'Yes, sir. Sorry, sir,' mumbled Toby, swallowing. He gripped Tiffany's upper arm, the huge fingers and thumb meeting. His shaven head had gone shiny with sweat. *He* couldn't be so afraid of Cobb, could he?

A blue Portaloo occupied one of the wings that branched off the main hall. The moment she was shoved inside, the door slamming behind her, Tiffany broke down in tears. She had never felt so wretched, so poisoned with fear. But she used the loo and dried her eyes. She had bought herself one chance. Now to use it.

Clever plans were a waste of time. Speed was her weapon. First bracing against the plastic sink for leverage, she hurtled out of the door and ducked Toby's flailing arms. Swerving sharply left then right, she ran. Her Mau body roused itself reluctantly. *I'm a cat*, it seemed to complain, *you've got to let me sleep*. She focused on Parda, the golden catra and the source of strength. Energy flooded her weary limbs. Toby's shouts echoed like thunderclaps.

She skidded round a corner into a wall of snapping jaws. Two black-and-brown demons reared over her, baying and snarling. Crying out, she shielded her face, tried to roll away and hit bricks. There was no escape. Curled in a ball she waited to be shredded.

'Fred! Ginger! Stand down.'

A tall shape stood over her, eclipsing the upper windows. Stanford whistled and the two huge Doberman dogs sat on their haunches, grinning like gin-traps. Limp with fright, Tiffany was dragged to her feet.

'Come on, you,' growled Toby. 'Just dare try that again.'

Avoiding Stanford's icy stare he carried her back to her cage.

'Next time, you use a bucket,' Toby sneered. 'I coulda lost my job.'

Tiffany lay motionless inside the bars, dimly aware of the argument that had broken out amongst the men, Cobb saying things about Toby, and Stanford making counter-accusations. Crushed with despair she ignored them. She'd wasted her only opportunity. She was too tired, too weak. And now her ankle was throbbing. Even if she got out again, she wouldn't be able to run.

An hour passed, perhaps two. Eventually she lost the will to weep. She heaved a sigh and felt a rumble in her throat. With it came a glimmer of warmth. That was Pur, of course – the cat's calming meditation. Often just a sound of contentment, cats could use it deliberately to handle pain and distress. Some people believed it could even speed up healing.

She shifted into the Sphinx crouch and let the rumble rise from her larynx. Soon it became automatic. Breathe in, breathe out. The purr sank into her like a padded drill, soothing her nerves and letting clearer thoughts through. Perhaps there would be more chances to escape. If and when they came, she would be prepared.

Then Cobb was standing over her.

'What are you doing?'

She stopped the sound. 'Nothing.'

'You were *purring*.' He squatted down. 'Is that one of your tricks? How is it done?'

Tiffany said nothing.

'I doubt you're happy. So what's it for?' Cobb wore a friendly smile, patting the cage. 'What else did that woman teach you?'

'If you let me out of here,' said Tiffany, 'I'll tell you. Just let me go home to my parents. I'll teach you everything I learned.'

She was so desperate, she half-believed it herself. Cobb, however, didn't.

'That's not a workable scenario,' he said. 'Besides, I've no desire to run across rooftops myself. All that interests me is the process. How does a simple girl defy physical laws?'

'How can a person kill his own mother?' Tiffany shouted at him. 'How can a human being keep animals in tiny cages and stick tubes in their guts?'

'These animals you love so much often kill their own relatives,' Cobb replied. 'And as for my treatment of them – you eat meat, don't you? You take medicines and wear make-up. All of it's been tested on animals.'

'But, no, listen –' Tiffany floundered. 'What you're doing is –'

'We can sit and have this pointless debate,' said Cobb, flourishing a piece of paper, 'or we can discuss . . . ha. This is familiar, is it?'

Tiffany, with a lump in her throat, found herself looking at a printout from the BBC's website. There was a photo of her dad speaking into a microphone. Beside him stood Mum, her heavily made-up eyes ruined from crying.

'So it is you,' said Cobb. A sound broke from Tiffany's throat. Cobb smiled. 'Tiffany Maine. And these are your parents. Yes?' He moved the picture further to her right, holding it in his claw-like hand. She followed it, magnetised.

'If you want them to see you again safe and well,' Cobb went on, in a gentler tone, 'then all you have to do is . . .'

There was a stirring in her peripheral vision. She turned sharply. Cobb's other hand was poking a hypodermic syringe through the bars.

'No! *No!*' Even as she grabbed at it, the needle jabbed into her shoulder. She fought in crazed fear, bashing herself against the cage's interior. Her struggles lasted brief seconds, before the pain faded in a cloud that dampened sound and turned the light black.

Ben's hands shook so much that he had to try three times to dial the right number.

'Hello, this is Safeline.'

Safeline. A nice name that surely fooled no one.

'H-hi. M-my name is Ben —'

'You don't have to say your name if you don't want to. This is a confidential line,' said the comforting female voice.

'I'm Ben Gallagher. I'm a friend of Tiffany Maine's. The missing girl. On the television.'

'Oh . . .' There was a short silence on the line. 'Good, Ben, go on. What do you want to tell me?'

'I think I know where she might be.'

Think? He knew it. Knew it with terrible certainty. When he hadn't been there to help, Tiffany had simply gone ahead without him.

'Go on, Ben.'

'I think she's been . . .' he felt ridiculous saying it, 'kidnapped.'

She had gone to that place. She had tried alone to free the animals. And, inevitably, she had failed. How could he have let this happen?

'Where are you at the moment, Ben?'

'In a phone box.'

'And how do you know about Tiffany?'

'I'm her friend.'

'Is she with you now?'

'No!' he snapped. 'I told you. I think some men have . . . abducted her. They're at the old factory in Stoke Newington.'

'Okay, Ben. Keep calm. I need to know how you know this.' Not even a bomb could have shaken this woman's calm. 'Can you explain some more? If we're going to alert the police, we need to convince them that no one's telling tales.'

'I am not making this up!' Ben shouted. 'Listen, if I'm lying, arrest me. My name is Ben Gallagher and I live at flat one, 12 Defoe Court. Come round and check. Okay?'

'Thank you, Ben.' Deftly the woman wound up the conversation. 'We'll look into it. Take care now.'

Ben put the phone down. His rush of relief lasted less than a second. Too late he remembered that flat one, 12 Defoe Court didn't exist any more. He punched the phone, sucked his skinned knuckles and tried to think. Who would believe him? Who in the world? There was no one. No sane person would spare him a second –

No sane person. Of course. He ran out of the phone box and down the darkening street.

The syrupy blackness began to ripple. Tiffany swam up against the tide of unconsciousness, to where voices echoed like water in a cave. She fought to open her eyes.

'If it had been left up to you,' someone was grumbling, 'the girl would be in a police station by now, telling them everything.'

'It was your thug who nearly let her escape.'

'Toby is my chief of security. You should be grateful I brought him.'

'And the dogs? I don't like dogs. You never said you were bringing dogs.'

With a mighty effort Tiffany prised her eyelids apart. She was lying on her back on the cage floor. Oh, no – had she been doped again? She felt sicker than ever. Merged into one blur, Stanford and Cobb stood talking close by.

'I won't let Fred and Ginger hurt you.' Stanford clicked his tongue. His two gigantic Dobermans sprang to their feet, tongues flapping. 'But if one of your monster cats gets loose, I want protection.'

'Do you now?' Cobb steepled his fingers. 'Let's suppose that a tiger such as Shiva did escape. Your ferocious dogs would have a life expectancy of, oh, approximately three seconds each.'

Stanford drew himself up. 'You'd be amazed at how far I can run in six seconds.' He hooked a finger in one dog's collar. 'Speaking of which, your cats had a job to do. Have they done it yet? Have *you* done it?'

Tiffany's heart clenched. She had forgotten their hideous plan. How they intended to dispose of Mrs Powell's dead body. All her sorrow flooded back, spilling fresh tears over her cheekbones. Again and again, in her mind, she saw Felicity fall, struck down by the bullet that smashed just below her right shoulder.

Cobb hesitated. 'I'll sort it out. Soon. Don't worry. No one will notice one more carcass in the meat locker. Now I've other things to think about.'

He advanced on the cage. Tiffany tried to draw back but felt as if she were pinned with paving stones. She could only loll her head and watch the scientist approach.

'John, my friend, share my excitement!' Cobb's eyes gleamed like ice. 'We could transform our manufacturing process. Panthacea is distilled from cat bile. Think how much time and money we might save if we could get it from a purer source.'

'A purer —?'

'The same basic product, already compatible with the human body. Here is the answer, handed to us on a plate!'

'You can't be serious.'

'It's a theory,' Cobb admitted. 'I should test it.'

From a pocket of his coat he drew a syringe that looked big enough to sedate a rhinoceros. He ripped a fresh needle from a paper sachet and fitted it. Tiffany's throat closed in terror. She didn't care for needles at the best of times, and this one was practically a bayonet.

'A bile sample is what I need,' said Cobb. 'Analysis will tell me if the right feline compounds are present in this girl's system.'

He knelt by the cage. Tiffany sucked air in gulps. Move, her mind screamed at her, move out of reach. It was no use. Her limbs refused to obey, lying lifeless as a mannequin's.

Stanford cleared his throat. 'Is this a good idea?'

Cobb slid the giant needle through the bars. 'It's finding the right spot that's tricky. My human physiology is so rusty.'

Tiffany bit hard on her own lip, trying to shock her body into life. Roll away, she had to roll away. Catras, where were her catras when she needed them? They floated out of reach, faint and cold as distant planets.

'Steady now.' Cobb levelled the needle over her left

• 253 •

side. 'The bile duct ought to be somewhere around *here* . . .'

'Cobb!'

Philip Cobb jerked backwards, the needle falling from his hand. Stanford had yanked him away by the collar. With a thump Cobb was sitting on the floor. He glared up at his associate in total bewilderment.

'No,' said Stanford. 'You make a mistake with that pig-sticker, what happens then? We call an ambulance? Why can't you just *leave things be?*'

Cobb stood. He straightened the creases in his coat, picked up the needle and dropped it into his pocket. Bringing his face very close to Stanford's he said, 'Don't ever touch me again.'

Tiffany lay still, her heart crashing in her chest. Cobb withdrew to his office chair. He rotated it so that his back was turned.

'Listen to me,' said Stanford. 'This girl. She isn't a slum kid. They're looking for her. We cannot keep her here.'

Cobb stayed silent. He appeared to be sulking.

'We can't!' Stanford insisted.

'But neither can we simply release her.' Cobb didn't look round. 'She's seen us. She knows our names.'

'Yes, thanks to you. What do you suggest?'

'You're the strategist, John. You tell me.'

'We'll have to leave the country,' Stanford sighed.

'Write off this mess while we still can. Hide out in Eastern Europe for a bit and start over when things have cooled off.'

'A delightful prospect.'

'You don't have to tell me!' Spit flew from Stanford's mouth.

'Calm down, John. You're forgetting we have an alternative.'

'*What* alternative?' Stanford lowered his voice, moving farther from the cage. Tiffany reached out with cat hearing and managed to pull their whispers into earshot.

'The other option,' murmured Cobb, 'is to make sure we're never found out.'

'And how do you propose to do that?'

'You know, John.'

Silence fell, so that for a moment Tiffany thought her power had failed.

'John? I want you to say it.'

'All right, I know,' Stanford breathed. 'By destroying the evidence. Like we're doing with the other. Our only other option is to kill her and feed her to the cats.'

19
Darkness and Day

A shining claw hung over Theobald Mansions. Ben slowed to a walk, letting his eyes fall from the new moon to the single lit window beneath. She was back from holiday. Relief soured to foreboding and he stood still on the pavement. It would be much easier to turn around, go home, sit on the sofa with Mum and Dad and watch late-night telly. For all he knew, his guess about Tiffany was quite wrong.

He stood for a minute, debating with himself. Then he was walking towards the block. The main door stood ajar, wedged with a copy of *The Times*. That was odd. He tried the lobby light – broken. He had almost forgotten what darkness was like. Blind, he groped his way up the stairs, missing more than ever the lightness of cat feet that would have carried him to the top in seconds. He fell against the last door and thumped.

'Mrs Powell! It's Ben. I need to talk to you.'

The door opened. Light dazzled around a dark figure.

'It's okay,' Yusuf called over his shoulder. 'He's come.'

Dazed, Ben stepped inside. 'What are you doing here?'

'Same as you, I think.'

In the pashki studio he found Susie, Daniel, Olly and Cecile, all kneeling in the Sitting Cat pose.

'Hey, man,' said Daniel.

Cecile glanced up, her face anxious. 'Hiya.'

Ben half-expected them to shout *Surprise!* and throw balloons about. 'Have you been waiting for me?'

'Kind of,' said Olly. 'We tried every other way to find you. Short of shining a cat-signal into the clouds.'

'Where've you been?' Daniel demanded.

'Well, for starters, my home got demolished.'

'Good excuse,' Daniel laughed. 'I'll use that next time I've got late homework. Seriously, Ben —' He stopped. 'Wait a second, you don't mean it?'

'Yes. Why?'

'You don't — you didn't live at Defoe Court?'

Ben, totally bemused now, nodded.

'Oh no. Oh *no . . .*'

Out of nowhere came the connection. What was the name of the building company that worked for

Stanford? Horton and Forrester? Daniel's surname was Forrester. His father, a builder.

'That was your dad's company? Your dad smashed up my home?'

He went for Daniel, who backed up against the window.

'I didn't know!' Daniel spluttered, holding his arms across his face. 'Nor did he. He was doing his job. How could he know you used to live there?'

'I was *still* living there. Okay, okay.' Ben shook himself free of Olly and Yusuf, who were pulling him away. 'Forget it. There's no point. Just forget it.'

A bitter taste stung his throat. He stared at a blank patch of wall. His rage at Daniel quickly ebbed. That wasn't why he'd come.

'Did Mrs Powell call you here?' He looked to see if she was spying from the kitchen.

'We don't know where she is,' said Cecile. 'She must be back from India 'cos there's new milk in the fridge. But Jim hasn't been fed for ages, he's half-starved. I gave him some cat food but now he bites if you stroke him.'

'And Tiffany's not—'

'No,' said Susie. 'You've seen the news?'

Ben nodded.

'Cecile rang me up,' Susie went on. 'Eventually I realised she was really worried about something. So we came here. We thought Mrs Powell might know what happened, but her door was locked.'

'But,' said Cecile, 'we found the key!'

'Taped just inside the cat flap,' Susie grinned.

Ben looked from one to the other, trying to keep up.

'To cut it short,' said Yusuf, 'we got together to work out what's going on.'

'We thought you'd disappeared too,' Daniel mumbled. 'When your phone was on the blink.'

Ben could feel it, like a weight around his neck. They were waiting for him to explain it all. He knew, they didn't, and it was torment.

'Listen,' he said, 'if Tiffany is with Mrs Powell, I don't think she can be in danger. But there's something you don't know.'

There was a lot they didn't know. The threats from Stanford. The bus-roof pursuit. The factory of caged cats. They listened in silence while he told them everything.

'That place . . . It really shook Tiffany up. She thought we might save those cats ourselves. She kept asking me to help.'

'But you didn't,' said Daniel.

'There was nothing we could have done,' Ben snapped.

'Maybe she didn't think so,' said Yusuf. 'When you

said no, she went to Mrs Powell. Is that where they've gone? To the derelict factory in Albion Road?'

'They might have.'

'They've been missing three days,' said Susie. 'Tiffany would have rung home.'

'Unless they're in trouble,' said Cecile.

There was a long silence. Then someone murmured, 'Well. There's no choice, is there?'

They all looked in surprise at Olly, who fidgeted.

'We've . . . we've got to go after them.'

Susie paled.

'He's right,' said Yusuf. 'We can't sit here doing nothing. And you can forget about the cops, because by the time we've explained everything . . . I'm afraid it's us or no one, my friends.'

His eyes raked over them. Cecile nodded quickly. Daniel stood up, pushed his glasses firmly onto his nose and clenched his fists.

'Count me in.'

Susie got to her feet.

'This is your worst idea ever, Yusuf,' she said, 'but if there's no other way . . .'

'If I think of one, I'll yell it out.'

Ben felt their stares on him.

'You can lead us in there?' said Yusuf.

'I can't –' Ben corrected himself, '*we* can't do this!'

'Tell me about it,' said Olly.

'Listen, if they've,' Ben could hardly get the words out, 'if these men have done something to Tiffany and Mrs Powell, what chance have we got? You – you can't imagine what they're like. I've had John Stanford in my home. He had my father beaten up. And as for the other one . . .' The hairs bristled on his neck. 'I'd do anything to help Tiffany. But if we go in after her we'll make things worse!'

'So your plan is . . . ?' Yusuf waited. After a minute he punched his palm. 'That's settled then. Olly. The gear.'

Olly unzipped the kit bag that lay at his feet and began dishing out black bundles. Susie and Cecile collected one each and left the room. Daniel and Yusuf took theirs into a corner of the studio. Olly tossed a bundle at Ben. It flopped against his chest and fell to the floor.

'Your uniform,' Olly explained. 'I got them printed, like I said. Only about twenty pounds each. You can pay me later.'

Yusuf and Daniel suited up. In their black outfits, emblazoned with Olly's striking cat whisker design, they resembled a cross between Japanese ninjas and acrobats from the Cirque du Soleil. Susie and Cecile reappeared, both changed and wearing their cat faceprints. No. This *had* to be a joke.

Yusuf looked at him quizzically through his own painted face.

'What's got into you, Gallagher?'

'Nothing. Yusuf, wake up! We're a bunch of kids. We are not superheroes!'

'*We* aren't,' said Daniel. 'But you are. You and Tiffany. What you can do —'

'I can't do anything!'

His voice rang in the silent studio.

'I can't,' he whispered. 'Not any more. I've lost it.'

A motorbike snarled up the street outside.

'How?' Susie whispered.

'There was an accident.' He could hardly bear to remember it. 'With pashki. Something happened.'

He told them about the face-off with Mum, the memory rising as a physical pain, a cramp like needles down his arm. 'And now I can't do it. The one time I tried pashki after that, there was nothing there.'

'What do you mean, "nothing there"?' Yusuf said shakily.

'The Mau body, or whatever you want to call it. It's gone. I can remember the moves but it's like, I don't know, trying to write with your left hand. It doesn't feel right.'

'You're just out of practice,' said Daniel.

'It makes no difference. The point is, you think I can lead you on some crazy rescue mission when I can't. You think I'm a cat warrior with superhuman powers, and I hate to disappoint you, but I am Ben Gallagher, a thirteen-year-old pinball addict with a headache, and I am not leaping any chasms tonight, tomorrow, or ever again!'

He stood, miserably defiant, in the middle of the studio. Tiffany might be in desperate danger but he couldn't help her. Nothing they said to him could make him feel more guilty than he already did.

'You know what I think?' said Yusuf at length.

Ben shrugged.

'I think you're afraid.'

'Really? Why would that be?' Ben exploded. 'Those men are insane. They *don't care* how much pain they cause anyone else. Yes, Yusuf, of course I'm afraid.'

'No.' Cecile looked at him in a strange way, as if seeing things no one else could. 'Ben, he's right. We're all frightened of those men. But you're afraid of something else.'

'Like what? Spiders?'

'Of what you can do. Of pashki. Your Mau body hasn't disappeared. It's just that you're keeping it locked up. Ben —'

He shut his eyes. 'Do you really believe I wouldn't help Tiffany if I could?'

'Fine,' said Susie. 'We'll go without you.'

'You won't come back,' said Ben softly.

For a moment he thought he'd got through to them.

'Maybe,' Yusuf answered at last. 'But I nearly didn't

· 263 ·

come back from that day in the woods. And Tiffany saved me. So if you don't mind, Ben, I'll do my best to return the favour.'

Opening the window Yusuf peered into the night. Olly hesitantly tapped his shoulder.

'Er, Yusuf?' he said. 'Maybe we'd better take the stairs. Just . . . until we've warmed up.'

'Good idea.'

'Think about this!' Ben pleaded. Yusuf ignored him, herding the others into the hallway.

'We may score only one out of ten as heroes, Benny,' he remarked. 'But that's way better than zero. Oh – one more thing. You might feed the cat while we're gone.'

The door slammed behind him. Ben was alone in Mrs Powell's flat. He sighed. They would come slinking back. As soon as they understood what they were dealing with.

A spider-web tingle settled upon his neck. As if he were being watched. He whipped around. Jim padded into the studio and considered him in a bored, oh-it's-you sort of way. Ben let out his breath. He followed the cat into the kitchen and poured dried food into its bowl. Jim jumped onto the draining board to lap the tap.

He bit his lip till it bled. There was nothing he could do.

Aimless wandering took him into a small lounge,

with a magazine table, a television and a lonely sofa. He picked up a newspaper but it was several days old. And it was hard to read the smaller text because . . . because the curtains were drawn and the room was pitch black. He grabbed at the lamp and light filled the room, revealing sofa, television, table. He froze. Had he just imagined seeing the words before the light came on? He must have. He couldn't have been reading in the dark.

His watch told him it was after ten. Mum and Dad would be worrying. He switched on the television.

' . . . in St George's, Bermuda, where hurricane Dianne continues to wreak devastation,' said a newsreader.

She wouldn't be on again. It wasn't a big story, one vanished girl. And what if this had nothing to do with Stanford and Cobb? Perhaps Tiffany really had walked out of a family argument and hidden at a friend's house. She was probably back at home this very minute, with hugs and tears and cocoa.

'East London police are widening their search for the missing schoolgirl Tiffany Maine,' said the newsreader. 'This afternoon her family made another emotional appeal for her return.'

Ben's finger trembled over the off switch. A young boy, chubby around the face, sat in a wheelchair. He gazed glassily out of the screen.

'I want, er, to ask anyone who knows where my sister is,' said the boy, 'to please tell someone. Tiffany. If you're watching . . . please come home. I'm sorry about what happened. I'll stop taking that medicine if that's what you want.

'I miss you. Mum and Dad miss you. If you come home you can have all my playing cards –'

Ben stabbed the power switch so hard that the television toppled and crashed to the floor. There was a yowl of terror. Jim, who had been lurking unnoticed in the corner, sped past him, brushing his calf. A violent shock thumped up his leg, as if he had touched an electric fence. The cat vanished into the hall. Ben knelt, rubbing the feeling back into his thigh.

Tiffany. Tiffany had been kidnapped. She was in mortal danger. What in the name of Anubis was he doing here?

He ran into the empty studio. The last of Olly's pashki uniforms lay in a heap. He pulled it on, heedless of where he flung his own clothes. He glimpsed his phantom reflection in the window. Something was missing.

Opening the last closed door he found Mrs Powell's bedroom. The single bed was an unmade mess. In her wardrobe he found a face-print he had not seen before, shaped like a cat's head, carved from a single chunk of ebony and set with yellow stones. He daubed the velvet pads with paints from the dressing table and pressed the mould on, wondering at the almost perfect fit. A picture hung above the mirror. Pasht, the Egyptian cat goddess, flanked by hieroglyphics. Ben could not read them but he knew what they said.

I heed no words nor walls . . .

He eased the print off his skin. Contours of black and red writhed on his cheekbones, drawn into the Mau pattern like flames up a chimney. He felt the rhythm of the words like a distant drum.

Through darkness I walk in day . . .

He lowered the ebony mask and a feline face stared out of the mirror, its eyes glowing with a dim amber light.

And I do not fear the tyrant.

20
No Way In

How much time had he wasted? If something happened to Tiffany because of him . . . Pashki skills he thought he had lost for ever were returning fast, his legs and arms re-learning each movement of their own accord, but anger at himself spurred him on even faster. Only when he skidded down a sloping roof and nearly plunged off the edge did he force himself to slow down.

The factory lurked beyond the fever-glow of street-lamps, a scab of darkness festering on the skyline. As he sprang from gutter to gutter his muscles complained like kids in September, pressed back into work after weeks of idleness. He took another spill on a patch of loose tiles; for one terrifying moment he was Ben again, an ordinary boy, messing around on a rooftop for some lunatic reason that his grieving family would never discover. Then his Mau body flickered back on, catching him like a safety harness.

Soon only a trace of human heaviness remained. It felt the same as when Dad had refitted his old bike with racing suspension. Barely fifteen minutes after he had leaped out of Mrs Powell's window, he was scaling the chain-link fence where his home had once been.

The crane stood sentry, like an evil bird. Four tiny figures were just visible against the factory's dark screen. A fifth ran from the shadows.

'No luck?' Yusuf's voice.

Daniel shook his head. 'This place is a fortress. It'd be easier to get in to watch Arsenal. I dunno . . . maybe Ben was right.'

'Maybe he was talking gunk, as usual.' Ben stepped into the midst of them, feeling his face redden with shame under the paint. Instantly he was mobbed with slaps on the back and someone let out a soft cheer, sounding strange in that grim place. He shooed them off, shaking his head in mute apology.

'So what's happening?' he asked. 'Are we going in after her or what?'

'That depends,' said Yusuf. 'Look.'

He'd never asked the most obvious question. How would they get inside? All the factory's windows were boarded over, some of them with brand-new planks. Daniel had already scouted all around the building for hidden entrances – there were none. Even the fire escape that he and Tiffany had used was now firmly locked. It was as if the occupants were determined to shut out every last glimmer of light.

'And no handy ventilation shafts,' Yusuf added, 'before you ask.'

'But there's got to be a door,' said Ben. 'How do they get in and out?'

'They have these new-fangled inventions called "keys",' said Olly.

Ben felt more powerless than ever. Could they really be thwarted by just a few feet of brick? Rumbling city silence pooled around them, a voice that whispered *It's no good. Give up. Go home.* The high walls mocked him and the building site seemed to join in, a JCB laughing at their plight with frozen jaws, the crane's wrecking ball hanging motionless overhead like the pendulum of a stopped clock.

Tiffany licked her arm where the needle mark still smarted. This time it hadn't been a sedative; Cobb had taken a blood sample, though she'd managed to take one from him in return while he struggled to hold her still. With his good right hand now wrapped in a bandage, the scientist had become so fractious that even the dogs were giving him a wide berth. He had set up a microscope at the far end of his office and was now peering at slides, mixing liquids and dripping her blood onto bits of paper and acetate.

'How long are you going to take with that?' Stanford, eyes raw from lack of sleep, prowled back and forth.

'As long as is necessary.'

'Sorry I asked.'

'There are particular substances, certain triphosphates, that one only finds in feline blood,' Cobb explained, as if he thought Stanford would be interested. 'If the girl has them, I must keep her for future study.'

'And if not?'

'Then she's no use to me,' said Cobb. 'So we can do it your way.'

Tiffany clutched the bars of her cage, using all her strength to see if they might bend. Some hope – they'd been designed to imprison jungle cats. Of her two impending fates she couldn't tell which would be worse: to be executed, or to live on as Philip Cobb's laboratory animal. A sudden, chilling vision of herself, years from now, a full-grown woman, wasted away in this very same cage, riddled with wires and tubes, hit her so vividly that her stomach convulsed. There was nothing to bring up. Since that flimsy sandwich she hadn't eaten at all.

Escape, she had to escape. But it was impossible. Beyond Cobb's private space the factory was still crawling with those green-suited guards, and she couldn't even get out of this metal box. She covered her face and wept. Mum and Dad would never know what had happened to her. Stuart would grow up thinking it was all his fault. That was the worst thing of all.

Memories tormented her. Visiting her brother in Lion Ward, the joyful weeks he spent at home, cheering him up with silly talk when he had to go back. All the family together touring Battersea Dogs' Home to find a cat, and immediately choosing Rufus. Rufus going mental inside his new cat carrier, scrabbling his forepaws through the grill and actually dragging the whole thing along the floor, making her parents roar with laughter . . .

Suddenly Tiffany was staring across the office, at the desk where Cobb usually stowed his keys. It was maybe fifteen feet away. No more.

Could she?

Tiffany made sure no one was watching. Hardly daring to try, she stretched both arms through the bars of her cage. One by one she summoned her catras, running through the sequence faster and faster, pouring her will into her fingertips. She got a grip on the floor and heaved. Her hands stayed fixed. Her forehead and shoulders pressed against the bars. She pulled until her temples throbbed.

The cage moved two inches.

Tiffany lay still, shattered. All that effort for so little. She'd never make it as far as the desk, never even get close. Wearily she let her eyes wander around. No one was paying her any attention. Cobb was bent over his microscope and Stanford was singing tunelessly to himself. They would have to peer over boxes to see her.

Just two inches. But that meant two inches less to travel. With nothing better to do, she tried again. Clawing at the ground for another agonising minute, she dragged the cage another inch. On her next attempt she hit a smoother patch of floor and managed to move her prison the length of her forearm.

Suddenly the desk looked closer. Suddenly she didn't feel so spent. In her mind's eye she saw the key to her cage, snug in the desk drawer. She saw herself sneaking it out, fumbling it into the lock. And then . . . She would do it, she decided. She would do it or drop dead from exhaustion.

'Surely that's inconceivable . . .' Cobb was whispering to himself. 'So the change *isn't* physical.'

'Progress?' Stanford gloomily inquired. Tiffany threaded her arms back into the cage and pretended to sleep.

'Quite the opposite. It appears,' Cobb stroked his chin, 'that there's nothing to find. Her blood is ordinary. Human, type B positive as it happens, but quite normal. She's no more cat than you are.'

He strode to his filing cabinet.

'And I was so hopeful. Well. So be it.' Out came his handgun. He slapped a fresh cartridge into the grip. For Tiffany the world went grey, like rain and fog, with only the jet black gun piercingly sharp at its dead centre.

'We're finished with her, John. Care to do the honours?' Cobb glanced at Stanford in an amused way. 'Ah, you'd rather not. Don't have the courage of your convictions, that's your trouble.'

He approached the cage. Tiffany stared up at him, unable to move or think. No, this wasn't right. She'd been going to escape. This couldn't happen.

'You were a funny thing, weren't you?' said Cobb. He cocked the gun's hammer.

'No,' whispered Tiffany. 'P-please. Doctor Cobb, don't do this. You don't have to.'

'It's not personal,' said Cobb. 'It's common sense.'

'Philip, please! Why are you doing this?' Tiffany wailed, as the gun barrel seemed to swell and swallow her like a tunnel. 'I know what happened to you. I know how horrible it must have been. It doesn't have to make you do things like, like, oh, please, James, *James, don't kill me!*'

'Do shut up,' said Cobb.

There was a deafening bang.

21

Cat and Mouse

Cobb stared upwards as the noise shook the factory, the gun still clutched, unfired, in his bandaged hand.

'What was that?'

'Thunder maybe . . .' It was clear from Stanford's face that he knew it wasn't. For a start, thunder wouldn't have sent a cloud of brown dust drifting down at the far end of the hall. His dogs leaped to their feet.

An insane wave of hope surged over Tiffany, making her head swim. Cobb rounded on her and his gaze was pure poison. 'I'll deal with you later.' He shouted at the top of his lungs. 'Frank! Round up the men. Protect the equipment. She wasn't alone!'

Dropping through the hole in the roof, Ben twisted to see the crane's wrecking ball rebound into the night in a puff of twinkling glass and plaster. He rolled aside to let Yusuf, Susie and Cecile jump through the caved-in skylight. The crane's slender boom tilted away, as if in salute, the steel ball swinging like a conker.

'Get clear of the hole,' Yusuf panted, as a slate fell close to him.

Ben scrambled across the rafters, feeling cobwebs brush his face. Fate, it seemed, had a weird sense of humour. It wasn't just that Daniel's father had driven the crane that destroyed Ben's home. Or that, having sat beside his father many times in the cab, Daniel had a fair idea of how the machine worked. It was that Daniel knew the combination for the door of the builders' mobile cabin – and that in the cabin was the key for the crane.

'Do you think they heard us come in?' murmured Susie sarcastically.

Cecile laughed shakily in the darkness. 'Well, we *tried* knocking.'

Yusuf waved through the hole. The two figures in the crane's cab gave thumbs-up signs. Olly had decided that Daniel needed someone to keep him company, and had quickly volunteered ('I'm not an avenging angel. I'm a graphic designer.')

'Ugh.' Ben peeled a web out of his hair. 'I knew there'd be spiders.'

What kind of room had they broken into? He could

only have described it as a kind of loft. On either side were great water tanks, sitting askew in a mesh of mangled piping. The air smelled of decay, the rafters of the floor sagging ominously. Ben almost put his foot through a fissure and glimpsed a metal walkway below.

Cecile took a sharp breath. 'Someone's coming.'

'More than someone.' Yusuf lay flat to peer through the hole in the floor. Running boots clanked. 'Below us. Three or four of them.'

'Everybody, hide.'

'No, Ben, they'll trap us. We'll have to rush them.'

'Where's a wrecking ball when you need one?'

The footsteps slowed, very close.

'We know you're up there!' shouted a voice. 'Down! Or there'll be trouble.'

'They're bigger,' said Yusuf, 'but we're faster. We'll distract them. You try and slip through.'

'That's not fair on you –'

'Argue about it later, Ben!'

Yusuf jumped with all his weight on a gap between two rafters and the flimsy plaster broke. He plunged, tearing a hole, and Susie dropped after him. Holding his breath, Ben stamped hard on a wide crack. For a moment all was choking dust. Arms wrapped around his head, he struck the metal walkway sooner than expected and the shock made his spine go numb. He crumpled, coughing out grit.

'Anything else you want to get wrong, Yusuf?' Susie gasped.

Through dust and watering eyes he tried to see. Four green-suited security men had backed up against the railing, but they were quickly realising that this wasn't the SAS, it was kids. Three of them drew police riot truncheons and advanced.

'Go carefully, lads,' breathed the fourth, a man with a beard. 'They're slippery. It was one of this lot who used her knife on me.'

Her. He could only mean Tiffany. She was here, somewhere.

'Scatter!' yelled Ben.

Hands reached for him and pashki took over. Wherever the Green Suits turned, grabbed or flailed, he wasn't there – he skimmed the fringes of their vision like a mote of dust floating on the eyeball. The leader went for Cecile and she slipped through his hands quicker than a bar of soap. Then Ben saw a truncheon swing at Susie's head.

She jerked back, the truncheon whistling by her nose. Ben froze, aghast. Couldn't this guard tell she was just a child? Couldn't he see that, in spite of the strange costume and war paint, he was trying to bludgeon to death a twelve-year-old girl? The nightstick struck a second time. Again Susie dodged, evading the blow by a finger-breadth, staying within range. The guard staggered, off-balance, and in a rage aimed a mighty swipe at her taunting face.

The stick brushed through Susie's hair and hit the chief guard in his generous gut. He folded up. Seizing their moment, the girls fled along the walkway and two guards gave chase. Yusuf ran in the other direction, drawing away the third. Ben found himself alone. Leaving the chief guard in a moaning heap, he ran to a stairwell. A frenzy of barking rose from the depths. Hesitating only for an instant, Ben slid down the hand rail, whooshing past two gigantic Dobermans that were galloping up the steps. Even as their jaws snapped at him, he slipped off the banister and dropped the last ten feet to the floor below.

The echo died and he had his bearings. He had landed in the lower of the two galleries, amid relics of machinery that lurked under dust blankets. Beyond a safety rail the factory floor yawned like a canyon, the once-empty space now a townscape of crates, buttercup-yellow. What could they be for?

The great curtain down the middle of the hall mostly hid the city of cat cages from view. It was a small mercy not to see the animals, though the foul stink of their suffering already filled his nostrils. The maze of crates tangled his eyes; he saw no sign of Tiffany. Then a sound on the edge of hearing caught his attention. At the foot of the rickety lift gantry stood Doctor Cobb's makeshift office. There, near the walls of cardboard boxes, stood a single, lonely cage. Something was hunched inside it. A panther. No. The shape looked slightly feline – but it was human.

'Tiffany!' Ben gasped. They couldn't, it was unthinkable. Nobody could be that sick. What had they done to her? In horror he cried out again, and this time it was the screech of a maddened cat.

'What's up? You hurt?' Yusuf skidded to a halt at his side.

Ben pointed, unable to speak. Yusuf said nothing but Ben knew that he had seen, too. His knuckles had turned white where they gripped the balcony rail.

'I'm going down for her,' Ben managed at last.

'You don't think that's a really, really dumb idea, then?'

Ben had managed not to notice that Tiffany's cage was the least of her problems. Even though Cobb's security men had their hands full chasing Susie and Cecile through the galleries, a hard core of Green Suits and leather-clad brutes had ring-fenced the office area. And they weren't moving.

'I can slip past them.'

'Maybe you can.' Yusuf held his arm. 'But can she? How are you going to get her away?'

'Like you said, we'll argue about it later.'

He pulled himself free and sprinted on, searching

for the quickest route to the floor. Yusuf matched stride, no doubt intending to grab him again before he could vault over the rail. Well, he was welcome to try. Ben's mind was made up. He just had to dodge a few men, all right, a dozen, then somehow get the cage open, then make it back up here with Tiffany . . . maybe carry her if she was hurt . . . The more he thought about it, the slower he ran.

'Ben, you're not Operation Desert Storm . . .'

'Ssh. I'm thinking.'

He stood still. If he simply went for it, he'd fail. A plan was needed.

'Yusuf, you're into big cats, aren't you?'

'I don't like the sound of that . . . I read up on them, yeah. A bit.'

'What if we let one out? As a diversion?'

'For one thing, my friend, you don't have the key, and for another, you *definitely* do not have a volunteer,' Yusuf scowled at him. 'We'd be dinner. I doubt pashki would protect us. If there's any way to pacify a mad cougar, *she* never taught us what it is.'

'Okay. Just a thought.'

Ben's eyes raked the factory floor, the length and breadth of the gothic brick edifice. Surely he could come up with something. All his life he'd had a weird ability to fathom a physical space in seconds, where others might take minutes. He'd only ever used it to play pinball . . .

What was that on the other side of the hall? Looked familiar . . .

. . . finding a machine's hidden quirks, so he could master it . . .

The goods- lift shaft, rising all the way up to the top gallery.

. . . but never yet had he tried to use it to save a friend's life.

He remembered Doctor Cobb ear-bashing a pair of dull workmen, snatches of talk about brakes and weights. The goods lift sat at ground level, barely twenty yards from where Tiffany lay captive. Two people could easily fit in there, maybe more.

'Yusuf. Follow me!'

A clear run took them past a clucking machine that was sticking labels on Cobb's Panthacea jars. Then they were at the lift gantry, a pylon-frame of rusty bars. Two parallel ropes ran from top to bottom, knobbly as goats' horns and giving off a musty smell. Ben leaned into the shaft.

'If I can get her into this . . .'

'It looks practically Jurassic. Is it safe?'

'Nothing's safe in here, Yusuf. But I know it works.' Ben searched his memory. 'They said something about getting the weight right.'

'That'd be the weight cradle up there.' Yusuf pointed at a shape like a stack of Jenga blocks, dangling high overhead on the second rope. 'You adjust that to match the load. It's a simple counterweight system. I did a physics project on this stuff,' he explained.

'Great,' said Ben. 'Reckon it'd lift me and her together?'

'Um . . . Depends. If we made the counterweight heavy enough, it might . . .'

'Get up there. See if you can find spare weights.'

'But Ben —'

'What?' He was climbing onto the balcony rail.

'The lift cable. It's just an old rope. And it stinks like my sock drawer. I think it's rotten.'

Ben balanced above the sheer drop to the floor.

'It doesn't have to hold for long,' he said.

Like a spectator he watched himself pitch forward into space, coolly as pushing off a poolside into the deep end. By now he was used to his Mau body making decisions faster than he could follow — even when they seemed suicidal. Sailing over a forty-foot drop, dimly aware of Yusuf's plaintive shout ('Ben, I only got a C for the project . . .') he finally worked out what he was doing.

At full Felasticon stretch he touched the central curtain. His claws scratched into the glossy vinyl and he slid down with a burning smell and a noise worse than fingernails on a blackboard. He dropped behind a pyramid of yellow crates as a hiding instinct kicked in. A dozen spines would have shivered at that sound; twenty-four eyes would have swivelled this way. He skulked in nooks and crannies while first a Green Suit then three Neanderthal heavies passed by. Ben slipped out through a pile of fork-lift pallets and dashed for Cobb's office.

Before he was ready, he was looking straight into Tiffany's eyes. He stopped still. Tiffany clutched the bars of her cage.

'*Ben!*'

'I said keep quiet, you!'

A man in a creased suit stepped from behind the cardboard wall. Ben felt the planet judder to a halt. For months now he had lived in fear of a monster who haunted his dreams. It was hard to remember that he was also a real person. A hundred times Ben had imagined what might happen if he ever met this man again. Now the only thing that stood between him and Tiffany was John Stanford.

Stanford noticed he had company.

'Who are you?' he exploded. 'What are you vandals doing in here? This is private property!'

Ben stepped forward. Nothing terrible happened. He took another step. His binocular predator's eyes fixed upon Stanford, holding his image like pincers between them. The arrogant scowl wavered.

'I'm warning you. You kids have thirty seconds to get out before —'

'Hello, Mr Stanford.' Ben clenched and half-opened his fist. 'I've been looking for you.'

He struck. Stanford reeled backwards and crashed with astonishing force into a tower of crates. It collapsed around him, containers bursting open to shed their loads across the floor. Stanford lay in the wreckage, blood on his white cuffs where he nursed his cheek.

'What . . . ?' he whimpered.

The wretched, bewildered face awoke no pity.

'You don't even *remember* me, do you?' Ben snarled. 'Ben Gallagher. Son of Lucy and Raymond. Ring any bells?'

Stanford looked too dazed to focus. Then recognition mingled with fear. He cowered.

'What you did to my mum. And my dad.' The memories rose like acid in Ben's throat. 'I ought to claw your eyes out . . .'

Then he was wriggling and kicking. Huge hands lifted him off the ground. Stanford's expression changed from terror to a savage smile.

'Toby! My excellent friend. Perfect timing. I'm sure I don't need to say this, but . . . beat him to a pulp!'

Ben's body locked in pain as his arms were twisted. He feared his shoulders would work free of their sockets. Claws were useless; even if he'd been able to summon them, Toby was pinning his hands. He cried out. Dreadful though the pain was, worse still was the glimpse of Tiffany's face before he lost the strength to raise his head.

'John! What's happened? Where is she?'

Doctor Cobb appeared in a fluster of camel-skin coat.

'Ahem.' Stanford picked himself up and smoothed out his jacket, taking care not to tread on any of the jars that had spilled underfoot. He dabbed his cheek with a silk handkerchief. 'The panic's over, Cobb. Thanks to my security man. Your cat isn't out of the bag just yet. And I seem to have caught another. Vicious little swine, too.'

Ben couldn't keep silent as Toby coaxed another crack out of his elbow joints.

'Don't damage him too much.' Cobb looked over-joyed. 'I might just decide to vivisect this one after all.'

'Can we get ourselves in order first?' Stanford rubbed at a scuff on his shoe. He touched one of the fallen jars. 'What have we here?'

'Panthacea, John,' said Cobb, 'naturally. The little pills that will make you a fortune. Why so surprised?'

Stanford frowned at the jar, the way people peer at a jigsaw when the final piece is the wrong shape.

'In all these crates?'

'Yes, of course.' Now Cobb looked puzzled. 'John,

you're rambling. You need some sleep.' He glided forward to take the jar away. Stanford drew it out of reach. The air between them seemed to tighten, suspicion a faint scent in the air.

'It's not labelled yet.'

'It's before shipping,' Cobb answered, impatiently.

'You told me Panthacea wasn't made here. You said . . .' Stanford measured each word, 'you said the cat bile was sent away for processing.'

'I scarcely think this is the time to discuss our manufacturing chain, John.'

'You said the pills weren't made here! Or shipped from here!' Stanford rattled the jar for emphasis. 'So what are they *doing here?*'

Cobb seemed at a loss. As if seized by a sudden, terrible insight, Stanford bent over the shattered yellow crate and rooted through the contents.

'Leave that!' Cobb ran over. 'You're making a mess!'

Stanford surfaced with a sheet of paper. Squirming in agony, Ben tried to see what it was.

'Paradise Supplements,' Stanford read aloud. 'Fifty-two of six hundred. Full strength daily vitamin boosters with glucosamine. Cobb, what is this? An invoice?'

'John . . . It's confusing, I know, but I can explain.'

'This stuff . . .' Stanford tipped the tablets into his

palm. 'These are vitamin pills, aren't they? Cobb! What the hell is going on?'

'Listen!' Cobb spoke through clenched teeth. 'I meant to tell you, at the right time. Panthacea, at present, doesn't exactly, um, exist yet.'

'What?' Stanford thundered. Ben looked up sharply, the pain in his bones forgotten. Tiffany was staring spellbound from her cage.

'I know it can be done.' There was only a slight tremor in Cobb's voice. 'Four thousand years of Chinese medicine can't be wrong. There is a healing substance in cat bile, and I *will* find it. The new laboratory will help. But John, I was running out of funds. I needed to get a product on the market *now*, or go bust. This was a temporary measure. A stop-gap.'

'You've been buying vitamins and relabelling them!' Stanford's face flushed so red that the claw-marks hardly showed. 'You've been taking my money and –'

'I never meant to deceive you,' Cobb pleaded. 'The new lab will change everything. I'll work round the clock on the cat extracts until I succeed in making true Panthacea. You'll be rich beyond imagining, John. The new lab–'

'To hell with your laboratory!' Stanford roared. '*Gottverdammt!* No one swindles me!'

He threw himself at Cobb, who had obviously been

anticipating this. Darting backwards, Cobb grabbed the gun off his desk. Stanford seized his wrist and the two men struggled over the weapon. Air squealed between Cobb's teeth. His eyes bulged like a reptile's.

Ben felt the grip on him slacken. Toby didn't know what he was meant to be doing. Ben jackknifed with all his strength and felt his hair stand on end, a crackle like lightning coursing down his spine. Toby let go as if he'd been stung. Hanging from one of Toby's oak-like arms, Ben swung head-over-heels and kicked the giant in the jaw.

Toby fell like an old chimney. Ben rolled clear, cradling his left shoulder, praying it wasn't broken. Crouched low, he wheeled, looking for Cobb and Stanford. They were gone. He heard, echoing through the arches, running feet, shouts and curses. Whatever was happening now, he guessed, it was between those two and no one else.

'Ben! Oh, Ben!'

Tiffany pounded at the bars with her fists. Ben ran to Cobb's desk and ransacked the drawer until he found a key. Tiffany burst out of her cage with a sob. Ben clutched her arm to steady her.

'Easy. You're safe now.'

'Out. Please. I can't stay in this place, Ben.'

'It's okay.' Ben tried to coax her to walk. 'I've got a plan. Yusuf's sorting it.'

'Ben. Don't let us die in here.'

'No one's going to die. Come on. Tiffany —' he pulled at her, 'you've got to help me. I can't carry you!'

At last she snapped out of it, enough to take a step forward, then another. Her nails hurt his hand as he pulled her towards the goods lift. Then his skin prickled and he knew eyes were upon them.

'There they are! Head 'em off!'

Green Suits were closing in. But the alarm had come too late. Four more strides would put them in the lift. Ben saw a lever, pushed up into Stop mode. Was it his imagination, or were both of the ropes quivering with tension?

'Get in!'

Tiffany stopped in the entrance. She had just escaped one cage — she wasn't stepping into another. She shook her head feebly.

'Tiffany, please!'

A guard burst from an alley of crates, swinging his night-stick. A great shadow was suddenly thrown against the office wall. Ben shoved Tiffany into the lift, yanked the lever down and dived in after her.

Yusuf had done his job well. With a whine the car shot upwards so sharply that Ben bruised his knee on the floor. Then the car tilted and a groan shuddered the mechanism.

Toby, white-eyed and foam-mouthed as a rabid Rottweiller, was clinging to the lift, climbing in. Tiffany screamed. Ben shrank out of reach as the huge arms grabbed at him. The car swung, rising in sluggish jerks against the man's great weight. Steeling himself, Ben swiped at Toby's hands and bloodied face. Instead of driving the monster back it only made him madder. Ben's Mau claws wouldn't come; it was like trying to strike wet matches. Then Toby was in there with them.

Ben would rather have been trapped with a bear. He feinted, kicked, squirmed and even bit, trying to use Ten Hooks to fend the brute off and keep him away from Tiffany.

'Come 'ere!'

A fist clubbed him to the floor. Stunned, he lay on his back and tried to rake his enemy with his feet. Still the car creaked higher. Toby picked him up and slammed him down, once, twice, once more. Sure he had been shattered to pieces, Ben hardly felt a thing as he was seized a fourth time, shaken like a rat and hurled out of the lift.

The world spun around him, bricks, ropes, girders, a grey floor rushing nearer. But every second was suddenly like five, as his mind shifted into that inhuman higher gear in which water-drips could fall slow as feathers and the fastest pinball drifted like a bubble. Ben pivoted automatically, putting his feet lower than his head, kicked clear of the gantry and rebounded off the wall. Heeding a tingle in his Mau whiskers, he snatched at something that checked his fall. Or not quite. He was still falling, just more slowly than before.

He'd grabbed a rope. The counterweight rope, rattling down as fast as the lift was rising. The car soared out of reach. Tiffany was in there with Toby. Ben stared up in despair. He had failed her. Fear had got the better of him. He'd let her down.

Let her down . . .

Below his dangling feet the ground was racing to meet him, three heartbeats away. No time to worry about that. Down there, bolted to the rope, was the counterweight cradle, stacked with enough iron ingots to outweigh the lift car and its occupants put together. There was one last thing he could do to save Tiffany, and he had half a second left in which to do it.

This time, when he tried, Mau claws erupted from his fingertips. He reached down and hewed at the rope. The taut cord exploded at his touch, scattering fibres like chaff. The weight cradle crashed to the concrete. Ben gripped the severed rope with both hands, knowing what was about to happen.

Shorn of its counterweight, the lift car stopped rising and hung motionless for the time it takes to blink.

Then it plummeted like a yo-yo. Ben, hanging from the other end of the cable, shot upwards. Down came the lift, unstoppable as a train. Ben let go with his left hand and stretched out as far as he could.

'Tiffany!' he screamed, not knowing if she could hear him, or was able to obey. '*Felasticon!*'

The lift twisted on the thrashing cable. Tiffany was suddenly there, throwing herself from its open doorway, reaching for his reaching hand. As the car plunged past with a whump of displaced air, his fingers closed on her wrist and she grabbed his.

A crash shook the gantry from top to bottom. The lift had hit the floor. Afterwards, Ben would have no clear memory of flying upwards, somehow clinging on with each hand, then tumbling through space as the whiplashing rope threw him off, his grip broken by Tiffany's weight. All he would remember was being sprawled face-down on the topmost gallery, feeling as if his arms had been torn off. He sucked a painful breath. Tiffany lay beside him, unmoving.

'Uuuuuuuhhhhhhh.'

'Woooo!' Yusuf danced above them. 'Ten out of ten all round, my friends!'

He helped them up. Tiffany seemed not to know where she was. Ben patted at himself, sure he was about to fall into two bits and wondering why it hadn't happened yet.

'Right,' he croaked, when he had the strength. 'Let's get out of here.'

'Hang on,' said Yusuf. 'Tiffany, you didn't come here by yourself? Where's Mrs Powell?'

Tiffany hesitated. Ben saw in Yusuf's face the same horrible thought that he'd just had. When Tiffany spoke it didn't sound like her voice.

'I'll tell you later,' she whispered. 'Let's just go.'

'Okay.' Ben shook off his sudden paralysis. 'Back the way we came in?'

He pushed Tiffany before him. Yusuf, bringing up the rear, glanced over his shoulder and let out a yell.

'Come on!'

First Susie and then Cecile erupted out of the stairwell, Green Suits breathing down their necks. The girls released the white bundles that they carried in their arms. The dust sheets unravelled and dozens of jars rolled out onto the walkway. Cecile and Susie sped away, leaving their pursuers to slip on the pills and fall in a tangled heap.

'Onto the roof,' Yusuf panted. 'We can signal to Daniel. Maybe he can move the crane and pick us up.'

'Crane?' Tiffany frowned.

In single file they scaled a ladder into the water tank loft. Cecile walked up a fallen beam and climbed through the hole in the roof. She and Yusuf helped Tiffany out onto the tiles. Tiffany gasped at the cleaner air and stood there, blinking foolishly.

'Say that again? Daniel's doing what?'

Ben followed them into the breezy night. It was beginning to spit with rain, cooling his rope-burnt hand. The streets of Hackney had never gleamed so beautifully.

'Yusuf's pulling your leg,' he grinned. 'What would we be doing with a crane?'

Something swung out of the darkness.

22
Eight Lives

Earth dare not hurt me
death's dart misses me
I breathe thunder
beware my wrath.

From 'Song of Pasht', Spell 13, Akhotep,
c. 1580 BC Trans. Matthew Toy.

The roof tiles rucked up in a wave beneath their feet and for an instant Ben knew how it felt to be a skittle in a bowling alley. By the time he had recovered enough to be sure he was still alive, he was lying upon damp slates, a boom ringing in his ears. A little way below him, yards from where they'd been standing, the factory's sloping roof was carved into a crater.

Yusuf rolled groaning on his back. Susie wobbled to her feet. Fighting dizziness, Ben looked up and saw the crane swinging its club like a giant.

'What are they playing at? Daniel!'

'That's not Daniel.' Cecile's voice was high and scared.

The cab's windows were steamed and rain-blurred. It was hard to make out the face of the man who now sat at the controls. Even without night vision Ben could have guessed.

'It's Stanford!'

Far below he saw the small figures of Olly and Daniel fleeing the crane in panic. The crane's boom jerked to and fro like the neck of some decapitated beast, wild and unguided, steered only by mindless rage. The wrecking ball swung around for another pass.

'He's trying to kill us!' cried Yusuf. 'Everyone, down to the ground!'

'You want to make a fool of me?' Above the engine's roar and inexpert grinding of gears, Ben's feline hearing could still pick out Stanford's furious screams. 'You think you're a genius, you think you're Einstein, you think you're *allmächtiger Gott* . . . You'd be nothing without me! I own you, and I can smash you!'

'It's not us he's after.' Ben felt a stab of delight. 'It's Cobb. They've fallen out big-time.'

'Come out, you *feigling*, you coward!' howled Stanford, grappling the crane's twin joysticks. 'Come out and face me with your fancy gun! Don't fancy this, do you?'

'He's just trying to destroy Cobb's factory,' said Ben.

'The factory that we're standing on, you mean?' Yusuf yelled.

The steel ball walloped the wall, drowning out his last words and shaking the roof.

'This way.' Yusuf waved them towards the chimney. 'There are drainpipes we can climb down.'

'Come on, Tiffany.' Ben took her elbow.

'Wait!' She hung back. 'The cats. They're trapped inside.'

Oh no, he didn't need this . . .

'We'll come back,' he promised. 'We can rescue them later.'

'Ben!' She knocked his hands away. 'He's smashing this place to bits! They'll be buried alive!'

She was right. Again.

'Ben?' Yusuf yelled.

'I'll follow you,' Ben waved him on. 'Take Tiffany. Get help.'

'I'm not abandoning the cats,' said Tiffany. 'I'm going back.'

To Ben's utter astonishment and horror she dashed for the hole in the roof.

'*Tiffany!*'

The wrecking ball clove the air between them,

forcing him to leap backwards and curl up to shield himself from flying slates. When he looked again she had gone. Had she lost her mind? Much more of this battering and the whole decrepit building would come down. On her head. Of all the stupid, ungrateful, moronic, heroic . . .

'Go on,' he shouted to the other three. 'You can't help now.'

Ben drew himself up, shaking off the rain. If there was an answering shout he never heard it. His world had shrunk to the weeping wind and the great steel ball. It rocked to and fro on its wire, gathering itself, feinting like a boxer. As if in answer, there appeared in his mind a cat's eye, smouldering six different colours. The ball rushed out of the night, an immense, solid ghost. Ben dodged aside, ran up the roof in its slipstream and leaped on.

She had promised. Nothing else mattered any more. She had come here with Mrs Powell to save the big cats and she was not leaving without them. Though how she would herd a pack of tigers, leopards, lionesses and pumas to safety, she hadn't the foggiest notion. Anyway, a pack? A pride? A pantheon? She hardly knew what to call them, never mind how to control them. But she couldn't let it all be for nothing. For Mrs Powell's sake, she had to try.

By now she knew the factory's layout better than the corridors of her own school. She wound her way down from gallery to staircase, guided as much by scent as by memory. The green-suited security guards had ceased to notice her; one of them even brushed past her in his frantic search for an exit that wasn't locked and bolted.

The thunder of the wrecking ball had abated. That was a tiny relief. Tiffany stalked down the last flight of steps into the hall of cages. She was in a nightmare playing on a loop. Ben had risked his life to save her from this place and now she was back. Maybe in her imprisonment she really had lost her mind. No. She was back because she had promised. She clung to that thought.

Gooseflesh on her arms and neck told her she was being watched. Half turning, she stared into the mahogany face of a tiger. It was Shiva, Cobb's first, oldest, most terrible acquisition. He squatted in his cage, the plastic tube pulsing weakly beneath his flank. Looking at her. The heat from those eyes could have set a forest on fire. Yet (she thought, numbly) they had never even seen a forest.

An amber blink. Her trance broke.

'Hold on,' she whispered. 'I'm going to take you away from here.'

'Don't get your hopes up, pussy cat.'

An arm hooked like a snake across her neck. A cold,

withered arm. She struggled as if drowning in a sack. Metal rammed against her temple.

'Keep fighting, why don't you.' Cobb dug the gun in harder. 'I've never shot anyone so close before. It'd be an interesting experiment.'

Terror sapped her strength. Cobb's grip was choking. This was supposed to be his weak arm.

'You think you're a match for me?' he hissed, as if reading her thoughts. 'Panthacea may not be ready yet, but I've been drinking a glass of cat bile every day for the past five years. I'm strong enough to break you in half.'

Tiffany writhed round and, instinctively, in sheer revulsion, spat in his face. Cobb recoiled with a cry of disgust, flinging her away. She crashed into a leopard's cage and fell to her knees.

'*You — revolting — beast*,' he howled. He raised the pistol and fired.

It had seemed such a simple plan in the split second it took to hatch. Grab onto the wrecking ball, climb up the cable, slide down the crane's steep steel neck and fall upon John Stanford like a thunderbolt. But it wasn't always good to have reflexes that worked quicker than common sense. Cat claws, he discovered, were no use for climbing wire. Ben had to resort to clumsy hands-and-heels shinning, as if he were ascending a rope in PE. A wet steel rope that hurt his burned right hand and thrashed back and forth like a live thing.

The building site swayed below him, a stormy sea. The hawser stretched up into the night, dividing into three separate cables. He'd climbed just a few feet. It took all his willpower just to cling on. Then, as if in one of his bad dreams, he was gazing down, down across the rainy void, into the triumphant expression of John Stanford. Stanford's face was lit with pure, demonic hate. If Cobb was his prime target, here was the unexpected bonus. He knew Ben, he knew what Ben had cost him, and now he had his victim just where he wanted him: jerking on a line with no hope of escape, waiting to be crushed like an insect. But was this such a surprise? Hadn't it always been this way, right from the beginning?

Ben gripped the hawser with aching hands. He could climb no further. The crane's neck turned and, casually catching up with it, the demolition ball knocked into the side of the factory. The shock of the impact almost shook him off. Slipping down the cable he grabbed at something, anything – and swung back over the building site hugging the wrecking ball itself.

A series of jolts almost shook him loose. Looking down (a bad mistake) he saw Stanford pummelling the levers like a man possessed. The wrecking ball swept up in a wide arc that passed right over the control cabin. A nasty instinct made Ben look behind him. At the other end of the arc, where the ball would soon be hurtling, was the factory's solid western wall.

Let go, an inner voice begged him. *Let go. Fall. It's your only chance.*

He couldn't. Weak though his grip was he physically could not unlock it. Could not, or dared not. What did it matter? Pounded into a wall or plunging fifty feet onto asphalt – either way he'd be dead.

No, no, the voice gibbered. The wrecking ball had paused on the upswing and was beginning to drop back. *Let go and you'll survive. You'll fall on your feet. Cats always do.*

But he wasn't a cat. He was Ben, and he knew that sometimes, when you fell, you just kept falling. There was no handy lake or bathing pond to save him here – only the crane's steel carapace and the even harder ground.

'Tiffany,' he whispered, 'you'd better be right.'

He let go.

Cobb levelled the pistol and took aim a second time.

'Impressive,' he sneered. 'Are you up to dodging five more?'

The gun roared again. Tiffany was already airborne, flipping herself over the leopard's cage. Touching down feet together, she rolled before the third bang, hearing the shriek as the bullet clipped the bars. She hadn't breathed yet. A tremendous crash made Cobb look round; the crane had torn down a strip of the western wall and the night was pouring in. Seizing her chance she ran, diving behind a drowsing puma that had woken with a snort of fright. Cobb jumped on top of another cage and fired down at her. Concrete dust bloomed close to her hand, leaving a white streak.

Which way? She was dizzy, utterly spent. She dragged herself out of view as another shot deafened her. And another. She crawled. No more, no more. Leopards turned their heads to follow her, crouching, in spite of the gunfire, eerily silent. Sobbing for breath she slumped against a pillar. Cobb advanced, pointing the gun. It was over. If another bullet flew she couldn't dodge it.

Wait a minute . . .

She got to her feet.

'You fired all six,' she whispered.

Cobb stood still. Then he smiled.

'Sorry. I lied. I had eight rounds left.'

The black hole of the barrel seemed to bore through her. She had no power to move. Before Cobb's sickening grin she shut her eyes and waited to be killed. The brickwork froze her shoulders. There came a strange sound. Creaks. A rumble. Mostly out of curiosity she opened her eyes. Cobb wasn't looking at her any more. He was staring around the hall in absolute terror.

Every door of every cage stood wide open.

The wrecking ball crunched into the factory's western flank, collapsing a section of brickwork around it like a wave striking a sandcastle. Ben noted this dreamily, as if half-watching a TV programme, while unbidden his head turned, his trunk twisted and his legs followed, pivoting his falling body on its axis until it locked, sure as a heat-seeking missile, in perfect line with the earth rushing to meet it.

But he wasn't going to hit the ground. In the split second before he struck, he registered that he was going to land right on the crane cabin's roof.

Both feet and hands took the impact, all four together. The shock travelled up the long bones and met in his spine, which melted in that instant into liquid rubber. All in all it felt no worse than missing a couple of stairs in the dark.

But the crane's windscreen crazed, the glass falling in like a sheet of frosted snow that splashed in John Stanford's lap. Then Ben was staring in and Stanford was staring out. Their eyes locked.

With a wail of fear Stanford scrambled out of the cabin. Flinging himself towards the metal steps, he tripped. Ben guessed correctly that, not being a cat,

Stanford was not going to fall on his feet. A moment later the businessman was writhing in the mud, suit glittering with glass, both hands clutching his broken hip. Ben stood over him, breathing hard, then more evenly, feeling the rain cool his head as, in inky drips and drabs, it washed the cat face print off his skin. Out of the night rose the sound of sirens.

The cages were open. Lynxes were slinking from their steel coffins. Wary pumas padded forth. A jaguar, sinuous sculpture of living granite, forced its body through the too-narrow opening of its prison. Cobb spun and spun again, aiming his gun everywhere and nowhere. On every point of the compass a big cat sat, stretching or scratching, and yet more moved with leaden velvet paces towards him.

Tiffany gaped, too astonished to feel fear. How had they got out? Tubes still jutted from their sides. Disconnected. Could the cats have torn these free themselves, with their teeth? No, someone must have set them loose. With a key. Someone . . .

'Get away! Get away from me!' Cobb fired his pistol at a lioness, missing. He caught Tiffany's eye. 'Call them off!' he begged. 'Make them go away! Tell them, tell them!'

The hall echoed with a roar. From between rows of cages glided something of fire and black, the size of a small horse. The tiger, Shiva. With a tail-swish he pivoted ninety degrees. Philip Cobb stood at the focus of his stare.

'Back!' Cobb shrieked. He fired. His shaking hand sent the bullet wide. The chamber clicked and clicked. All eight rounds were spent. He turned to flee and met a fence of bared teeth. No way through. He ran back the other way. Shiva came on. Cobb screamed.

'*Help me!*'

Tiffany fled across the factory floor, her heart hammering not with fear anymore but with a fierce, mysterious joy. The snuffling sea of cats parted to let her pass, as if at some intangible signal. Ahead, through the break in the wall, flashes of blue light were tinting the rubble. Far behind her, Cobb's dreadful cries rose to the vaulted roof and then, abruptly, they ceased.

23
The Final Curtain

His fur ruffling in the breeze, Rufus lay draped along the arm of the bench, surely the most uncomfortable bed he could have chosen other than the barbeque itself. Supporting a column of shimmering air, the grill rocked on its legs as Peter Maine turned the chicken wings.

'That one's mine.' Stuart prodded the brownest one with a fork.

'Hands off,' said his father. 'These have already been reserved.'

'Stuart, you'll be burnt,' warned his mother.

Huffing, Stuart trudged back to his wheelchair.

'It's not fair being the youngest. You always have to wait your turn. I wish I was an only child.' He stopped, appalled in the sudden silence. 'Sorry, I'm sorry, I didn't mean . . . that was horrible.'

'It's all right,' said Tiffany. 'Anyway, I know exactly how you feel.'

Stuart looked relieved. Then he scowled. 'Oi! Now you're being horrible!'

Tiffany fetched her food off the barbeque. Her dad smiled, kissing her on the forehead for the fifth time since lighting the charcoal briquettes.

'We're so glad to have you back, Truffle,' he murmured. 'Whatever any of us say.'

'Dad! Don't call me that.' Reddening, Tiffany glanced over her shoulder.

'Hotdog, Ben?' Peter grinned.

'Cheers.'

Tiffany's eyes glittered in an *if-you-ever-mention-that-name-to-anyone-you're-dead* kind of way. Ben filled his face with roll to keep the laughter in. Peter looked at him seriously.

'Mr and Mrs Gallagher,' he said. 'Your son probably saved my daughter's life. I won't ever get tired of saying that. You should be proud of him.'

'We know,' said Dad, taking Mum's hand. 'Don't we?'

'You did a great thing, Ben.' Gently Mum drew her hand back.

'If you hadn't called that helpline,' Peter went on, 'well . . . I'm not even going to think about it. It's thanks to you that the police found her.'

'Not that it matters,' said Tiffany's mother, 'but how did you know where she was?'

Ben made a big show of chewing.

'I told him the day before,' said Tiffany. 'I'd heard a stray cat mewing near the old factory. I said I was going to see if it was trapped.'

'Right.' Ben picked up the cue. 'I guessed she'd been there. So I called Safeline and told them.'

'Thank goodness they followed it up,' said Mum. 'The police never took as much notice of me, did they, Ben?'

'He turned on the old Gallagher charm.' Dad nudged her. Mum smiled, a bit thinly Ben thought, and went to look at the sizzling kebabs.

Ben followed Tiffany into the corner of the garden where Rufus drowsed on his bench. The loud music from the kitchen stereo masked their conversation.

'So how's it going?'

Tiffany shrugged. 'Weird.'

'Yeah. It's funny. What exactly do your folks think happened?'

'Fran told them something about warring criminal gangs and some kidnapping racket. Fran's the officer who I let find me,' Tiffany explained.

'And the police believe that?'

'Probably. Even if John Stanford tries to tell them the truth, they won't swallow it. Fran says he's got a criminal record as long as a street. Ten years ago he was Jacques Saint-Claude, selling people chateaux in France that didn't belong to him. They're almost sure his real name is Jaeger Straubhaar. Either way, when he comes out of hospital the German, French and British police will be fighting over him.'

'And what about . . .' Ben felt reluctant to say the name.

'They found Cobb.' Tiffany picked at her chicken wing. 'There wasn't a scratch on the body. The cats never touched him. Fran wouldn't talk to me about it, but I overheard her saying that she'd never seen anyone who'd truly died of fright.'

Ben gulped at the shandy Dad had made him. It was too strong. He heard Stuart arguing over how many burgers he was allowed in one bun.

'You should have let me stick around,' said Ben. 'I know you wanted to keep everything secret but . . . I'd have liked to watch the police trying to round up fifty-odd jungle cats. What did they do, call in London Zoo?'

'I asked them about that.'

'And?'

'Fran just looked at me. Like she thought I was ill. They didn't find any cats in there, Ben. Not a single one.'

'What?' He said it too loudly. Cathy Maine turned

to look at them. 'That makes no sense,' he whispered.

'Lots of things make no sense,' said Tiffany. A strange smile appeared. 'How did the cats escape in the first place? Who let them out?'

'But . . .' Ben was floundering. 'You said . . . Cobb shot her. You saw it happen. You told us Mrs Powell was dead.'

'I asked about that, too.' The sparkle in Tiffany's eyes didn't fade. 'I asked the police to look in the cold room at the back of the factory. I begged them to. Fran told me to rest and not get upset. All they found in that meat locker were sides of beef, going bad. Someone had disabled the freezer unit.'

Ben struggled to get his head round it all. 'That stuff about cats and nine lives . . . it's not really true.'

'No. But they can fall out of high-rise flats. Get trapped in washing machines. Have car wheels go right over them, and still recover.'

'Yeah, look at me. Beaten up, thrown down a lift shaft, fallen off a crane, and I didn't even get a sick note for the first day of term.'

'Bad luck. I've got two weeks off.'

Ben had to laugh. He checked to make sure they weren't being overheard.

'So Mrs Powell is alive?'

'That's what I believe,' said Tiffany. 'She must have used Pur. I tried it myself when I was hurt, to get my strength back. She'd be a lot better at it. Maybe good enough to keep from bleeding to death.' She chewed on a thumbnail. 'I went round her flat but no one was there. The thing is, neither was Jim.'

'He might have wandered off.'

'No. She took him. Just like she took the big cats. I've no idea how she did it, how she made them follow her and escape detection like that . . . but I think there were lots of things she could do that she never told us about.'

Ben watched his parents, sitting on garden chairs placed slightly apart.

'After getting us into ten kinds of trouble, she just melts away into the night, without even saying sorry. Nice.'

Tiffany sucked her empty glass. 'I'll miss her.'

Ben would too. The subject was suddenly painful and he forced it away.

'Something else I don't understand. That Panthacea.'

Tiffany nodded. 'I know . . .'

'If those pills were only vitamins with new labels on, how come they worked on your brother?'

'Maybe —' Tiffany paused. 'Maybe because we believed they would. Maybe because my mum and dad stopped quarrelling at Stuart's bedside. Because we were all happy for a change. And so he got better. It wouldn't be the strangest thing, would it?

'Suppose not.'

'He's not cured, you know,' said Tiffany. 'Even taking those tablets he had bad days. They just didn't bother him as much.'

'What'll he do now? No more ONO, no more miracle pills. Even if they were fake.'

'Oh, he'll get by,' said Tiffany. 'The world's never going to be perfect, is it?'

That was true. Mum and Dad were still chatting to Tiffany's parents, but they were hardly saying a word to each other. Ben had been so sure they would get back together. For a time it had seemed like it might happen. Yet it hadn't. All this heartache and they were still as far apart as ever. What did he have to *do*?

'I meant to tell you,' said Tiffany. 'We're re-starting the pashki classes on Thursday. The others are keen.'

'Who's going to teach them? You?'

'Both of us could. To start with. We can find out more stuff on the internet. You really have to search for it, but it's there. We've only just scratched the surface.'

'So to speak.'

'Daniel says his dad might hire us a room somewhere, so long as we tell him that the class is actually tae kwon do. What do you think?'

Ben sat on the bench. Sleepiness had come over him.

'Mrs Powell trained us for a reason,' said Tiffany. 'She'd want us to carry on.'

'A reason. Right.' Ben looked at Mum, laughing and joking with Cathy Maine. The bruise he'd made on her cheekbone was no longer visible, but he could still see it. He would always see it. Glaring at a dying dandelion, he wished for a moment that he'd never heard of Mrs Powell.

Tiffany laid a hand on his, and he knew that she understood. *I'm scared too*, the touch said. Her other hand stroked Rufus's coat for reassurance. Ben considered the cat, lying on his impossibly narrow bed, a picture of bliss. There was smoke, thumping music, a barking dog next door and fleas twitching in his fur, but in spite of all this Rufus had found a moment's pure peace, before the next rain shower or lawnmower came to disturb him. Perhaps that was enough. As much as anyone could hope for.

'I think your brother's feeling left out,' said Ben. Stuart sat by himself, shoveling spilled onions back into a hotdog.

'I'm going to eat till I'm sick,' Stuart announced as they approached. 'And then I'm going to eat some more. It says they're best taken with food.'

He popped something in his mouth and gulped it with ginger beer. Ben spotted a jar by his side.

'Hey . . .' Then Tiffany trod on his foot. Peering at

the jar's label, Ben read: *Paradise Supplements. Everyday Multicomplex formula.*

'It's the same stuff as Panthacea,' explained Stuart. 'Tiffany found out the company's been taken over so it's got a new name. Still tastes horrid, though.'

Ben glanced at her. Tiffany gave a little shrug. Had she done right? She didn't know, and nor did he. You could say it was still a kind of deception. But things were never going to be perfect.

Orange flashed in the corner of his eye. Rufus was disappearing over the fence, already off again on some mysterious mission of his own. Stuart seemed tired as he toyed with a strange pack of playing cards.

'What's the game?' Ben asked.

'Superhero Top Trumps,' Stuart mumbled. 'It's no fun anymore 'cos I always win.' His face lit up. 'Don't suppose you two want to play?'

Tiffany smiled and knelt on the grass in front of him, looking, just for a second, remarkably like a contented cat.

'Deal,' she said.